SCAM

JACK STROKE

SCAM

JOIN MY MAILING LIST

Don't lose touch.

Sign up for my mailing list and get free books,
occasional updates and fun stuff.

As well as free content, member are always the first
to hear about my new books.

See the back of the book for sign up details.

SCAM

JACK STROKE

DEAR READER

T hank you for taking the time to pick up a copy of *SCAM*.

Please note, this is a story about uneducated Aussie criminals. They tend to swear, sometime excessively, so if you are offended by occasional coarse language this may not be the book for you.

Also, *SCAM* is written in Australian English, which is not quite American or British English, but somewhere in-between. I have included a glossary over which may be of help (any errors or typos you find maybe chalk them up to Aussie English).

Thank you and enjoy.

GLOSSARY OF AUSTRALIAN LINGO

The following is a list of slang and expressions for those unfamiliar with speaking 'strayan (Australian).

ACCC - The Australian Competition and Consumer Commission.

Arse – Ass. Bottom.

Arvo - Afternoon.

Bathers - Swimsuit.

Boot (as in car) – Trunk.

Brekky - Breakfast.

Chadstone – Reputably the world's biggest shopping centre.

Choof - Smoking dope.

Ciggies - Cigarettes.

Cricket – A dull game with bats and balls that at its worst can go for five days without a result (honest to God. Five whole days and it still ends in a draw).

Crim – A criminal or Aussie gangster.

Dunno – I don't know.

Dunny – Toilet.

Fair Dinkum/Fed 'inkum – Who the hell knows? A pointless Australian phrase people use when they want to sound Australian. Something to do with fairness.

Flat – A small apartment.

Fluro – Fluorescent.

Fucken – Fucking. Not as in having sex, but as an adjective to describe something bad. For example – *This fucken thing is fucked* (This stupid thing is no longer working).

Gonna - Going to.

Jesus Strap – The handle in a car you hold onto when someone is driving erratically or too fast.

Lift - Elevator.

Number plate – Licence plate.

Neighbours - A long running Australian soap-opera, perversely popular in the U.K. Where actors like Russell Crowe and Naomi Watts got their start.

O Week – Orientation week for university (college) students.

Pash - Kissing the way horny teens do

Piss – Several meanings, context dependant:
    To have a piss – to urinate.
    On the piss – drinking alcohol.
    To be pissed – to be furious about something.
    Piss off – Please go away.

Ranga/Bluey – A person with red hair.

Reckon - Think.

Storey – The floor of a building.

'Straya - Australia.

Trackie Daks – Tracksuit or sweat pants.

TAFE - Apprenticeship and trade training.

Trolley – A shopping cart.

Turnbull – One of the endless stream of Prime Ministers we have had over the last ten years. They never tend to last more than a year or so.

Tyres - Tires.

Ya - You.

Uni – Short for university. College.

Somewhere in Melbourne, 2008

(Maybe late 2007. I can't remember)

1

For the third time Jonathan raised his hand to knock and yet still couldn't bring himself to go through with it. Completely irrational fears fluttered through him. He was going to die. Why was he doing this? Such a bad idea.

No. He was being silly. He wasn't going to die. He would more than likely cough though. With these two guys, a violent coughing fit could blow the whole deal. So then, the rational side of his brain told him, don't cough. And if he did, who cares? If only it were that easy.

He loitered outside the crappy downstairs flat, trying to will himself to knock on the door. Come on. Just knock. Jonathan hadn't expected to be nervous. Probably because he hadn't thought too much at all. The plan had just materialised in his head, fully formed. So he hadn't given a whole lot of consideration to the specifics of what getting it into play might entail. The specifics of the action.

He wandered away, giving himself a little pep talk. This was a rare opportunity in life. A chance to roll the dice and get ahead for once. A chance to play instead of being played. He could do this. It all came down to the story. The story was solid. All he had to do was hook them. They'd get hooked just like he was hooked.

So he knocked.

THE DOOR swung open and Stevo appeared with that '*Who the fuck are you?*' look, although maybe it wasn't a look, maybe it was just his face. If you told a little kid Stevo was a vampire they would believe you one hundred percent, with his greasy black hair and pasty white skin that rarely saw the sun.

It was difficult to tell if Stevo even recognised him. Jonathan opened his mouth to introduce himself when Stevo said " 'bout fucken time." and walked off.

JONATHAN FOLLOWED him through the flat to the little room out the back. The room was a design quirk. Not really big enough to be anything, its sole purpose to bridge the gap between the kitchen and laundry.

The boys had squeezed a couple of beaten up old couches in there and deemed it their smoking room. Jonathan suspected they probably smoked elsewhere in the house too but having a specific room for smoking seemed almost civilised.

Daz was waiting in the smoking room, his bulky Maori frame taking up more than half of his couch. He greeted Jonathan with a broad smile but didn't bother to get up.

"Jonathan, the man with the plan."

They were an odd duo, Daz and Stevo. Daz built like a tank, Stevo all skin and bones.

Fresh nerves tickled Jonathan's insides. He wasn't sure where he was supposed to sit, what the protocol was. Not wanting to put himself in the wrong place, he waited for Stevo. When Stevo took the other couch, Jonathan helped himself to the only seat left, an old kitchen chair, the vinyl all cracked and scratchy. He didn't care. He would prefer to be upright and alert for this, not sunken into a couch.

They were all good to go.

A bong sat waiting on an upturned milk crate with a bunch of other smoking paraphernalia. A bowl and a pair of red handled crafts scissors and a lighter and an ashtray and a pack of cigarettes. Daz pulled out a metal box, removing a large bud of marijuana.

The ritual was about to begin.

Okay, Jonathan thought. *Go time.*

"So... I heard this great story the other day."

Part 1 - Jonathan's Story

2

Jonathan's voice had a slight nervous twitch to it. He doubted either Daz or Stevo would notice though. Or hoped they wouldn't. They didn't probably know him well enough to pick up on it.

"You ever go to that club, Loft?"

"Can't fucken stand that rave shit," replied Stevo.

"Not really our scene, bro," said Daz as he prepared for the smoke. He had the prep down to a fine art. A well practised ritual. He used the craft scissors to chop up the marijuana, slicing tiny pieces off the bud, catching them in a small round film canister.

"Yeah, but you know the club?"

"Heard of it," Daz said with a shrug, putting the remainder of the bud back in the silver container for another day. Or more likely, knowing Daz and Stevo, in about two hours when they decided they were due for another smoke.

Daz swapped the scissors for a lighter and a cigarette. He used the flame to lick the sides of the cigarette, enough to toast it, while not letting it catch fire.

"So, I met this chick the other night, right? She works there."

Carefully cracking the browned paper, Daz spilled the lightly toasted tobacco into the canister with the dope.

"Works where?" Stevo asked impatiently, unable to take his eyes from Daz, mesmerised by the chopping up.

"The club, Loft. Get this - she works in the toilets. Imagine that. Imagine spending seven hours a night stuck in a nightclub dunny."

'*Dunny*' wasn't a term Jonathan used regularly but he felt it might play well to this particular audience. Daz picked up the scissors again, sticking the blades into the film canister and chopping the mix.

"What, she's like a valet?"

"What the fuck's a valet?"

"They hand you towels and shit when you wash your hands."

"So, they just hang around the toilet? That's creepy."

"Nah, she's not a valet," Jonathan cut in. "She's a dealer. Party pills."

The images unfurled in Jonathan's mind as he relayed them. The girl hanging around near the basins in a grimy nightclub bathroom. Loud muffled bass pounding through the walls. Someone approaching her. The surreptitious exchange of money for a couple of pills.

Daz leaned back in his couch.

"Hurry up," Stevo told him.

"Chill." Daz in no hurry. Enjoying the ritual and the control.

Man, it was roasting in the little room. Jonathan perched on the edge of the seat, not quite able to get comfortable. A decent puddle of sweat was pooling in his arse crack. He hadn't envisaged sweating as being an issue. Having come straight from work, Jonathan was still in his work suit and he was beginning to regret his choice. The back room temperature, added to the nerves, was wreaking havoc with his body temperature. Now, he was stuck. He couldn't take off his suit coat without revealing the enormous sweat patches under his arms. Best just to ride it out and hope he didn't sweat too much more.

The stupid part was there had been easily enough time to go home and get changed. He hadn't because somewhere in the back of his head he had thought the suit might give him the upper hand. A position of power. Well, he misjudged that. Look at what these two idiots were wearing. Daz's hairy Maori legs were sticking out of a pair of patterned shorts, as usual, while Stevo was in trackie daks. What had he expected? Shorts and trackie daks were all these guys ever wore. Why had he imagined they'd be impressed by a suit?

Fleetingly Jonathan wondered if his suit was cursed. He needed the suit for work and a mate of a mate at The Drake organised to set him up with one. It wasn't entirely clear where these suits had come from although the implication was that they were hot. It was still more than Jonathan would have liked to spend, but the suits seemed to be a massive bargain, far less than retail.

Jonathan and several mates all bought them. At first, Jonathan was thrilled with his purchase, feeling decidedly slick. As he got around in it Jonathan was certain he could feel eyes on him. Strangers impressed by his sense of style. Unfortunately, after a few weeks, the knees and elbows started to go shiny and it became apparent the suits weren't stolen, merely cheap knockoffs.

Not surprisingly the mate of a mate at The Drake was long gone, never to be seen again.

Ignoring the sweat and his cheap suit Jonathan ploughed on with his story, aiming his pitch squarely at Daz.

"So, this girl, right, the thing is, she's fully sanctioned by the club."

Daz nodded, still chopping.

"The fuck does that mean, *'fully sanctioned'*?"

Jonathan wasn't sure how much of Stevo's aggression was aimed at him or how much was frustration they weren't smoking yet.

"She's like an employee of the club. She may as well be working behind the bar or some shit. Every night, right, just before the club opens, she has to go to the office and they give her a big bag of pills."

He glanced about for a reaction. It was hard enough trying to tell whether Daz and Stevo were even listening, let alone whether he had them hooked.

"You believe that? The club supplies her with the drugs to sell."

This was the part of the story that had most amazed Jonathan when he'd heard it. Daz and Stevo appeared much less amazed.

"Clubs pull that shit all the time," Daz told him. "Have their own dealers."

"So, at the end of the night —"

"Know what else?" he interrupted. "You can't bring your own pills from home either. Club like that, they pat everyone down on the way in. If they find any pills on you, they bin 'em. So you either buy from their dealers or you take all your pills at once before you go in, which would be fun, but possibly not real smart, 'ey?"

"Fucken scam," Stevo said.

"And God help anyone else who tries to deal in their

club. They catch you dealing, the bouncers take your pills and your money and beat the shit outta ya out back. Not like you can go to the cops, 'ey?"

"Fucken need pills to listen to that shit," said Stevo, doing a remarkably plausible impression of techno music. *"Doof, doof, doof."*

Jonathan waited to regain control of the conversation.

"Happened to that guy we used to know. What was his name?"

"Anyway, at the —" Jonathan tried.

"Guy we used to smoke with."

"Guy?" said Stevo, no idea.

"Not Guy, that guy."

"Anyway," Jonathan continued. "At the end of the night the girl has to —"

It was of little use. They weren't listening.

"Adam? Something?" Daz asked, looking at Stevo.

"I dunno what the fuck you're on about, Daz."

Finally, Daz finished, pouring the new finely chopped mixture from the film canister into a bowl, which he held up, presenting it to Stevo and Jonathan for their approval. Jonathan wasn't sure what Daz expected. No, not good enough. Chop it some more? It already looked better chopped than any mix he had ever seen. For most people chopping up was a fairly quick, rudimentary process. A means to an end, leaving a rough mix of tobacco and oversized chunks of bud. Not Daz. Here the entire thing was a pretty mix of tiny of green and brown flakes. Jonathan settled on giving Daz a little nod.

Stevo snatched the bowl and grabbed the bong from the upturned milk crate, packing himself a cone.

"At the end of the night, this girl has to hand back any leftover pills and the cash. It all has to add up. Anyway, this chick was telling me, it costs like twenty bucks to get in, then with drinks and drugs and shit the average person ends up spending between fifty and a hundred bucks."

The images flashed into Jonathan's mind once again, just as they did when he had first heard the story. Long lines of people waiting for entry. People handing over money to get their hands stamped on their way in. People handing over money to buy drinks at the bar. People handing over money to buy drugs in the toilet. Money, money, money.

The sound of the bubbling bong filled the small room. The sound always left Jonathan feeling a little uneasy, scaring him somehow.

"All this cash just gets dumped in a big safe out the back."

Jonathan could see it. A great big old metal safe, overflowing with cash.

"What do you wanna do, fuckface? Rob a nightclub?" said Stevo, attempting to talk and hold in a lungful of smoke.

There was a guy like Stevo at work and Jonathan could not stand him. Same ten cent head. No filter. Couldn't stop himself blurting out whatever stupid thoughts appeared in his brain.

After a moment Stevo blew the smoke out. "Fed 'inkum, you're as dumb as ya fucken look. Clubs have cameras. Security."

"Are you going to shut up and let me finish the fucken story or you wanna make up your own story?"

Daz chuckled, offering Jonathan the bong. Jonathan waved him away.

"You go. So, the same guy who owns Loft also owns Energy 57 and The Palace.

"Faaark," said Daz packing a cone.

"Right? All three of those clubs, enormous."

"How does that work?" butted in Stevo again. "That's gotta be anti-competitive behaviour." He looked about for agreement. "Get the ACCC on his arse."

Daz chuckled. "Still getting mileage out of your tafe degree, 'eh Stevo? Imagine how much you would know if you hadn't flunked out after two weeks?"

"Fuck off, Daz. It's true. It's anti-competitive."

"Yeah, but, that shit doesn't apply to nightclubs, 'ey?"

The fine mix of dope and tobacco ignited in the cone. Daz pulled his bong, drenching the air even more with the sickly, sweet smell. Fuck. Jonathan only had the one suit. He had to wear it again tomorrow for work. Would that matter? Dope smoke smell didn't hang around, did it? Not like cigarette smoke. Just another reason why Jonathan should have gone home and got changed. Stupid.

Already the secondary smoke was making him feel lightheaded. He wasn't really a smoker. I mean, compared to Joe Blow off the street who had never touched dope in his life, he was a smoker. He enjoyed the occasional joint, especially at a party or something. But he wasn't a smoker like Daz and Stevo. These guys were serious. Like they were in training for the bong smoking Olympics or something. Morning, noon and night. Actually, Jonathan doubted Daz had seen a morning in a long time. Noon, night and later at night.

No joints here though. If Jonathan was going to prove himself one of them, he was going to have to smoke a bong. That was given. He had known that coming in and was fine with it. He would just have to do his utmost not to cough. Having a bong was no problem. He just wanted to get the story out first. Get them to buy in.

"Biggest nights for clubbing." He extended out his

fingers to count off the nights. "Thursday night, uni students. Friday, Saturday, weekend crowd. All three clubs —"

"What about caterers?" said Stevo, reaching across and snatching back the bong off Daz.

"Caterers?"

"Fucken hospitality and shit. People who work weekends have their own nights out."

"Fine," Jonathan responded essentially ignoring him.

"What? They're big nights too."

Jonathan raised a hand, still focused on Daz. "Stevo, I believe you, just not what I'm talking about."

Stevo muttered something and focused on packing another cone.

"All three of these clubs have an average of a thousand people every Thursday, Friday, Saturday. Lines around the block. Crowds inside, all drinking and dancing and taking pills. Reaching for the lasers and whatever else. Right? And all three clubs have the exact same process. Their own dealers in the toilets, all the money going into a big safe out the back."

He could see Daz listening now, intrigued as to where the story was going.

"That means for all three clubs combined, there is somewhere between half a mil and a million dollars coming in. Every weekend."

Daz nodded, impressed. Stevo less so.

"Yeah, but that's not pure profit though. You've got to pay wages, buy the alcohol. Fucken lasers aren't cheap."

Jonathan didn't bother to look at him. "Again, all good points. Not what I'm talking about. This is purely about the cash coming in. Now, the owner has a problem..."

"What? Counting his fucken money?" said Daz with a smirk.

"Exactly. The club closes at seven. At two P.M. the armoured truck turns up, to take the money to the bank. All the money. Entry, bar and drug money. Problem is all the money is mixed together, but only some of it is legal."

Jonathan could sense Stevo opening his mouth again.

"No, I'm not stupid enough to suggest we rob an armoured truck. Just listen. First thing the bank does is count it. Except no way does the club owner want the bank or anyone else knowing how much cash is actually coming in. So, what does he do?"

"Just fucken swipe a chunk off the top," said Stevo.

"He's running a business here. Besides, what if he gets audited? Has to be consistent and look legit under scrutiny. Apart from that, he needs to know if the drug dealers are ripping him off in the toilets. That the bar staff aren't slipping money out of the till. He needs to be across everything."

"So, what does he do?" Daz asked, looking at Jonathan quite seriously now and Jonathan could not help but smile. Right there he had them. Hooked. Or at least he had Daz and really that's all that mattered.

3

A pain in Jonathan's shoulder warned him he must have been scrunched up. All tense. He could relax a little now though. He eased back in his seat.

"So, what does he do?" Daz asked again, an intense flickering in his eyes, competing against the dope.

"Saturday morning this guy comes. Van Damme. Van Damme visits all three clubs, picking up the cash —"

"Van Damme. Good choice," Stevo muttered.

"What?"

"Good choice. Van Damme. He's fucken tough. No one's gonna fuck with him."

Daz joined in. "Getting a bit old though now, isn't he? He'd be what? Sixty?"

"Still be able to beat the shit outta ya. He'd still be cut."

The unexpected turn in the conversation bewildered Jonathan. "You realise it's a nickname. It's not the actual guy from the movies."

"Could be the guy from the movies."

"What?"

"True. He did an ad for that breakdown company last year. Lube Mobile or whatever it was," Daz said.

"Heh, heh," Stevo chuckled to himself. "Lube Mobile…"

"So what if he was in an ad?" Jonathan asked Daz.

"So, I'm just saying, he hasn't made any movies for a while. Maybe he's a bit hard up 'ey?"

Jonathan shook his head. "Guys, it's not him. They just call this guy Van Damme."

"Even so, even if it is not the actual dude from the movies, there's gotta be a reason why they call this guy that."

"Maybe it's ironic. Like calling a ranga Bluey," Jonathan said.

"Or when anybody calls you brains, Stevo," Daz added with a smile. Stevo didn't find this nearly as amusing as Jonathan and Daz did. He kicked Daz in the shin and went back to his bong.

"So, Van Damme visits the clubs, picks up all the cash for the three nights and takes it to a house and counts it…"

The images unfurled in Jonathan's mind once again, like a movie. Van Damme stopping by all three venues, leaving with a big duffel bag full of cash, going to a house. The house must have one of those money counting machines Jonathan decided. Had to. There is no other way they could count the money quickly enough. Maybe it has a few. Jonathan could hear the money machines clicking and purring as they shuffled the notes.

"Once Van Damme knows the total, he figures how much each venue should have, and he goes back to each of the three clubs and dropping the money off in time for the official pickup."

What would it be like to be Van Damme? Sitting there in a house with huge piles of cash, all stacked up in front of him in? One for each club and the drug money on top?

"Hold up," said Daz, breaking Jonathan's train of thought. "Why take all this cash to a house? Why not count it out one of the clubs?"

"Yeah, why not, dickhead?"

"I dunno," said Jonathan. "Maybe it's safer. Maybe they are more likely to be caught if they count it at the club. Maybe —"

"Bullshit," said Stevo.

"Look, it's not me. I'm not a guy, okay? I don't own the clubs, I'm just telling you what happens."

"Why doesn't Van Damme just fuck off with all the money?" Stevo asked.

"Probably scared," said Daz.

"Nah, he's a pussy."

"So, this guy, Van Damme..."

Jonathan could see the cogs turning Daz's brain. Now was the time. He grabbed the bong and the bowl. Time to show these guys he was one of them. Just a small cone. That would be all right.

"Good weekend," Jonathan said. "He's walking around with close to a million dollars. Cash."

"Jesus." Daz shook his head wistfully. "Doesn't matter though. There'd be no getting near him. He would have a machine gun and a whole crew of big arsed motherfuckers. Fierce looking dudes with suits and sunnies and high-powered assault weapons."

Jonathan shook his head, suppressing a slight smile. This was the best bit. "Nope. No security."

"Fuck off."

Jonathan could feel Stevo's eye him, wanting him to hurry up with the bong. Fuck Stevo. Jonathan was in control now. He had no intention of hurrying. In fact he paused, taking even more time.

"Think about it. A crew of big dudes turn up at these clubs every Sunday, clearly some sort of security, pretty soon someone is going to twig as to what is going on. They can't do that. They have to be discreet."

"So this fool is just wandering about by himself with close to a million in cash?" said Daz.

"That's the genius part. It's a Sunday morning. Nobody has any idea who this guy is, what he's up to. There is no reason to target him."

Daz nodded, impressed. " 'magine that. Just a normal street on a quiet Sunday morning. Maybe a jogger. An old lady walking a dog. And Van Damme with a million bucks. Sheesh."

Jonathan clicked on the lighter. He was about to pull his bong when Stevo spoke up.

"Well, that's a stupid fucken story."

"What?"

"It's a stupid fucken story. What's the point? Some dude somewhere is carrying around a whole bunch of cash. So what?"

"Stevo, Stevo," said Daz. "You're forgetting who we're talking to, 'ey? This isn't just anyone, right here. This is Jonathan, the man with the plan."

"Yeah, well, at the moment he's just a guy with a story," Stevo replied. He turned on Jonathan. "You got no idea who Van Damme is, do you?"

Jonathan shook his head, hiding a small smile.

"And you dunno what he looks like?"

"No."

"Stupid fucken story then, cockface."

Jonathan shrugged, taking his time. Enjoying his moment.

"You know somethin', though, don't 'cha?" Daz asked.

"Yeah, I know something. I know exactly where Van Damme will be on Sunday morning and what time he will be there. And I don't think he'll be too hard to recognise."

Daz nodded appreciatively. He leaned forward just enough so he and Jonathan could bump fists. Now was the time. Jonathan lit up and smoked his cone. Dope had never tasted so sweet. He didn't even cough or anything.

4

Fuck! Where the hell were these two idiots?

Jonathan looked at his watch for the hundredth time in the last two minutes. Ten past nine. Still. He had made it clear they were leaving nine on the dot. Should he text again? He grabbed his phone and reread the last message from two minutes ago.

Coming.

Well, come on then! Holy crap. The whole plan was going to get blown because these two couldn't get themselves out the front door.

He checked his watch again. Nine-fifteen, Jonathan decided. If it hits nine-fifteen I'm going in. Part of him wanted to leave without them, although that wouldn't work on a practical level.

Deep down Jonathan had the desire to be cool. Joe Cool. Like the old Snoopy comics. Chill and able to handle anything that came his way. The problem was that gulf that there often is between how you want to be and how you actually are. And lots of times in life you really don't know how you are until you are tested. No matter what you might want, the situation will determine your response.

On the casual Sunday morning of the robbery the situation had Jonathan totally on edge. He tried to tell himself it was simply the excitement. All lies. As he waited outside Daz and Stevo's flat, he worried the nerves that jittered through every part of his body were going to eat him alive. He would be much better, he felt, once he had something to focus on. Something to do. He needed to relax. He reminded himself they had plenty of time, which they did. It didn't help.

He barely slept the night before, going over the plan again and again and when he did sleep his dreams were fulfilled with variations of the plan and everything that could possibly go right or wrong.

Nine-fifteen, I'm going in. At least that is what he told himself. Except he knew nine-fifteen would come and go and he would still sitting there like a fool.

How could Daz and Stevo possibly be late for this? In his day-to-day life Jonathan often ran late for things, but most things in day-to-day life don't matter. This was a once in a lifetime, life-altering event. Too important to fuck up. If it were up to him, he would have been there already. Problem was as soon as he introduced Daz and Stevo into the mix he lost that element of control.

Jonathan and Daz were sort of friends. Daz was a buddy of a mate who turned up at enough social engagements that he and Jonathan became friends or friendly at least. Daz with that New Zealand charm, the sort of dude you couldn't help but like, warm and infectious. Problem was, with Daz came Stevo, like a package deal.

Nine-fifteen. Fuck. It was nine-fifteen right now. Should

he text again? No. Just go. Pull them both out by the hair if he had to. What if he waited and they never showed?

Butterflies swarmed his guts as he opened the car door to get out when he heard their front door slam. Finally. Thank fuck.

DAZ WAS BARELY OUT of the flat when the early morning sun assaulted him like a blow to the head.

"Fuck, that's bright, 'eh, Stevo?"

Stevo said nothing, struggling as much as Daz with the early morning hour. This was ridiculous. Daz couldn't recall the last time he was up this early. Years ago probably, when he had to get up for school. That was about it.

The two of them had almost overslept too, him and Stevo. Almost. Made sense. It wasn't natural to be up at this early and on a Sunday of all days. It wouldn't have mattered if they had overslept anyway, so long as all three of them hadn't. If Stevo hadn't come and bashed on his bedroom door and told him to get up, he was sure Jonathan would have.

They stumbled down the driveway to where Jonathan was waiting in a sparkling white car. Daz could feel his brain scraping against his forehead with every step. Fuck. How do people do this every day of our lives? Jonathan had a job. Daz was going to ask him how he coped, getting up like this, day after day, except by the time they made it into the car it was clear Jonathan was feral. Was he angry or nervous? Probably both.

Daz hopped in the front, Stevo in the back.

"All right, Jonathan," Daz said. "Let's do this."

Daz glanced at Jonathan but it looked like he was giving

them the silent treatment. They were barely even in the car before Jonathan took off.

"Whoa, slow down, Schumacher," complained Stevo from the back. "Haven't even got my seat belt on yet."

THE CAR HAD a nice purr as it glided along the quiet streets.

Daz ran his hand along the window panel upholstery. It wasn't sticky or anything.

"This is a nice fucken car, bro. I don't think I've ever been in a car this clean." He turned to Stevo who was gazing about, lids at half mast. "You ever been in a car this clean, Stevo?"

"Nah. There's not a single piece of rubbish," agreed Stevo.

"I know. And look at the interior. It's been vacuumed like immaculately. Stevo's car you can't even see the floor, 'eh? You're up to your knees in Slurpee cups and chip packets and God knows what else. Never know what you might find. I get scared something is gonna bite me."

"Fuck off, Daz."

Daz turned to Jonathan. "Is this your car?"

"Course it's not my car," Jonathan said, under protest. "It's a hire."

"Phhhfftt," said Stevo from the back. "Hire car? It's coming out of your cut."

Jonathan eyeballed him in the mirror.

"I'm not paying so you can swan around in this shit."

"Yeah, you're right, Stevo. I should have used my car."

"Why not?"

"What if Van Damme sees the plates? Or somebody else does? Use your fucken head."

Daz turned away amused. "Yeah, Stevo," Daz said,

unable to help himself and causing a flutter of giggles. Stevo leaned forward and whacked him in the shoulder. That didn't help. Soon they were both giggling.

Slamming on the brakes Jonathan brought the car to a screaming halt in the middle of the road. He glared at Daz, then Stevo and back to Daz. Shock and disbelief etched on his face.

"What?" snapped Stevo.

"Are you fucken stoned?"

"Brekky bongs, man. Essential," Daz told him. "It's fucken early, 'ey?"

"No. It's late. It's twenty past nine." Jonathan fired the car back up as angrily as he could manage.

"What's your problem, spunkrag?" Stevo asked.

"This is a big thing we're doing. You need to be at your absolute best and you two are bent."

"Hey, I am at my best when I'm bent, bro," said Daz.

Stevo sniggered in agreement. "Fucken A. I'm like a fucken ninja when I'm stoned."

It was true. Brekky bongs evened everything out. Daz was struggling as it was. No way would he have made it this far this early without a morning pick me up. Now he was ready.

Jonathan drove on. The hire car cruised along the lifeless suburban streets. A quiet Sunday morning. Very few people about.

THE CAR EASED to a stop in Brown Street. A road intersected it, ending Brown Street in a T-junction. Jonathan parked with a clear view of the road in front. Soft music floated from the speakers.

"See?" Daz smiled. "Plenty of time."

"We said nine," Jonathan replied, doing his utmost not to sound as snippy as he felt. They were probably right. It probably didn't matter. Yet Jonathan remained annoyed anyway.

He had to leave it. Move on. They had a job to do and more important matters to focus on. What would happen next? Van Damme would appear. They grab the bag. What was he missing? What hadn't they thought of?

Stevo leant forward from the back seats.

"Okay. Who wants what?" He handed over two rubber kids' masks.

"What the fuck is this?" Jonathan asked.

"The masks."

The masks were the cheapest, nastiest pieces of crap you could imagine, barely even recognisable as whatever animals it was they were supposed to depict.

"You were supposed to get balaclavas."

"You said masks."

"Balaclavas. Ski masks."

The cheap material gave off a revolting chemical latex smell. Jonathan turned one the masks over in his hands. It wasn't sticky exactly, but it gave the impression of coming away in his fingers as he touched it.

"I don't even know what these are supposed to be."

Stevo pointed. "Giraffe. Frog."

Jonathan attempted to force the mask onto his face. The elastic was cutting off all circulation. Like sticking his face in a vice. He glanced in the rearview mirror. The mask barely covered his features.

"He's right, bro," Daz said. "Shit masks."

"You get the fucken masks next time then, fuckbag."

Daz turned. A Buzz Lightyear mask sat on the back seat

next to Stevo. Buzz was moulded plastic. Still a cheap mask, but a billion times better than the latex animals.

"Why do you get to be Buzz Lightyear?"

"I got the masks, I get to choose."

"Why didn't you just get three Buzz Lightyears?"

Daz and Stevo glanced at one another and cackled.

"Can't all be Buzz Lightyear," Daz said.

"Idiot," Stevo added for good measure.

Somewhere deep inside Jonathan a voice questioned whether Daz and Stevo were the right choice for this job after all. It was important to contain his annoyance. Much as he wanted to yell and scream and rant and rave, they were here now. The decision to bring them in long since made.

"At least tell me you got the gun..."

"Better," Stevo said, pulling out a little black box. At first, Jonathan thought it was a dictaphone.

"What the hell?"

"Taser," said Daz. He and Stevo smiled and nodded, looking most pleased with themselves.

"We agreed," Jonathan pleaded. "A gun."

"You try getting a gun on short notice, cockspank."

"I don't have to," Jonathan spat. "I'm not the one who said I could get a gun. *'Yeah, done, yeah, easy, I'll get the gun,'* you said."

"Listen, fuckstick, we were in the states, I could get you a gun like that." He snapped his fingers. "Easy. But this is 'straya."

"Were we not in Australia when you said you could get a gun?"

"What?"

Jonathan waved him away, becoming aware of a throbbing in his head. A throbbing that could easily become a pounding.

"Hey, Jonathan? Relax," Daz told him. "This is better anyway, 'ey."

Jonathan shot him a look like he was criminally insane.

"You wanna shoot this guy? No. What if he's a hero? We shove the gun in his face, tell him to give us the bag, he says no. What then?"

"Yeah, what then, dickhead?" Stevo joined in.

"This way, we taser him and take the bag. Doesn't matter if he's a hero or not."

Jonathan couldn't help but turn away, muttering to himself.

"Dude, you gotta chill," Daz went on. "I wanna ask you something. Why did you come to us?"

Jonathan was asking himself that same question.

"Experience. You came to us cos you wanted someone with experience in pulling this kinda shit. Someone who knew what they were doing. Well, that voice of experience says 'Relax'."

Stevo leaned between seats and snatched the taser.

"You know what the vital factor in any robbery is?" Daz went on.

"Sticking to the fucken plan?"

Daz shook his head. "Attitude. It's all in the vibe. If you are uptight and tense, you'll cock it up. If you're relaxed and cool, you can handle anything."

Stevo leaned forward again. "How do I tell if this thing is on?"

"Holy fucken crap..." Jonathan muttered.

"Did you turn it on?" Daz asked.

"I dunno. It's not clear."

Daz leaned over. The two of them turned the taser about in their hands examining it closely.

"We need to test it on something," Daz suggested.

"Test it on Jumpy" Stevo said, indicating to Jonathan. "Calm him the fuck down."

"Can't test it if you can't turn the fucken thing on."

"You're doing a lot of muttering there, Jonathan. You need to check that shit, bro. The muttering under your breath. Bottled up aggression? It's no good for your health, 'ey?"

Daz and Stevo fiddled with the taser, their manner a little too lackadaisical for Jonathan's liking. He glanced up. No sign of Van Damme, thank God. There would be, any second now. Then what would they do? Maybe he would hand over the bag if they asked nicely.

He returned to watching Daz and Stevo, not really much else he could do. One of them must have pressed something, because all of a sudden the taser deployed - two electrodes shooting out of the end, barely missing Daz.

The electrodes might have missed Daz however they made a direct hit into the car CD player where they attached, causing a flash and sparks then a slow drone as the radio and the car went dead.

"Cool. It's on," stated Daz.

"Jeez, I hope it doesn't need recharging."

Jonathan stared from the radio to the taser to Daz and Stevo, mouth agape. He wanted to say something, except there weren't any words to say.

"Hey, fuckface, is that Van Damme?"

Across the road a man strode towards the car, moving fast and clutching a large duffel bag. The man wasn't much to look at. Just an ordinary guy, nothing like his muscular, martial arts trained namesake, yet it had to be him. The place, the time, the bag. It was Van Damme.

"Fuck!" yelled Jonathan.

5

Jonathan sprinted for his life. His lungs hurt and his chest felt like it was being crushed in the fist of a giant. He couldn't stop running though. Not yet.

They must have looked a sight, the three of them running along like this on an empty Sunday morning.

"Hey, Jonathan," puffed Daz. "I don't know what your plan is here, but I can't keep running like this, 'ey."

Running was not a long-term strategy. Jonathan was aware of that. At least he played indoor cricket most weeks, but he doubted Daz or Stevo ever did anything remotely physical.

"Just a bit further," Jonathan said, with no idea what his plan was either. They simply had to get away.

To say the theft of the bag had not gone entirely as Jonathan had envisaged was a massive understatement. The possibilities of what might have happened with Van Damme had played over in his head many times, but never quite like how it eventuated.

Upon seeing Van Damme coming the three would be assailants had tumbled out of the hire car and bumbled along, Daz and Jonathan struggling to force the tight stinky latex masks over their faces as they ran at Van Damme. Stevo had little trouble getting his superior quality mask on but was completely focused on trying to figure how to retract the electrodes back into the taser so they could fire it again.

Despite all this, they were quiet enough that Van Damme didn't notice anything until the trio were almost upon him. He barely had time to look up and see his attackers before he was zapped. He fell hard to the road, unable to fight the overwhelming surge of electricity, doing his best to cling to the bag, without much luck.

Duffle bag in hand, the frog, the giraffe and Buzz dashed back to the car.

They jumped in. Jonathan fired up the engine... At least he tried to. Nothing.

"Get out of here, fuckhead."

"I'm trying."

He turned the key again. Nothing. It wouldn't turn over, the car not even pretending like it was going to go.

"It won't start."

Jonathan turned the key a bunch more times in vain.

There was nothing else for it. The three of them abandoned the car and took off on foot. Jonathan could see Van Damme watch the trio dash off with the bag from his position, lying prostrate on the side of the road.

HENCE THE RUNNING. They had to keep running too. Until they were clear. Until they found a way out of this mess. A way to escape.

"Look," Jonathan puffed with relief as they turned a corner. There was a train line up ahead.

"What?" said Stevo, angry as always.

"Train tracks. There must be a station around here somewhere."

"Whoop-di-fucken-doo."

"Come on. We just need to follow the tracks."

"A random train station is not going to do us any good, cockhead. Not if we don't know what line it is."

"All train lines go in and out of the city. We'll catch one into the city and one back out to the hideout."

"Great. We should be there by Wednesday then."

Jonathan ignored his griping and hurried off again, Daz and Stevo trailing reluctantly behind.

SURE ENOUGH, as predicted the train tracks led to a train station. Just what they need. They settled on the platform to wait and catch their breath, only to realise after five minutes they were on the wrong side and waiting for a train out of the city (which for whatever reason Stevo blamed Jonathan for). They quickly switched platforms.

The other side of the station was better anyway, in that it had a shelter. So while Daz and Stevo slouched in there, Jonathan prowled the platform anxiously. He mashed the green announcement button on the wall.

"*Good morning, passengers. The next train on platform one will depart in forty three minutes,*" an automated voice informed him. Forty three minutes? Bloody Sundays. Still, if it were a weekday, they probably would have had to contend with a station full of other passengers. As it was the platform was deserted.

From somewhere behind Jonathan heard Stevo whinge. "Forty three minutes? Lucky we fucken ran all that way."

Once again Jonathan told himself to ignore Stevo. Not

worth it. He gazed about. It wasn't much of a station. Two long concrete platforms on either side, enclosed by cyclone fencing. The small shelter the only protection from the elements. God, Jonathan hated trains. They reminded him of school.

He fretted about the hire car. It wasn't terribly smart to abandon it like that. They'd left the doors open and everything. Yet what choice did they have? Could he go back and retrieve it later? How would he know if it was being watched?

Jonathan froze, his blood turning to ice. Footsteps. Someone was coming. Oh God, it was Van Damme. He found them somehow. No, not found, followed. Of course the stupid taser hadn't done its job properly. What did he expect? Why would he think otherwise? Van Damme had recovered and given chase on foot. It would have been easy to follow them. Why hadn't Jonathan even thought to look back?

A swarm of nerves swallowed him. One look at Daz and Stevo told him they were thinking the same thing.

Stevo pulled out the taser, cradling it in his palm. The shelter limited Daz and Stevo's view. They couldn't see much, except Jonathan. Their eyes followed him intently, getting their cues from him. Jonathan shot them another quick glance and gave a small nod. Get ready, he said with his eyes. Van Damme was almost upon them.

A second sound mixed with the footsteps. A scraping. What the hell was that?

Van Damme was dragging something. A weapon.

Jonathan tensed, hands balling tightly into fists. If it was Van Damme, bring it on. Weapon or no weapon. There was three of them and only one of him.

Except it wasn't Van Damme at all. It was an old lady, dragging an old lady shopping cart.

Jonathan almost laughed. His shoulders slumped. Of course Van Damme hadn't followed them. How stupid was he?

What happened next was a point of some conjecture between the three of them. About the only thing they managed to agree on was that the old lady made a strange sort of quacking sound when Stevo jumped out and screamed "Die, you fucken mother fucker!!" and shot her square in her frail old chest with the taser.

6

"I'm just saying it's not fair, 'ey? He's got to fire the thing three times, I haven't got to fire it once."

"Tough. Luck of the draw."

"You'd be furious if it was me that got to fire it three times and you hadn't got a go, 'ey?"

"Guys, focus. We got bigger problems than whose turn it is with the taser."

They had grabbed the old lady from where she lay on the platform, dragging her into the shelter. She didn't appear to be dead but after moving her none of them wanted to get close enough to find out for sure.

"Fuck off," Stevo said, backing away quickly when Jonathan told him to go check if she was still alive. "I'm not fucken touching her."

"Me neither, bro. Old people are terrifying."

So it was left to Jonathan to shove his fingers under her nose. He was pretty sure he felt breath. Breathing equalled not dead, surely. He placed her trolley alongside her, not really sure what else to do with it.

"She made a noise like a duck, 'ey? I would never have expected that."

"Yeah, that's just the noise people make sometimes when they get tasered," Stevo said, suddenly an expert on the subject.

Jonathan wasn't interested in the noise she made when they zapped her. It was the noise she had made hitting the concrete that concerned him. Especially that horrible crack her skull made when it smacked the ground.

Stevo turned on Jonathan, suddenly full of fury. "Why'd you tell me to zap her, cockface?"

"I didn't. I was very clear. I nodded, as in '*Its cool*'."

"Nah. You nodded as in '*Do it*'."

"He's right, bro. You need to be clearer with your signals."

Arguing was as tempting as it was pointless. Jonathan's mind raced in a million different directions.

"What do we do now?"

"We wait for the train."

"No, I mean, about her."

"Ahh, the old dear just needs to sleep it off."

The old lady did appear quite peaceful prodded up against the side of the shelter.

"It's not like she's had a few too many sherries. We might have killed her."

"You might have killed her you mean, with your unclear signalling," Stevo said. "Doesn't matter whatever."

"It doesn't matter?"

"Look at her, she didn't have long anyway."

"Jonathan, I can't believe I need to be telling you this again, bro, but you need to chill." Daz placed a firm hand on his shoulder. "Come on, breathe with me. Nice, deep, calm breath. That's it."

Jonathan shook his shoulder free. He was breathing fine. He didn't need Daz's help.

"If she is dead, someone will find her here in the next few days. If she is not dead, she'll wake up and it'll all be fine. Nothing to stress about, 'ey?"

"If she's dead, they're gonna come looking for us."

"Who? The old lady police?"

"The regular police."

"No one is gonna come looking for anyone."

"You can't just kill people..."

"Even if she is dead, no one is gonna know she was killed."

"When they do the autopsy —"

"Autopsy... phhfft," snorted Stevo. "What do you think this is, fucken CSI Melbourne?"

"What on earth are you talking about?"

"This isn't the fucken movies, dickbrain. They don't do that shit in real life. At least not for anyone over the age of... sixty. They don't need to."

"They'll want to know how she died."

"No, they won't. They'll take one look at her and how old she is. Case closed."

"That's not how things work."

"Oh, and you'd know, would ya?"

The truth was Jonathan was not entirely across police procedure for such a case, he just knew Stevo was talking shit. There was no arguing with Stevo though.

"We can't stay here with her." He pointed at the old woman, a little drool seeping down her chin.

"Why not?"

"What if someone comes?"

"They'll just think she's asleep, 'ey?"

"What if it's a friend of hers?"

"A friend?"

"Yeah, like if she's meeting someone here."

"You get that old, you don't usually have any friends, 'ey? Besides, if she was meeting someone here they would be here already."

"We don't know that. What if she's early? What if it's like her husband and he just dropped her near the gate so he could go and park the car?"

Daz and Stevo scoffed.

"Now you're just being silly," said Daz, wagging a finger at Jonathan.

"If they have a car, what the fuck are they catching the train for, idiot?"

Daz shuffled past and took a quick look down the platform.

"Jonathan, are you worried about her being in the shelter? Cos we could put her on the other side of the fence if you like."

"You want to throw the old lady's body over a fence?"

"I don't want to, 'eh, but I'm not the one who has a problem with her being in the shelter."

"Fine," Jonathan said attempting to shake the stupidity from his head. "We'll leave her. We've gotta get the fuck outta here."

"We are getting outta here," said Daz. "We're waiting for the train, 'ey?"

"The train?" Jonathan said, eyes in danger of bursting from his head. "No. We can't, after this. We'll get to the hideout some other way."

"What other way? Your stupid hire car won't start."

"The hire car wouldn't start because you tasered it."

"Yeah, whatever," Stevo scoffed. "Don't try and blame me for your fuck ups. The point is the hideout is a long way. That's why we needed the car in the first place. It's not like we can walk."

"We get a taxi then."

"We're in the middle of nowhere," said Daz. "There aren't no taxis around, 'ey?"

It was true. Well, not the part about being in the middle of nowhere, they were deep in suburbia. But the part about taxis was right. The quiet streets had houses and parked cars and the occasional shop (closed at this hour on a Sunday) but Jonathan hadn't seen a single taxi anywhere. They could be lucky and happen across one, although the way their luck was running today they have more chance of coming across a police convention. Jonathan didn't have a taxi number in his phone. There had to be a taxi somewhere. He wondered how far to the nearest main road.

"I'm not paying for any fucken taxi anyway," said Stevo. "Too expensive."

"We've got a bag full of cash," Jonathan implored. "You won't even notice —"

Stevo made a lunge for the bag, swinging it out of Jonathan's reach. "You touch this fucken bag, I'm gonna break all your fingers."

"Fine. I'll pay for the taxi. Let's just walk until we find one or..." He could tell from Stevo's scowl he was fighting a losing battle.

"You want to waste money on a fucken taxi, go for your life. I'm catching a train. So is the fucken bag."

Jonathan looked to Daz for reason, getting nothing.

It wasn't the easiest of choices for Jonathan. Risk jail time for killing some old lady versus risking never seeing

Daz, Stevo or the bag ever again. In the end though, there was no choice. Not really.

The train seemed to take an eternity to arrive, but it did come eventually and left again without incident.

Not surprisingly the old lady didn't make it aboard.

7

The train ride to the city brought Jonathan little relief. The old lady was pretty much forgotten once he stepped in the safety of the carriage, other concerns overrunning him.

Sunday morning peacefulness ensured the carriage was virtually empty with only four other commuters. The issue was that every one of them seemed to know what Daz and Stevo and Jonathan were up to and what was in the bag. It wasn't possible they could know and yet somehow they all did. They stared at Jonathan, evil intent in their eyes, biding their time, waiting to steal the bag. Jonathan knew it was his mind playing tricks on him, not that the knowledge helped.

Walking around with a bag full of this much cash sure gave you a different view of the world. Of course he was nervous. Shit, Jonathan would get nervous with one hundred dollars in his pocket. This was a hell of a lot more. A little paranoia was to be expected. That's why they shouldn't have been anywhere near a train with the bag. They should have been in the damn hire car. And by now at the hideout already.

More of a concern than their fellow passengers was how Stevo was looking at him. Paranoia as well or was there more to it? Daz was looking at him funny too... Had Jonathan served his usefulness? Was the taser destined to fire one more time? Daz hadn't got his turn yet. Daz was a mate and Jonathan trusted him. Kind of. Stevo though, Stevo was a wildcard. Being the man with the plan isn't much use once the plan was done. Part of the issue was they had been vague on what happened from here. All of their forethought had gone into how to get the bag, not what to do once they had it.

Every moment that passed sharpened Jonathan's acute awareness about the amount they were dealing with here. There was a fuckload of money in Van Damme's bag. Even though he doubted Stevo could count, he still presumably knew splitting the dough in two ways was a far better deal for him and Daz than splitting it into three. At what point did he become expendable?

Jonathan sighed, pushing the paranoia way down deep inside. They had done it. They had stolen the bag. There was nothing to worry about. At least that's what he told himself.

FINALLY, after changing trains and suffering through another forty-minute wait Daz and Stevo and Jonathan trekked the twenty-minute walk from the station to the hideout.

Jonathan did his best to keep his mania in check, staying as alert as possible just in case. How would Daz and Stevo do it, if they were going to turn on him? Running away was definitely out. Daz had only just caught his breath from the earlier burst of running. No, if it was coming (and Jonathan continued to remind himself it probably wasn't) it would be the taser. He made sure he stayed behind Stevo, keeping his eyes fixed on him.

After following for a bit, Jonathan realised there was something else going on. Stevo looked as angry as ever, but both he and Daz were both thoroughly cooked. How long since either of them had done this much exercise or seen this much daylight? The brekky bongs had well and truly worn off leaving a tired, testy duo.

Not exactly sure where the hideout was Jonathan followed, hoping it was soon. Eventually, they stopped outside a supermarket.

"Oh, thank God," exclaimed Daz, sinking into a bench out front.

"What are we doing here?" Jonathan asked.

"We need supplies, 'ey?" He looked at Stevo. "I'll get the ciggies, you get the food."

Before Jonathan had a chance to argue Stevo nodded at Daz and disappeared inside. They were splitting up. Jonathan's brain almost folded in half trying to keep up. Were they intending to lose him here somehow? Jonathan couldn't see any possible way and yet maybe that was his problem, attempting to apply logical thought to Daz and Stevo's actions.

Desperately as he wanted to stay with Daz, every fibre of his being told him not to lose sight of Van Damme's bag. It was entirely possibly Stevo planned to do the dirty on both of them. He dashed into the supermarket.

THE UNLIKELY COUPLE of Stevo and Jonathan walked the aisles. Foolishly Jonathan had assumed food meant you know, actual food, when in fact it meant stoner food. The shopping trolley quickly filled with blocks of chocolate, chips (both Doritos and a twin pack of salt and vinegar), several two litre bottles of Coke, chocolate biscuits (Mint Slices, Tim Tams and Squiggle Tops), a ten pack of Whiz Fizz and a cheap and nasty selection of frozen dim sims and spring rolls.

"That's all the major food groups covered then?" Jonathan said with a smile.

Stevo turned on him aggressively backing Jonathan into a shelf. "Shut the fuck up. You lost the right to talk to me."

Jonathan did as he was told.

STEVO DUMPED it all on the checkout belt and a bored woman with dead eyes rung it up.

"Thirty-seven dollars and eighty cents please," she said.

God, thirty-seven dollars eighty on nothing but crap. Jonathan realised the woman and Stevo were both staring at him.

"You're paying, moneybags."

Jonathan opened his mouth to protest.

"If you can afford to piss money away on taxis and hire cars that don't even fucken work, you can afford this."

Although he didn't recall actually wanting any of this junk Jonathan saw no point in putting Stevo further off side.

FINALLY, after far too much laborious travel and waiting around Jonathan, Daz and Stevo made it to the hideout, an empty third-floor apartment in a cheap block of flats Stevo had sourced.

Still jittery and nervous, Jonathan pushed his way in, ignoring the overpowering stink of mould and cat piss, just pleased to have made it here despite the issues. Yes, they were several hours later than expected, however they were here.

Except at least when they were travelling, they were doing something. Stopping, all Jonathan's temporarily abated fears came roaring back.

The two stoners sauntered in behind him, appearing entirely unfazed by the way the day had panned out. Jonathan waited for them to make their move but nothing happened.

Daz and Stevo didn't attack him or pull out weapons or anything. They sunk into the tattered couches, just like they were at home. As though if they had been forced to take even one more step it may have killed them.

Jonathan hovered awkwardly for a second before disappearing to the bathroom to figure out his next move. Just because they hadn't done it yet didn't mean they weren't going to. Maybe their exhaustion was a scam. His hands shook under the stream of water. His reflection stared back, telling him the day had probably taken several years from his life expectancy.

The filthy bathroom walls closed in around him. Jonathan chided himself for never thinking this part through. God, why hadn't he? It could all go so wrong, so easily. He whacked himself across the face, attempting to jumpstart his brain. All the three of them had to do was split up the cash.

"Umm, Jonathan?" came Daz's voice from the other room.

"Just a sec."

Oh crap, this was it. Think, God dammit. Stevo was the problem. Jonathan could reason with Daz if they turned against him.

"Oi, Jonathan."

"I'm coming."

He had no weapon. No way to defend himself. No, he was being silly. He didn't need to defend himself. They were on his side. It was simply paranoia.

"Jonathan, get the fuck out here now, cockspank."

He had to move. Don't get tasered, he told himself. It was all he could think of. Don't get tasered.

Jonathan crept out on his guard, expecting to see Stevo holding the little black box and ready to dive out of its way.

Except Stevo wasn't holding the taser. He was holding two pillow sized ziplock bags, full of some kind of crystallised brown powder.

"What's that?"

"You tell us, fuckbag. This is what we just stole."

8

Jonathan stared at the two bags in disbelief.

"What we just stole?"

Almost tripping over the coffee table in his haste, Jonathan fumbled through Van Damme's now empty duffle bag, somewhat pointlessly turning it upside down and shaking vigorously.

"But... Where's the cash?"

His eyes flicked from Stevo to Daz. Was this some kind of set up? Had they hidden the money somewhere? Swapped the cash for this whatever it was? They couldn't have. There had been no time. These two hadn't moved that fast. Not today, maybe not in their entire lives. No, they had sat down on the couches and Stevo had opened Van Damme's bag and...

"Fuck."

Jonathan stumbled backwards, mind launching into triple speed.

"Now, Jonathan, I think you would agree Stevo and I have been pretty patient up to now," Daz said diplomatically. "A lot has gone wrong today. And while I am not saying it is all your fault —"

"Fuck that. I am," interrupted Stevo. Daz held up a hand to keep him quiet.

"But this is a pretty major issue, 'ey?"

He waited for a confirmation nod from Jonathan before continuing.

"I think you need to tell us what's going on. Right now."

Jonathan barely heard him, lost in his own mess of thoughts.

"She lied to me..."

"Who lied to you?"

Jonathan bit down hard on his bottom lip. Hard enough to draw blood.

"Kelly."

9

The entire mess started, at least for Jonathan, a little over a week ago, on a Friday night. In Jonathan's world Fridays meant one thing. The Drake.

The Drake was Jonathan's favourite pub. It was low-key and chill without the pretension other pubs seemed to have. It wasn't a place to be seen or to listen to the hippest music or be told you weren't allowed in without big tits or the right shoes. It was an ordinary place for regular people who wanted a quiet beer after work.

Jonathan and his crew met at The Drake every Friday night to play pool and drink and just be. It was Jonathan's place, especially now. After the turmoil of his love life over the past few months, The Drake and his mates were an essential part of his recovery.

On this particular Friday Jonathan had been thinking about George all day at work. Sounded funny - thinking about George. George, Georgie, the bartender at The Drake. George was a bit of a tomboy. She had short dark hair and didn't take any shit from anyone. A colourful sleeve of tattoos ran down her left arm. Rumour had it she had a matching set on her right leg, although Jonathan was yet to see any evidence of that.

Jonathan had wondered more than once if George had a crush on him. She and Jonathan had a friendly flirty banter going which he noticed she didn't appear to have with anyone else. He thought she was fun. Cynical and good value. Her body was thick, more solid than voluptuous and she had the most neutral looks Jonathan had ever seen. Neither good-looking nor ugly, just a person.

The reason he had been thinking about George on this particular afternoon was Jonathan had decided it might be time to see if he could turn their flirty banter into something more physical.

There were a couple of reasons for this, other than, you know, she was female and she was there. Firstly she gave Jonathan the impression she would be a grateful lover, which would probably result in quite a pleasant sexual experience. Also, she had fairly large breasts, so even if the sex was terrible, he could at least focus on those and it wouldn't be a total loss. And finally, George seemed like a nice, easy way to get himself back in the saddle so to speak after the disaster that had been his love life over the last few months.

The Drake was only beginning to warm up when Jonathan and crew had arrived, immediately settling into a game of pool. Being a bit loud maybe but not bothering anyone and no one was bothering them. Until Raj return from the bar with five points and a worried look.

"What's up?"

Raj didn't say anything, he merely indicated towards the tables across the room.

Sitting there by herself was a stunning young woman dressed to kill in a revealing red dress.

Kelly.

To the uninitiated Kelly looked like a mirage. A model plucked from a magazine and dropped out of context into the dank grunginess of The Drake. To Jonathan and his mates, she looked like the devil herself.

Kelly glanced over and glanced away again, completely impassively, not remotely phased by the angry glowering glares of the five young men in their cheap knockoff suits.

"This is not right. I'm gonna go over there," Raj stated, his voice creaking slightly, shattering any illusion of toughness. "Tell her to get the fuck outta here. This is our place. She shouldn't be here."

Jonathan grabbed his arm. "Nah, it's cool, Raj. Just leave it. She can be here if she wants."

"What are you going to do?" one of the others asked.

"Nothing," Jonathan told them. "Just ignore her. She'll get bored and fuck off."

They returned to their game, although not quite as boisterous, the spectre of Kelly like a wet blanket.

About an hour later she hadn't moved.

"I'm gonna go over," Jonathan announced.

"Don't do it, dude," Raj warned him, but with four beers into him Jonathan wasn't worried about anything Kelly might say. He stomped over and leaned aggressively on her table.

"What?" he demanded.

"What?" Kelly said, with a twinkle in her eye.

"What do you want?"

Her face settled somewhere between innocent and coy. "I'm just sitting here. You came over to me."

"Get the fuck outta here, Kelly." It felt good. Not quite as good as telling her to fuck off or get fucked, both of which he had practised in his head many times, but good all the same. Of course, a great many things had run through his head involving what he would say or do if he ever saw Kelly again, including, in some of his weaker moments, begging her to take him back. Not that she would ever know that.

Pleased with himself Jonathan turned and strode away.

"It's nice to see you," she said, stopping him in his tracks.

"Stay, go. I don't care. We're done, Kelly. I'm not playing your games anymore."

Undoubtedly his words would have had a far greater impact had he kept walking. He didn't. He stood there looking at her, intrigued as to what she might say next.

"Buy me a drink?" That playful look flickering in her eye.

Jonathan shook his head, unable to quite believe her and yet at the same time thinking same old Kelly. One thing was for sure. She would want to be careful how she moved in that outfit. Bits of her could easily come popping out. The backless dress with its material stretched across her chest made it clear she wasn't wearing anything under there and gave a tantalising hint of side boob. Was it possible she had nothing on underneath at all? His eyes found the smattering of freckles leading to the valley between her breasts. No doubt about it. Kelly looked goooood.

"Thanks, George," Jonathan said as she placed down two shots in front of him, Kelly's presence totally expunging from his mind whatever he had been thinking may or may not happen with George tonight.

As he picked the shots up she clamped a protective hand onto his wrist.

"Be careful."

Jonathan winked at her. He was born careful.

Kelly watched them from across the room, a determined, focused look in her eye.

10

Susan had an over active imagination. She always had, for many years. Prone to what her mother politely referred to as flights of fancy. If someone was ten minutes late she would start to worry.

If they were twenty minutes late she was certain there had been a serious car accident and prayed that they were okay.

By thirty minutes she was writing the person's eulogy in her mind and wondering what life would be like without them.

The fact there was always a reasonable explanation and people were almost never running late because of car accidents, serious or otherwise, didn't make any difference to Susan's overactive mind. She still fretted away.

She had read a term for it once - *error thinking*, and while she appreciated the term the book in which she read it was useless in helping with a solution, seriously suggesting the way through was simply not to allow your mind to think like that. Fat chance.

Telling herself she was being silly might work for a few

minutes however the unease would come roaring back, sooner rather than later.

The proliferation of mobile phones made things better, or so she thought at first. In the last five to ten years, the 2000s essentially, everybody had got a phone. Even her parents. Susan began getting text messages from her mum and dad. Brave new world. But if anything mobiles only made her anxiety more acute. Now if she texted somebody and didn't get a response her reaction was far worse. Why weren't they texting her back?

Which led her to Jonathan. She and Jonathan had loose plans to go to the market together this morning. They had agreed to discuss it further last night. Susan had texted Jonathan and got nothing in response, and whereas in the past this would be expected, it was most unusual now. He had never been a reliable texter by any means. However since his problems with his personal life and the amount he had leaned on Susan he clearly felt a sense of owing her. These days he always got back to her texts, at least within the hour.

As such when he didn't respond Susan followed up with four subsequent texts, all of which went unanswered and another two this morning.

With the passing hours Susan's mind arrived at the conclusion Jonathan may have done something stupid. The logical part of her brain told her it was unlikely he had done anything really stupid, certainly not the utterly ridiculous scenarios that leapt into her mind, but that part was overrun by the part that saw nothing except drunken bar fights, drink driving or even, God forbid, self harm. It had been a tough couple of months for him. And now with the alcohol and drinking and who knows what else, what if he was feeling down and it all got too much for him?

With the morning marching on, rather than simply waste her time texting him again and fretting when he didn't respond, Susan made the decision to be proactive.

She drove her sensible little car over to his place. It was difficult to articulate how much she loathed his apartment block. With its exposed staircase and outside corridor leading to the rooms it was like a seedy motel you might see in movies. All that was missing was a buzzing neon sign and a pool with a body floating in it.

She flat out refused to come here at night, certain she would be attacked or robbed or worse. Her body dumped out the back near the bins, eaten by the rats. (There definitely were rats. Susan had spotted them on more than one occasion.) Coming over during the day wasn't a whole lot better than at night however this was important.

The doorbell was sticky and resistant to touch. Looking out over the neighbours' yards it occurred how Susan much she wouldn't miss this view. Jonathan would move soon, as he inevitably did and she would be thrilled never to set foot here ever again.

The second ring of the bell finally roused some movement from within. The door opened revealing a slightly nervous and uncomfortable Jonathan.

"Where have you been? I texted you a bunch of times last night."

Susan made to walk inside as usual, except Jonathan blocked her path. What the heck?

"We were going to go to the market today, remember?"

"Oh, right. The market. Yeah."

Something was definitely up. Susan could feel it before she heard the noise from within the apartment, informing her there was another person was in there. Jonathan's face fell, settling somewhere between abject terror and guilt.

Susan looked past him inside. Kelly sauntered out of his bedroom (his bedroom!) and down the hall wearing nothing but one of Jonathan's shirts. Kelly and Susan's eyes met for the briefest of moments and for the first time in Susan's life her overactive worry had been completely justified. Something dreadful had happened to Jonathan and it was far, far worse than anything she had imagined.

A guttural sound emerged from somewhere deep inside of her. She threw a shocked look at the hapless Jonathan before trying to force her way into the apartment. Had Jonathan not being there to hold her back Susan would very likely have killed Kelly.

Part 1a - The Kelly plan

11

The fresh morning air swirled up under Jonathan's dressing gown, caressing his junk. Had he known he would have worn underwear at least, except he hadn't planned on standing out here, outside his apartment, in the morning breeze.

Susan appeared to have calmed marginally from the manic cyclone of swinging arms and legs that tried to force her way in and attack Kelly, however it might be a ruse. It still seemed wise for Jonathan to remain positioned between her and the door of his apartment, just in case.

The smell of bacon frying wafted from one of his neighbour's apartments, making Jonathan hungry.

"You're an idiot," Susan said eventually.

"You're right. I am."

"Shut up. You're not supposed to agree with me."

"Why not? You're right, I'm an idiot."

"Wrong strategy," Susan said with a snarl.

"What?"

"Trying to pacify me by agreeing with me. You're just making me angrier."

"I'm not just agreeing with you to agree with you. You're right. I'm an idiot. It's cool though."

Susan let out a sigh of total exasperation. "It's not cool, Jonathan. In no possible way can it be cool. Let's go in there and hurt her. Together."

Jonathan chuckled, aware Susan was totally and utterly serious.

"Stop grinning at me. Are you really this much of an idiot?" she said, eyes narrowing to slits. "Don't think you can come and cry on my couch again night after night. Do you not remember? This girl ripped your heart clean out of your chest and showed it to you, while it was still beating."

Jonathan remembered all right. What else had he thought about these last three months?

"I know."

"Of course you know. The question is how can you be dumb enough to be back in there with her now? How can you even go near her? It will happen again."

"Not this time," Jonathan asserted confidently, an evil glint in his eye matching the near-manic grin landing on his face. "You should have seen this dress she was wearing last night."

"Oh, God..."

"She was putting on a show. Using herself, her body, as bait."

There was nothing but disdain in Susan's eyes.

"She was trying to trap me."

"Exactly," Susan tried, but Jonathan ploughed on over the top of her.

"Don't you see?"

Susan didn't see.

"She came to me. She wants something."

"So?"

He grabbed Susan's arm and pulled her a little further from his doorway and prying ears.

"So, I'm going to get her," he whispered, the evil glint flaring in his eye. "Whatever it is, whatever she wants, whatever she is planning, I'm gonna fuck it up. It's payback, baby."

Susan sighed as forcefully as possible. "That's all great, Jonathan. But if you get bitten by a snake, you don't go back for a rematch."

"Yes, you do," he said, gripping her arm a touch too tightly. "You go back with a shovel and decapitate the fucker."

"You got a shovel? Come on. She's trapped in there. Let's decapitate her right now."

"Why would I have a shovel?"

"It doesn't have to be a shovel. Just something blunt and heavy we can beat her to death with."

"No, no, no," he insisted. "We don't need violence. This is far better, slow and painful."

Susan shook her head, refusing to make eye contact.

"I appreciate you looking out for me, but I know what I'm doing."

"Yeah, you're inviting this bitch in to fuck up your life again."

"Suse, I know what I'm doing. Trust me."

"You're an idiot."

WITH SUSAN ON HER WAY, mollified if not convinced, Jonathan headed back inside to find Kelly sitting and waiting for him in his pokey, poor excuse for a kitchen. The morning after, just woken, no makeup and she still looked damn good, especially in his old Bingtang beer shirt, that barely reached the top of her legs. A perverse thrill ran through him. He was going to fuck her up. Fuck her up good. Actually both. Fuck her and fuck her up.

"I don't think your sister likes me very much."

"Susan?" Jonathan said, unable to take his eyes from her legs. "She was talking about coming in here and decapitating you with a shovel."

"I can see that. Thanks for stopping her."

Kelly waited but Jonathan didn't go on. "What did you tell her?"

"About what?"

"About me. Being here."

Jonathan shrugged, doing his best Joe Cool. "I told her you hadn't told me what you want yet."

"Why do you think I want something?"

"Come on, Kelly," Jonathan said, finally meeting her eyes. "I'm not an idiot. You're not here because you love me or because you want me back. You're here because you want something."

Kelly peered through him, weighing it all up in her mind. "All right..." She sat up perfectly straight. Serious now, almost formal. "I heard a great story the other day. Ever go to the club, Loft?"

Jonathan shrugged.

"I met this girl the other day who works there. In the toilets..."

And so Kelly told Jonathan the whole story about the three clubs, the three biggest nights for clubbing, the dealers in the toilets and them being sanctioned. And about Van Damme and the big bag full of unprotected cash ripe for the picking. Almost word for word the story Jonathan would go on to tell Daz and Stevo, except Jonathan claiming it was he who had met the toilet dealer and heard the story first-hand.

And Jonathan ate the story up. As he listened he couldn't believe his luck. This was perfect. Better than perfect. Revenge and a great score all rolled into one. What could be better than that?

12

"So... We're gonna rob this Van Damme guy?"

"That's the plan," Kelly told him. "There are two possible places where we can hit him."

She took Jonathan to a large empty car park. The sun beat down on the black bitumen, giving things in the distance that wavy mirage look. Tall, grey concrete buildings hemmed in the area, accentuating the seclusion.

Jonathan spun slowly in a circle, taking the whole space in.

"This is out back of Clarence's Discount Safari. It's good because it's secluded. That time of a Sunday morning there will be absolutely nobody about."

The possibility played out in Jonathan's mind like a movie. Van Damme walking through here with his bag full of cash and no idea. Jonathan and Kelly sneaking up and robbing him, Bonnie and Clyde style. Über classy. Badass.

"It's also not so good, because it's secluded. There's nowhere to hide. Van Damme could see us coming."

Jonathan nodded, taking one last look around before they jumped back in the car.

They drove the small distance to the second location, the Brown Street T intersection.

"This is our second potential robbery spot. Brown Street T. Easier to blend into the suburban surrounds. The problem might be people."

Getting out of the car Jonathan took everything in. There wasn't a whole lot to see, just an ordinary suburban street.

"Anyone could be walking past," Kelly went on. "Much higher chance of a witness or a hero or both."

See, right here was where Jonathan caused all of his troubles by trying to be too clever by half. Had he been thinking clearly he could have questioned why Van Damme would be walking through the empty car park out the back of Clarence's Discount Safari at all or why he'd be walking here, at the Brown Street T for that matter and how that fitted into the overall narrative about a man carrying a large amount of nightclub takings.

Instead, he was attempting to be smart and position himself two steps ahead of Kelly. So when she said "I say we take him at Clarence's..." he was all like "I agree. The car park. Definitely," when in his head he was thinking *'You have fun by yourself in that big empty car park. By the time you've figured out what's going on, I'll have robbed Van Damme at Brown Street.'*

Yep, no doubt about it, the plan was genius. In Jonathan's head at least.

LIFE WAS FUNNY, Jonathan decided, as he lay flat on his back in bed, Kelly naked on top, gently thrusting. If anyone had suggested to Jonathan he would be in this position with Kelly ever again he would never have believed them. And yet here he was. It was the third time they'd had sex in the last few days, although this time the sex seemed almost incidental, both of them far more engaged in the conversation.

"When are you going to steal the car?" Kelly asked.

Steal the car? He tried to stare back in a noncommittal manner but his face gave him away.

Kelly sighed. "You can't use your car, Jonathan."

"Of course, I know... But why not?"

"What if Van Damme sees your plates?"

Oh yeah. Of course. He nodded.

"I'll hire a car then."

"Fine," she said, struggling to contain the frustration in her voice. "Have you got a fake ID?"

Silence. Kelly sighed again. The façade was unravelling. She had been on her best behaviour with him. Nice and friendly, not busting his balls at all, but with every passing moment the effort to keep that up seemed to be more and more of a challenge.

"Three seconds."

He didn't understand.

"That's how long it will take them to find you if you hire a rental car under your real name." The patience in Kelly's tone stretching to its absolute limit. "You going to be able to do this?"

He scowled back at her.

"You are hardly Mr Cool in a crisis. You get nervous in tense —"

"I'll be fine," he huffed.

Kelly closed her eyes, maintaining the gentle thrusting. The silence of the room swallowed them both. Jonathan stared up at her, wondering where she was. She certainly wasn't here.

"Why me, Kelly?"

Her eyes crept open.

"Why choose me? There must be plenty of other men you could have roped in to do this. Why me?"

Kelly arched her back, facing the ceiling. Her voice came from somewhere above him. "I trust you."

Not silly enough to claim she loved him. Jonathan couldn't help but smirk happily to himself. You trust me, hey? Let's see where that gets you.

ON THE MORNING of the robbery Jonathan sat in the hire car outside Daz and Stevo's flat. It was five to nine and he was nervous but content. He was here in good time. Nothing had gone wrong. Yet. As he waited for Daz and Stevo to emerge he received the text he had been waiting for.

All clear. We're good to go.

Jonathan beamed, very pleased with himself. The thought of Kelly sitting alone, at the car park behind Clarence's Discount Safari tickled him.

"Oh yeah, we're good," he said out loud, with emphasis on the *'we're'*, meaning him and Daz and Stevo, rather than him and Kelly. Not that there was anyone else in the car to hear him. Anyway. It was payback time. Kelly was about to get a nasty surprise.

Feeling most pleased with himself he wrote back:

On my way.

13

Jonathan stood in the middle of the lounge room in the hideout, cat piss and mould assaulting his senses. The two bags of whatever the brown stuff was stared up at him. Mocking him. He shook his head. Sure, he might have been the man with the plan, but he had absolutely no idea what to do now. Probably the best thing would be to stop and think, except panic and confusion were overrunning his brain to the point he didn't seem to be able to think at all.

Daz was speaking and it was about all Jonathan could do to focus on that.

"Wait a minute... Kelly? As in your ex-girlfriend Kelly?"

This only added to Jonathan's confusion.

"The girl who smashed your heart into a million tiny pieces? That Kelly?"

"How do you know about Kelly?"

"Bro, everybody knows about Kelly. You were a borderline shut in for months."

Stevo stood watching, head snapping back and forth between them like he was at a tennis match. "Wait... Who the fuck is Kelly?"

"His ex-girlfriend. Broke his heart bad. Fucked him up real good. The way only a woman can. That's where Jonathan got the story."

Stevo was a few laps behind. "Your ex-girlfriend sells drugs in a nightclub toilet?"

"No," said Jonathan, furrowing his brow so hard it threatened to make a permanent crease. "I never met anyone who worked in the nightclub toilet. Kelly told me the story."

"What the fuck...?" Stevo turned on Jonathan, about ready to blow a gasket.

"None of this matters," said Jonathan, struggling to assert control. "How can it possibly matter where I got the story from?"

"How can it matter?" Stevo snatched up one of the bags full of brown powder. "This look like cash to you, ya dumb fucken cock sucking fuck?"

"Stevo, chill," instructed Daz. Stevo had no intention of chilling. He whipped out a flick knife from his back pocket.

"Don't fucken tell me to chill, Daz. Whether he knows it or not this idiot's been lying to us the whole time."

Daz got up and stood between them, heading him off. "Stevo..."

"The guy's name probably isn't even Van Damme. Nah, this is all fucked up. All bets are off. I say we gut him like a fish."

With Stevo it was probably all show. Still, Jonathan was pleased to have Daz's bulk keeping them separated.

"Stevo, stop being a dickhead, 'ey? Go sit down."

Still surly and pouting Stevo did as Daz instructed, without putting his knife away.

"Okay," Daz said, turning back to Jonathan. "Let's go through this, nice and easy. Just to make sure we've got it all sorted out and everything straight. This bag we stole, it was supposed to be full of cash, yeah?"

"That was my understanding, yes."

"So, where's the money?"

Jonathan struggled to process everything. "I don't know."

"The fuck do you know then, ya fucken —"

Daz quietened Stevo with a simple raise of his hand. "So, given we thought this was going to be full of money and it is actually full of what would appear to be a drug of some description, is it fair to say your ex-girlfriend Kelly lied to you? Would that be an accurate representation of the situation?"

Jonathan nodded haplessly.

"Which leads to the obvious question, what do you reckon we do now?"

"What does he reckon we do now? Daz —"

"Stevo, shut it."

Stevo did, although clearly under protest.

Suddenly very tired, Jonathan pushed the heels of his palms into his eyes. Had he been this tired earlier and simply not realised?

"I don't know. I just... I just need time to think."

"Yeah, yeah," yelled Stevo from the couch. "You go and think, Einstein."

Stumbling towards the door Jonathan paused. He glanced back at Daz.

"Don't do anything until I have thought this through."

Daz nodded.

"I'm serious. Do nothing."

"What would we do? We're just gonna have a choof, 'ey?"

Satisfied, Jonathan turned and trundled out the door.

. . .

Daz watched Jonathan mope off into the other room. Poor little blighter.

"I almost feel sorry for him, 'ey?"

"Feel sorry for him?" said Stevo about ready to explode. "The fuck? I can't believe you're just gonna let him get away with —"

Daz indicated for Stevo to keep his volume down. "He's trying, poor little guy. He's just out of his depth. It's what happens when ordinary blokes try and get involved with crime. They need to leave it to the professionals like us."

"Exactly. I mean, I know he's a mate of yours, but fuck, this guy..."

Daz picked up one of the bags and examined it.

"This shit's outta control and he deserves a good slap just for fuckin' everything up. And friend of yours or not, I'm gonna fucken give it to him if we don't start gettin' some answers soon."

Daz ignored him, more concerned about the bag.

"This isn't like you, Daz. This is soft. You're not soft."

"Hey, what do you think this is?"

"Drugs," Stevo said.

"Course it's drugs, Stevo. What type?"

"Who cares?"

"Oh, Stevo, you just don't see the big picture, do you?"

Stevo screwed up his face, not responding.

"Look at the size of it. There's a lot."

"So?"

"So, I think we've just come in a step too early. Yes, it's not a bag full of cash, but what if someone was about to swap the drugs for a bag of cash?" Daz gave the bag a shake. "We've done the hard work. We stole something of value."

"How the fuck does that help us?"

"I reckon we sell it. Could be worth a bit."

"We dunno what it is, Daz."

"Don't have to. We can blag it."

"You reckon?"

"For sure. We don't have to know what it is. As long as whoever buys it knows, we're sweet."

Stevo ran this over in his head, evidently not coming up with any objections.

"What about fuckstick in the other room?"

"Jonathan? Like you say, he's already fucked everything up pretty majorly to this point. You wanna give him the chance to fuck it all up again?"

Stevo shook his head.

"You call, I'll chop," Daz told him.

AND SO WHILE Stevo got on his phone and Jonathan did God knows what in the other room, Daz did his favourite thing in the whole world, prepared for a smoke. The way Daz saw it they were minutes away from a choof, nothing could be that wrong in the universe.

He laid everything out ready; the scissors, the ciggies, the film canister, the bong and most importantly the dope. The ritual of chopping up relaxed Daz. Made him feel good. Just the knowledge a smoke was imminent was almost as good as the smoke itself.

Taking his time, Daz methodically worked his way through each step. Prepping the bud, roasting the cigarette, cutting it all up. Chopping up was an art form and he was the master. Too bad they didn't have that shit in the Olympics. He would win every gold medal for sure.

As he sliced and diced, Daz could just make out Stevo's muffled voice and footsteps clomping up and down the corridor outside the hideout. He stuck his nose in the film canister. The bud's sweet scent smelled good.

"Yeah... Yep..." Stevo said, sticking his head through the hideout door. "Hey, Daz." He placed his hand over the receiver. "You ever hear of The Sharks?"

"Football team?"

"Nah," Stevo said. "Dealers."

Daz shook his head. Stevo shrugged and disappeared again. Yep, this was gonna be a good smoke.

14

The warehouse appeared to be as big as it was dark. Saxon doubled back and rechecked the address, even though he knew this was the right place. Why the fuck would she want to meet here? And yet, he knew immediately. Because it was Emily.

Saxon had been selling drugs for some time now, about ten years, since school and he had seen all types of unexpected buyers in that time. Teachers at his old school. Parents of the kids. The odd cop. But no one was quite as unusual as Emily.

These days uni students were his bread and butter and for a dealer like Saxon the ideal customers. Sure, the blokes always acted tough, thinking that was the way to go, while the girls were all flirty and touchy-feely, like they could seduce the drugs out of him, but they all bought and almost always came back for more.

People go to uni to experiment and spread their wings, that was the whole point of it. If you were going to try five pills in one night and see where that got you, university was the time and place. And thanks to the explosion in

Melbourne's suburban universities, there was an endless supply of potential customers with disposable income and the desire to experiment with getting fucked up.

Like lots of marketing, the key to shifting drugs was networking and not looking as though you were trying to sell anything at all. In his early 20s, Saxon made a plausible uni student. All he had to do was hang about a few O Week activities and make a few friends and the gear sold itself. Soon you become the go-to guy if anyone needed anything. He had a fake student card and number although he never needed it. Saxon found sports gatherings the best - the rowing clubs and footy clubs and pretty much anything to do with Uni Games.

Recently Randall had suggested Saxon expand and set up business at a second campus. And why not? Sure it made for some busier times getting things going during Orientation Week but once he was set it should mean double the business.

As such Saxon was hanging around his fourth pub night in two days when he met Emily. Emily was a different beast entirely to anything Saxon had dealt with before. Short with thick glasses and hair that looked as though she may have cut it herself, Saxon's first impression was Emily was a grade A dork. So when she first approached him, sidling up and whispered in the least subtle way possible "I'd like to buy some drugs, please." Saxon's jaw just about hit the floor.

"You sell drugs, don't you?"

"Maybe…" he responded, cautiously on his guard. It felt like a trick. "You're not wearing a wire, are you?"

"I don't think so," she said, and she honest to God looked herself over as if to see if she was or not.

"You don't need to check," Saxon told her. "I think you would know."

"I think I would too. In that case, some drugs please," she said with an enormous smile.

Saxon couldn't help but smile back, although he was smiling at her, not with her. "What drugs would you like?" He was tempted to add 'young lady' except how old was Emily? Mid-thirties maybe? What was she doing hanging around an O Week pub night? Then again, she wasn't alone, with a wide variety of ages frequenting the venue. Maybe only fifty percent of the people around were your typical uni students.

"What drugs would I like? Ooh, good question." Like this had never even occurred to her. "What types do you have? I've always liked the sound of party pills. They sound like fun." And with that, she did the dorkiest dance Saxon had ever seen.

She glanced about. "I have the money. Where should we do this?"

"Just here is fine. As long as we're discrete."

Disappointment filled Emily's face. "Oh, I thought we would go out to a seedy laneway or something. I guess this is okay."

Emily ended up buying five pills right then. When she sought him out for ten more a few days later he decided a few questions were in order.

"You know I'm a dealer, don't you, Emily?"

"Derr. How else would I be buying drugs off you?"

"It is just you seemed to get rid of the previous lot awful quickly, so I can only assume you didn't take them all yourself. Makes me think you are on-selling them."

"Maybe. Could be I am buying them off you to get them off the street."

Saxon smiled. "Could be. I didn't think of that. Are you?"

"No."

"What the fuck do I care? Look, I am not trying to bust your balls. All I'm saying is I think there is potential here. If you have a steady line of buyers, I am happy to sell you whatever the fuck you like."

"Okay then," Emily said, rubbing her hands together. "Let's talk bulk,"

Emily was like a revelation. Saxon tended to focus on the cool kids and sporty types, but she possibly had access to an entirely previously untapped market. Dorks. And why not? Dorks need drugs too. Plus haggling didn't appear her strong suit. She seemed content paying way over what she should be for this size deal. It was all upside.

The only issue was Saxon foolishly let Emily suggest a place they should meet. Saxon wasn't one for making house calls, however in a moment of weakness he decided to make an exception for Emily given her potential. Which led Saxon here, to the warehouse. At a guess she was trying for somewhere appropriately atmospheric.

DISUSED AND BOARDED UP, there was no apparent front door. With a little searching Saxon managed to find his way in. The old warehouse had been used to manufacture something back in the day but had been dormant for years, panels missing from the roof, holes punched in the graffiti-covered walls.

"Hello?"

Several rooms in Saxon finally found Emily waiting at a table with her male equivalent.

"Here you are," Saxon said.

"Hi, Saxon," Emily said enthusiastically. "Thanks for coming. Isn't this the perfect place for a drug deal? Oh, this is Ian."

"Hi," said Ian with equal amounts of enthusiasm, an outstretched hand lunging at Saxon. Tall and rake lean, Ian could probably spot an error in your computer coding at ten paces all while giving you an in-depth history of Dungeons & Dragons, Saxon guessed. He might not have encountered many girls like Emily in his life, but he had met plenty of blokes like Ian. Just not generally in his line of work.

"You her protection?" Saxon asked, looking Ian up and down and rejecting his shake.

"I'm... her brother," Ian stammered, somewhat uncertainly.

"You here to look after her?"

"We look after each other," Emily told Saxon.

Saxon shook his head. "Emily, I'm not planning to fuck ya, but if I was, he wouldn't be much use."

A look of confusion covered Emily's face. "My brother wouldn't be much use if you were planning to fuck me?"

"Physically..." Ian said, snarling like a tiger, his fingers curled into claws. "Grrr." Next to Emily's party pills dance it was about the most pathetic display Saxon had ever witnessed.

"I'm not planning to fuck ya..." he muttered under his breath.

Emily glanced between the two of them. "No, sorry, I'm still lost. Why are we talking about you having sex with me?"

"No, fuck you as in rip you off... Never mind."

Emily rolled forward on the balls of her feet and whispered like an excited schoolgirl. "Did you bring the drugs?"

Saxon gave the two of them his best death stare and pulled a brown paper bag out from the back of his pants, tossing it on the nearby table.

"For future reference, I don't make fucken house calls either."

"Good thing this isn't a house," suggested Ian, goofily laughing at his own inane joke as he grabbed the bag. He opened it and stuck his nose inside.

"Is this good gear? Primo stuff?"

The words sounded all wrong coming out of his dorky mouth.

"Shit," Emily corrected him. "I think you say shit. Primo shit."

"Primo shit," Ian repeated with a nod. "Well, I guess I'm done for the day. I might as well go home." He raised his eyebrows at Saxon expectantly. "You know, they say you learn something new every day? I may as well go to bed."

Emily chuckled. God, these two. Saxon expected them to start reciting 'The Holy Grail' any second now.

"Yes, that's good gear. Good as your gonna get anyway." Saxon turned to Emily. "It's quite a bit. You sure you can move all that?"

"Oh, certainly. Don't worry about us." She tried to take the bag but Ian wouldn't give it to her. He held it over her head, out of her reach.

"Ian," she whined. "Not fair. I wanna hold it. Ian. Give it."

She poked him in the ribs causing him to titter. He handed over the bag.

"All right. We'll be off," Emily said. "Good to see you again."

Saxon couldn't quite believe what he was witnessing, watching the pair of them totter off together.

"Oi…"

Ian and Emily stopped and turned back.

"You forgetting something?"

It took them a second, and then Ian chuckled. "Birdbrain! You forgot to pay."

Ian and Emily appeared to find this far more amusing than Saxon did.

"Whoops. Pay the man, Ian."

"I don't have the money," Ian replied with a straight face.

"Ian, this is no time for silly buggers. Give the man his money."

"Ems, I don't have it. Seriously."

"Well, I haven't got it."

Saxon took a step towards them. "See, I can't tell if you're fucking around and you think this is funny. Some kind of dork humour."

He casually pulled out a large knife. "But if one of you doesn't produce my fucken money right now, I will fuck you up."

Emily raised herself so she was standing perfectly straight. It didn't make much difference. She was still tiny. At first Saxon thought his threat was getting through to her. The giggling gone, Ian and Emily suddenly very serious.

"Now, now... There is no need for profanities."

Saxon took a step towards them, brandishing his knife. "You think I'm playing, shitbrain?"

"Don't talk to my brother like that, Saxon," said Emily. "We've all been introduced. If you wish to address us, use our proper names. Ian and Emily —"

Saxon lurched forward menacingly. "You think I give a fuck —"

Ian and Emily didn't take a backward step. "Ian and Emily Shark."

The words hung in the air, taking Saxon a moment or two to process. He stopped dead in his tracks. The knife clattered loudly to the floor as Saxon took off, running for all he was worth.

The warehouse was too damn dark. Where the hell was the exit? Fear and panic impeded any logical sense of thought.

Just run. Get out. He could think later.

15

I an and Emily stayed where they stood, side by side, no need to move. They could hear Saxon's footsteps echoing about the warehouse. Could footsteps sound terrified? If they could his certainly did.

"He seems fun," Ian commented.

"Hmmm," said Emily.

They smiled pleasantly at one another. Moving as slowly and as stealthily as he could manage Ian leaned towards Emily and poked her in the ribs. Emily squealed.

"Ian!"

She did her best to poke him back.

"It isn't fair. You've got those long, lanky arms." She gave poking him back a good go anyway. After a few moments they composed themselves. She would get him back later, when he least expected it.

Soon Saxon returned, although not of his own volition. He was carried by Nuke. Saxon wasn't a small guy by any means, but Nuke had absolutely no difficulty carrying him, cradling Saxon in his arms like a baby.

Behind them, Three shuffled in.

Now Three, Three was a big boy. Muscles on muscles. Like pantyhose stuffed full of peanuts. That type of look. But there was something far scarier about Nuke.

Nuke dumped Saxon at the feet of Ian and Emily and the brother-sister combination grinned down at him. Not happy grins, their faces contorted into wild, manic expressions.

SAXON WAS BEGINNING to have second thoughts. Thus far he had managed to keep his mouth shut. He hadn't said a thing when they interrogated him. He hadn't said a thing as they taped his hands to the old chair with electrical tape or when they bound his legs together. And he hadn't said a thing as they taped his mouth shut. Now, of course, he couldn't.

He was being loyal. To Randall. Although if he was completely honest loyalty was only one factor. A big part of his silence was also fear. Fear of what came next. The information they wanted was all he had. Once he told them what they wanted to know he would be of no use to them and it scared him what they would do then.

And part of it was just pure shock. Shock at the turn of events that made any potential words swell up and catch in his throat, refusing to come out.

Now, with Ian standing there, staring at him bug-eyed, flanked by the menacing bulk of Three on one side and Nuke on the other Saxon wondered if it would have been easier just to tell them everything and take his chances.

He squirmed in his seat, although the electrical tape meant he really couldn't move much except his head. The tape was going to hurt when it got ripped off and yet that was the least of his problems. His chair was sitting on clear plastic drop sheets. The type you might put down when you don't want to make a mess. The only thing likely to make a mess was Saxon and that was a terrifying thought.

What were they waiting for? The three of them had been standing there staring at him for ages.

"Sorry, sorry," Emily said, tottering in, lugging an old-fashioned, black leather doctor's bag. The bag made a heavy crunch as she dropped to the floor a little to the right of where Ian and Nuke and Three were standing.

Emily sat cross-legged on the concrete behind the bag. Looking at Saxon she rubbed her hands together with unbridled glee before opening the deceptively large bag.

"Do you like living here? In Melbourne? I don't mind it..." Ian told Saxon.

The first item out of Emily's bag was a large potato peeler.

"Hey," Ian said, trying to regain Saxon's attention. "I asked you a question."

"Oh, Ian, don't be so mean," said Emily halfway between a scold and a snigger. "You know he can't answer."

Ian tittered, amused by his own joke. "I know. I know. Sorry. Anyway, living here. People say it's a big city and it is. It's certainly very..." He clicked his fingers, trying to think of the word. "Very..."

"Sprawling," said Emily, holding up the potato peeler up close to her face, closing one eye, looking from the peeler to Saxon.

"Sprawling. It sprawls all right. But in other ways, the city is quite small," Ian went on.

Poor Saxon didn't know where to look, his eyes wide and terrified, flashed between Ian and Emily.

"For example, in the business we are in you can barely step one way or the other without treading on someone's toes."

Emily removed a small felt bag from the larger bag. What the fuck was that? The felt bag darted about in her hand. There was something alive inside the felt bag, moving about. Emily raised her eyebrows and nodded at Saxon, a look of excited anticipation on her face. Saxon felt increasingly sick. What else she could possibly pull out of her bag of tricks?

"Now, you've been a very silly fellow, Saxon," Ian went on. "A very silly fellow."

"He has just been loyal, Ian," Emily interjected. "Loyalty is a very commendable trait."

"It is," Ian agreed. "Loyalty is a rare commodity. But in this case it has done Saxon a great deal more harm than good."

Emily removed a thin coil of wire from the bag, making a disgusted face.

"In life there are chances," Ian went on. "Moments you must seize. Have you heard that expression '*Carpe Diem*'? It's French."

"Latin," Emily corrected, not realising Ian was joking.

Ian tittered, amusing himself. "It means '*seize the day*'. When you have these moments of opportunity, you must take them. Unfortunately, you missed yours. We gave you one such opportunity to talk and you didn't."

Next out of Emily's bag were a couple of lemons. Her mouth formed a silent 'Oooh'.

"Now we find ourselves in somewhat of a conflicting position," Ian said. "Cos, Nuke here and Ems, they don't want you to talk. See, these two enjoy making life uncomfortable for people."

"Oh, please," said Emily. "You can't compare me to Nuke. It's just a hobby for me. He's the pro."

Saxon's eyes found Nuke and Three. The two of them

hadn't moved, a silent, menacing presence behind Ian. Three glowered at Saxon. Nuke though didn't appear to be paying attention.

"You are getting pretty good yourself, Ems."

She unfurled a role of Japanese chef's knives. "I'm trying. I'm learning. Nuke is sensei. I am merely his student."

The steel handled knives looked brutal. Emily pushed the tip of her finger down on the razor-sharp point of one.

Ian returned his focus to Saxon. "Very, very soon you are going to be a whole world of pain, my friend. Worse than anything you could have ever possibly imagined."

The last item out of Emily's bag was a car battery and jumper leads. She placed them on the floor with the rest of the items, the torture devices forming a semicircle around her. Saxon's eyes couldn't move from Emily's assortment of items, puzzling over which would be used and for what.

"And as the minutes, hours, even days drag by you are gonna wish you had talked."

Saxon stared back. His mouth would have been agape were it not taped shut. If their objective was to scare him, mission accomplished. He felt a terror light years beyond anything he had previously experienced in his life.

"About your only hope is that Nuke and Ems get bored somehow and maybe you get another chance to talk."

Oh God, they didn't have to do this. Saxon contemplated trying to scream through the gag. Rocking back and forth in the seat urgently, letting them know he was ready to talk. Right now. Except he didn't. He just sat there, staring.

Emily bounced over to join her brother.

"But until then get ready, because you are about to have a very long, very bad day."

An unexpected lull took over the room.

Nothing happened.

One by one Three then Emily then Ian glanced over at Nuke. Nuke however was away with the fairies.

"Nuke?" Ian said. "Nuke."

The distracted Nuke snapped out of his daydream, surprised to discover everyone looking at him.

"Oh, yep? Sorry."

Ian extended out a hand towards their guest. "It's time."

"Right," said Nuke, taking a step forward.

Without a moment's hesitation he pulled out his revolver and blasted. The unexpected shot reverberated around the empty warehouse. The force of the impact sent Saxon flying backwards.

Saxon and his chair landed heavily on the plastic sheeting behind.

Silence quickly asserted its control over the room contrasting the blast of the revolver. With the quiet came a sense of surprise and shock.

"I like the ... vigour," Ian said eventually. "But what happens now?"

Three shook his head. Nuke wasn't following.

"We're supposed to be getting him to talk," Emily said. "How is he supposed to talk now?"

"Oh, right," Nuke said. "Sorry."

Emily skipped over and examined Saxon's body.

"I think you had better clean this up quickly, Nuke. It would be preferable if he didn't die here."

"Okay," Nuke nodded. "Three —"

"You take this one, Nuke. Ian and I need to have a chat to Three."

16

T hree could feel a headache coming on. A nasty one, right behind his eyes.

At this moment he had two possible options and neither was terribly appealing. Ian and Emily asking to talk to him without Nuke was highly unusual. It wasn't how things worked. He had no desire to be stuck in a small room with them. At the same time, he didn't really want to be cleaning up Saxon's mess with Nuke either.

Three knew Nuke shooting Saxon was his fault. At least partially. He could have pre-empted it. He had noticed, that was the thing. He had seen that Nuke looked distracted and had thought nothing of it. What should he have done? Whacked him? Told him to pay attention? Of course, he would have done something if it had occurred to him Nuke would shoot Saxon like that.

He pressed a finger into his eye, trying to push the pain away. Despite the turn of events Ian and Emily maintained their usual happy, smiley demeanours.

"Goodness," Ian said. "That was dramatic."

Three nodded, on guard. He didn't know The Sharks exact age, figuring them to be late thirties or early forties. That only made them ten to fifteen years older than him, and yet meetings like this always felt like getting in trouble. Being hauled in to see a schoolteacher or an angry parent or something.

"Is everything okay with Nuke?" Emily asked. "He seems a little distracted."

"We can't have Nuke distracted. It gets messy."

"Messy is bad. We can't do messy."

Three took a moment, in no hurry. "Nuke is working through a few things at the moment, but it's cool." He paused, choosing his words carefully. "Nuke is Nuke. You can't have a lion as a pet then complain when he bites someone."

"Really? Then what are you for?"

"Gee, thanks."

"Awww" Emily said, accompanying it with a patronising rub of Three's arms.

"Come on, Three. Don't be like that," Ian said. "We've all got our jobs to do. You have made a career of sticking close to Nuke. You're like a package deal."

"A two-fa."

"A team. The dynamic duo. Can't have one without the other. He's a lion, you're the lion tamer."

"No Nuke," Emily said, "you are just a funny looking dude with a whip and a chair."

"Great," Three said.

"You're looking at this all wrong," said Ian. "You're looking at this like it's a bad thing when it's not. We've all got our roles to play. Get his focus back, everyone is happy."

"But," Emily said, "things remain messy, we have to start

thinking about making some changes. Change isn't good. For anyone."

Yep, no doubt about it. The headache Three could feel coming on wasn't going anywhere anytime soon.

Part 2 - Nuke's Woes

17

The warehouse bathroom was in keeping with the rest of the space - rundown and barely functional. There was running water though, enabling Nuke to wash Saxon's blood off his hands and arms.

Three opened the door and stared at him in the mirror with a look of resigned disappointment.

"I know, I know. I should have counted to five."

Nuke and Three were working on a new tactic to help Nuke rein in his temper. On those occasions when his anger threatened to get the better of him Three suggested he count to five in his head, as a form of impulse control. If after the count he still wanted to act so be it, but the idea was to blunt some of Nuke's more impulsive actions. Give him at least a little control, so he wasn't so much a slave to his emotions. It is hard to remember these things in the moment though and so Three had suggested Nuke think of him.

"Think of me and count to five." That was the general idea anyway.

"Yeah, I don't know how much counting would have

helped in this situation," Three told him. "This was more to do with you not paying attention."

"You're probably right," Nuke said, going back to scrubbing that pesky blood from his knuckles.

THE CANARY YELLOW Mustang piloted its way through the quiet industrial streets with Three at the wheel and Nuke in the passenger seat, staring out the window.

"You've gotta get your head back in the game." No response. Three glanced over. "Nuke?"

He was miles away. Again.

"You've gotta stop obsessing over it. You're doing your head in. You're just going through a thing. A rough patch. It happens."

Nuke shook his head sadly. "It's more than that."

The apartment building came into view, pressing against the horizon. Nuke tried to spot the twelfth floor. She was up there somewhere. His beautiful wife, Wanda. Probably in the kitchen cooking. She was and always had been a strikingly beautiful woman. As beautiful today as when Nuke first laid eyes on her. Suited by age and maturity unlike so many other older women. Slim and elegant.

Nuke would be with her in ten minutes and experience told him exactly how things would play out.

He would enter and watch her, surrounded by all her things, all the pricey designer labels he had bought for her. All the hideously ugly and hideously expensive modern art she liked covering the walls. And for a moment, maybe two, Nuke would be able to watch her moving about their apartment, and pretend she was still the woman he married. Until she noticed he was there. And then her body language would change completely. She would stiffen up in the shoulders, all rigid and tense.

He would say *'Hi'* and maybe go to the fridge and grab a beer, while she pointedly ignored him. Perhaps he would even hang about and lean against a cupboard and take a swig and hope that they would be able to talk, like they used to, except it wouldn't work. A horrible tension would clog the air, infecting them both. He would watch her for a while, wanting to say something, but never ever sure what to say. Not anymore. Not like before, when conversation and laughter flowed freely between them.

Eventually, he might try something basic like *'Are you okay?'* and she would nod, except it would be the most unconvincing nod ever seen. And she would stride out leaving Nuke by himself and sad and lonely. Leave him wondering what it was he had done and what it is he had to do.

"It's not supposed to be this way," Nuke told Three as he eased the car to a stop at a red light.

"She loves you, man. She does," Three told him reassuringly.

"Maybe once..." He stared at the building off in the distance. "Hey, let's not do this. Let's go do something."

"Like what?"

"Dunno," Nuke said. "Get a drink or something."

18

"Come on," Nuke scolded. "Keep up."

"I am, I am. I'm drinking."

In truth Three wasn't. He was only pretending. He had accompanied Nuke to the bar, not to drink, but as a mate.

Recently Three was experimenting with a new diet. Or eating pattern more than diet. It seemed pretty good so far. He could eat whatever he wanted within a specific eating window. The window closed quite early, so he was having nothing but water after four P.M. and that made drinking even harder.

Three wasn't much of a drinker anyway. He wasn't one of those *your body is a temple* type guys, however he was careful about what he put in his system and alcohol was simply empty calories. He was quite happy to have a drink on special occasions. Nuke drowning his sorrows on a Wednesday evening was neither special nor an occasion.

Besides, the plan was to hit the gym at four thirty A.M. whatever, so the way he saw things he could either hit the gym feeling okay or hit the gym in a self-induced state of feeling like shit. All of these factors combined meant overindulging here now with Nuke was in no way worth it. There was no saying any of that to Nuke though. In any case, what Nuke really needed was a sympathetic ear, not a drinking buddy, whether he knew it or not.

"I'm a good person, aren't I?" The slightest of slurs creeping into Nuke's words.

"Ummm..."

Nuke swung around to face his partner. "You don't think I'm a good person?"

"No, I mean, yes and no," said Three, treading carefully. Nuke's grim stare compelled him to clarify. "That dealer today, Saxon..."

"Yeah, what about him?"

"I'm not sure who would agree you're a good person. If, you know, he was still with us."

Nuke waved Three off dismissively. "Who cares? I'm not talking about some piece of shit drug dealer. Let me rephrase." He took another stiff drink. "I'm a catch."

He signalled the bartender for a refill.

"A catch?"

"I'm a good husband."

"I think so," said Three. "From what I see you are, sure."

"My point is I'm not some fucken Tony Soprano. Like tonight, we're here at a bar, we're not at some strip club or massage parlour or whore house, are we?"

"Why did he kill Christopher? I never understood that. Adriana, I get..."

"What?"

"Tony. You remember, he killed his nephew that time —"

"No..." said Nuke abruptly, sticking his hand in Three's face and swaying ever so slightly on his stool. "You're missing my point. What I'm saying is you see all these gangsters in movies and TV and whatever they've all got mistresses and girlfriends and they're sleeping with strippers. I haven't slept with anyone since I've been with Wanda."

Nuke swung the hand about wildly to emphasise his point, the drink exaggerating the movement.

"Anyone."

"Yes, I know. You're very —"

"No, wait. What's her name blew me a few times, but that was before Wan and I were engaged, I think... Wasn't it? Before we were married certainly. Who cares. I haven't touched anyone since we've been married. Absolutely." He turned on Three again. "So, what the fuck?"

Three could do little more than shrug. They were entering dangerous territory.

"I'm a catch. She gets to live in that amazing apartment, with million dollar views."

"It is a great apartment."

"Hasn't had to work a day in her life. Gets to buy whatever the fuck she wants whenever she wants. Women would kill for what she's got. I'm not some fuck who has completely let themselves go. I'm in shape. I'm mean, I'm not you, but I'm fit. I'm a good-looking guy."

He glanced at Three for some kind of affirmation.

"Sure you are," Three responded diplomatically, wondering how much of this he would remember come tomorrow. "If I was a hot chick, I would totally be into you."

" 'xactly."

While Nuke disappeared into his head, Three checked the room for potential problems. Nuke wasn't always the best drunk, particularly in this frame of mind. Alcohol didn't mix too well with his somewhat combustible temper. He wasn't likely to start anything but he sure as shit would finish it. All it would take would be someone to bump into him or get a little mouthy. Fortunately the place was reasonably quiet tonight.

"Why not an ugly chick?" Nuke asked.

"Why not a what?"

"You said you'd be into me if you were a hot chick. What if you were ugly?"

"You think I'd be an ugly woman?"

"The fuck do I know? Maybe. You're fucken all muscle now. If you were like that as a chick..."

Three shook his head gently. "Nothing wrong with a woman who is in shape."

"Depends what shape. Those body building chicks, who are all muscle. That's not a good look. If you looked like that you'd be an ugly chick. But answer my question."

Even considering it made Three's head throb. "Yeah, I guess I would be into you if I was an ugly chick. I never really thought about it."

He snuck a quick glance at his watch. How long was this going to go on for? Maybe he could push the gym until five A.M. tomorrow.

"Good-looking chick, ugly chick, doesn't matter to me. I don't wanna be sexist.... No, Looks... Looks-ist."

"No, you don't want to be looks-ist," Three agreed. A thought struck him. Maybe there was something here. Maybe Nuke's sexual frustration was the issue. Maybe getting him a good fuck would solve all their problems.

"I just want her to be happy, you know?"

"Sorry?"

"Wanda. I just want her to be happy. That's all I want. All I've ever wanted."

19

The wind blew at Nuke's face. Enough to feel it, yet not enough to be annoying. Crisp air, straight off the bay.

Reclining in his chair Nuke rotated his large black mug slightly in a clockwise direction. Not for any reason. Merely something to occupy his hands. The coffee was as tasty as always. Somehow it seemed tastier from these mugs at his outdoor table than it ever did takeaway.

This was a new Sunday routine which had been evolving over the past few months. One Sunday they had run out of coffee at home and Nuke had happened upon Byron's by the Bay.

Byron's wasn't the sort of place he would usually frequent, too hip and trendy, however the coffee was delicious. Nuke began coming more and more, switching from a takeaway coffee to grabbing an outside table and staring at the sea across the road. Something about the waves rolling in relaxed him. Byron's seemed to be one of the few places he could go and not think. Not think about work or Wanda or The Sharks. Not think about any of it.

And so he had developed this nice Sunday ritual of

going and sitting and not thinking about anything, until life called him back, which it generally did by his second coffee. The phone would ring and that would be that. However the twenty minutes, half an hour or sometimes even an hour of nothing before that was most pleasant.

On this Sunday Nuke didn't even make it through his first coffee before life intervened. Unusually it wasn't the phone which took him away on this occasion. Nuke glanced up and spotted a couple of men approaching from the street. He didn't have to see any badges to know who they were. Not specifically but the general occupation. They flashed the badges anyway.

Nuke sighed but didn't make a scene. What was the point?

THE TWO MEN escorted Nuke to a surveillance van parked close by. In another life the large van had been some kind of campervan, now it had all been repurposed.

There was a table in the middle which three of them sat around. Nuke on one side, with the other two opposite. Two policeman or plainclothes detectives or something. What did it matter? Arsehole cops of some sort.

Behind them sat another two tech guys, operating the equipment. The equipment was just crazy. The van was full of screens and gear and wires running every which way.

"Hey, which of you two unlucky fucks has the job of working out what all these wires do? What a nightmare," he said, addressing the two tech guys up the back. "I didn't even set up the TV and DVD player at my place. Easier to pay someone to get it done properly. Am I right?"

The two sitting at the back pointedly ignored him. It was fun fucking with them like this. Cops always had a plan of attack. They would have themselves all organised with one guy who was meant to do all the talking. No way the tech guys were supposed to say anything.

Right on cue one of the cops at the table sitting opposite Nuke opened his mouth.

"You wanna talk, you talk to me. I'm Agent Harris." A toothpick hung from Harris' lip. He looked too handsome to be a cop. "This is Detective Hunt."

Hunt, the other cop at the table, a big bruiser of a guy, said nothing. He passed Nuke a card.

In one motion Nuke took the card and flicked it away flippantly unconcerned. The card span through the air, hitting the metal wall of the van and falling to the floor.

"So, let me guess, you don't speak?" Nuke asked Hunt. "Is that your schtick? He does all the talking, you just sit there looking scary."

Cops always had a shtick of some sort.

"Am I supposed to be scared of you? You're a pretty big guy. Most people probably would be, wouldn't they?"

Hunt didn't respond to his goading.

"Hey, can I ask you something?" Harris doing his best to get Nuke's attention away from Hunt. "Do your eyes hurt?"

"What?"

"Your eyes. Do they hurt? I reckon my eyes would hurt if I was up to my eyeballs in as much shit as you."

Nuke stared back impassively.

"See, we know all about what you're up to, all your shit. Every last tiny piece of bullshit, *Nuke*."

He emphasised Nuke's name with ridicule. Nuke didn't react. Harris shook his head and elbowed Hunt.

"Look at this fucken guy. Tough guy. Flip the situation, I am there, you're here," Harris widened his eyes. "I'd be shitting myself. But not you. Mr Cool. Mr Lucky."

Nuke sat stony-faced, unsure where this was headed.

"Mr Lucky. You are lucky. But luck's a fickle river. Sooner or later she always runs dry. You know it and I know it, amigo."

Nuke sniggered. "They teaching poetry in detective school now?" He knew it was probably best to keep his mouth shut and yet he was unable to resist. Something about dealing with dickhead cops. They brought out the smartarse in him.

"Luck's a fickle river? That's very pretty. 'cept you keep talking like this you're gonna have to lend me a thesaurus so I can keep up."

As Harris studied Nuke, Hunt leaned over and whispered something in his ear. Harris nodded, taking his time, his eyes never leaving Nuke.

"Here's what we are prepared to do for you, Nuke. Total immunity from all of your past crimes. Your numerous sins and offences. The slate wiped clean, just like that, if you come downtown with us right now. You help us, we absolve you of all your sins. Pretty sweet deal. What do you say?"

Nuke fixed his face with the most ponderous expression he could manage, taking his time. Eventually he mimed casting out a rod and reeling in a fish.

"You like fishing, Agent Harris?"

The cops glanced at one another, uncertain.

"No? Cos that's what this is, a fishing expedition and a pretty shit one at that." He treated them to a faint smile. "Honestly, this is about the worst shakedown I've ever seen. You think I don't know if you two halfwits actually had anything on me, even the smallest little thing, you would bring me in, slap me around, use it as leverage. You think this is my first dance?"

Harris maintained his steely stare, while Hunt appeared vaguely uncomfortable.

"This is pathetic," Nuke went on. "A desperate shot in the dark. You're embarrassing yourselves. You know it and I know it, amigo."

He stood, leaning on the table with both hands. "So thank you very much for your kind offer but I am afraid I am going to have to tell you to get fucked."

The cops stared back, nothing to say.

Nuke strolled from the van. He didn't expect to be challenged although he couldn't be sure with these jokers. They clearly had no idea what they were doing.

As he ambled down the street he wondered where they had come from. The Sharks had some pretty high level contacts in the force, who generally kept them out of trouble. But dealing with law enforcement agencies was like an endless game of Whack-a-Mole. Between all the different agencies and departments and task forces and agents and detectives and regular police, it was impossible to keep all of them in check.

Still, whoever these guys were, they didn't seem too much of a threat.

20

Nuke woke from restless sleep and a bad dream. Someone was trying to tell him something important. Someone or something. It was right there, except he couldn't quite grasp it. Who was trying to tell him what? A giant bird maybe? What could a giant bird have to say that was so important? The dream had been quite vivid, only to slip away the moment he awoke, like trying to grasp water in your hands, leaving a general unsettledness in its wake.

He swung his legs off the edge of their large bed.

The uneasy sensation remained, momentarily obscuring the fact something was wrong. Different.

No Wanda. He was alone.

"Wanda?"

Shuffling out of the bedroom in his boxer shorts Nuke found his wife at the dining room table. She was texting someone, her face lit by the phone screen's pale glow. Completely focused on what she was doing. He watched her and wondered. Who could she be texting at this time of night?

"Wanda?"

His voice startled her, causing her to drop the phone which clattered noisily onto the wooden table. It only took Wanda a fraction of a second to regain control and to glare accusingly at Nuke, like he had done something wrong, giving her a fright like that. But in that moment, as the phone dropped from her hands, he saw it. A look of guilt. A look that said he had caught her doing something.

"What are you —?"

"I couldn't sleep," she said, a harsh edge in her voice to match the *don't fuck with me* look on her face. It was too late though. He knew what he had seen. Anger raged in Nuke like a sea of boiling lava. But he didn't need to count to five. This was a different type of fury.

"If she's playing a game then she's a fucken hypocritic."

"Hypocrite?"

"Whatever."

Nuke was sitting behind the wheel of his black Jaguar, with Three in the passenger seat. They were parked in an unassuming street, not quite city, yet not suburbia either. Office buildings and shops on both sides of the roads. It was relatively early, with a steady stream of people on both sides of the road heading to work. As usual, Nuke wasn't quite as focused as he should have been on the task at hand.

"Whenever she catches me on the Xbox she gives me that look like she's walked in on me wanking over porn."

Three focused on the passing foot traffic. "You're missing my point. Games are just one of a number of possibilities."

"That she was doing, on her phone, in the middle of the night."

"Phones do a lot."

"What's that supposed to mean?"

Just then a scruffy looking kid appeared, shuffling down the street. Kid meant in the loosest sense of the word. He was early twenties, clutching a can of Red Bull and looking a little worse for wear. The fact his suit was about two sizes too big for him merely exaggerating that boy in a suit appearance.

"Hey," Three said. "There's Tom."

They gazed out at their target.

"He's gonna run, isn't he? Why do they always run? We've found him once, we can find him again." Three shook his head. "They must know we will catch up with them eventually and if they run they will just piss us off. I guess it's human nature."

Silence was his only reply.

"Nuke?"

"Yeah?"

"Jesus... Focus, Nuke." He clicked his fingers in Nuke's face.

"What? I'm focused."

Yeah, like shit you are, Three thought. With a slight nod Three got out and Nuke drove away.

THE ANGRY RAP music blaring from Tom's headphones was audible around the block. Foolishly loud. It had to be hurting his ears, if not now then down the line. Three stepped directly in the young guy's path. It took Tom a second to notice. He froze, assessing his options. Then he ran.

Actually, seeing Tom up close like this Three knew well why he ran. Trying to put himself in someone like Tom's shoes it must be scary to see a person like Three coming at you, someone who could break you in half with one hand.

Not that Three had ever experienced this sort of fear himself. He was used to being the biggest. When he was thirteen the old man took him aside and told him he was always going to be big but he had a choice. He could be big by design or big by default. As in muscular or fat. Three went for muscular and started lifting weights from that day forward. The old man, big himself, taught him how, initially supportive but growing increasingly bitter as age dragged him down while Three went from strength to strength. Literally.

Tom bolted into an office. Whether it was his office or just an office didn't really matter to Three. He doubted a little shit like Tom would have too many friends anyway. No one would make a scene.

Out front near the entrance a secretary sat at an island desk, isolated from the rest of the office. Tom dashed straight past without a word, leaving her looking somewhat bewildered. Three followed suit, giving the secretary an expansive smile, which only confused matters further.

As they hit the main part of the office Three was confident this wouldn't take long. He had chased down plenty of people in his time, and he could tell this guy wouldn't give him much trouble. The big advantage he had was their mindsets. While Tom darted between desks, shoving chairs out of his way in a wild, terrified panic, Three followed with a detached but determined calm. He also had physical prowess on his side. A misconception about Three (and most big guys) was the assumption he would be lumbering and slow. It wasn't the case. Three prided himself on being fit and agile, incorporating cardio and yoga regularly into his training.

There were only half a dozen people in the office, most of them too caught up in their own worlds to even notice what was going on. A few turned when Tom hit a wall divider, sending it crashing noisily onto the desk behind.

It slowed him up. Three almost had him. Tom threw a chair in Three's path hoping to impede his progress, however Three sidestepped the chair with little difficulty.

Close enough to see the whites of his prey's eyes Three lunged. Tom anticipated the move, scrambling over an unmanned desk, temporarily boxing Three in and sending a computer screen and telephone crashing to the floor.

Dodging a few co-workers Tom bolted through the kitchen area and towards the rear exit. The little piece of separation boosted Tom's confidence. With a triumphant smirk, he gave Three the finger and ran straight out the door...

"Hi, Tom."

... and into Nuke, who stood directly in his path next to his Jag, boot open and waiting.

There was barely time for Tom to crumple with defeat as Three scooped him up and stuffed him into the car boot. Nuke slammed it shut.

"What if she is seeing someone else?" Nuke asked Three, right back into it. They walked to their respective sides of the car.

"Now you're just being silly."

"Why is that silly?"

They got in and Nuke fired up the engine.

THE JAGUAR'S tyres squealed on the concrete as it zoomed up the circular ramp of the deserted car park. The calm conversation at odds with the car's speed.

"Let's say she was texting," Three said, hand firmly

gripping his Jesus strap. "Why would she bother doing it in the middle of the night?"

"She thought I was asleep."

"Why take the risk? You're out 12 hours a day. If she is gonna text, do it during the day when you're not home. Texting when you're there is just dumb and Wanda is not dumb."

"Who the fuck knows why women do anything?"

The car sped towards the open air, top level of the car park.

THREE SIGHED. No matter what he said he couldn't seem to deter Nuke from the discussion. Even here. Standing on the edge of the building Nuke wouldn't let it go.

"I still don't get what that is supposed to mean. You keep going on about apps —"

"This isn't the time," Three said sternly. "We'll discuss it later."

"No. We're discussing it now."

With a reluctant sigh, Three pulled out his phone. "Look at this thing. I can watch videos, take photos, listen to music, go on the Internet —"

"So what? Not relevant."

"Phones can do a lot. That's all I'm saying. Just because you don't —"

"She was in the lounge room with the stereo and the TV and the computer. If she wanted to watch TV, she would have watched TV."

"My point is —"

"Yes, I get it. But she wasn't doing any of those things. She was texting."

Three shook his head. "Like arguing with a revolving door," he muttered.

"Let's ask this guy."

Nuke pulled his arm in from where he had been holding Tom dangling over the edge of the building. Tom's wrists were bound behind his back, his feet desperately scrambling to find purchase on the ledge. They were about six storeys up. Far enough for the ground to seem like a long way below.

Nuke moved Tom closer and ripped the strip of tape from his mouth. "Middle of the night, I find my wife in the lounge room, right?"

"I'm not scared of you," stated Tom brazenly, although his tone suggested something entirely different. In both a brave and foolhardy manner he spat in Nuke's face.

To the untrained eye, Nuke didn't seem all that angry at Tom's action. He merely re-taped Tom's mouth with one hand and let go of him with the other.

There was no time to intervene. Three could do little except watch the whole thing play out more with frustration than concern.

After a couple of seconds there was a sickening crunch as Tom's body merged with an abandoned shopping trolley on the footpath below.

"Jesus, Nuke. Count to five, remember?"

Three peered over the edge. Down below what was left of Tom was a crumpled mess. Body parts protruding at wrong angles, like he had been assembled incorrectly. A pool of blood seeped out from under the trolley.

"We're only supposed to be scaring him. You're a fucken liability at the moment."

"He shouldn't have spat at me."

"You're supposed to think of me, remember? I'm standing right here."

"Oh, yeah. It didn't occur to me."

"How is he supposed to pay now? He only owed a couple of grand."

Nuke wasn't listening.

"You need to get your head back in the game or someone is gonna get hurt," Three said. He strode back to Nuke's car, muttering to himself.

Nuke watched him go. "Why is it so hard for you to accept that she was texting someone?"

"I UNDERSTAND THE CONCERN. But there is no way Wanda is cheating on you. No way," Three told Nuke as they leaned against his car in a vacant lot, shovelling down burgers, fries and shakes. It wasn't the most inspiring of places to eat. The view consisting of weeds pushing through the concrete and piles of junk.

Nuke's response struggled against a mouthful of food. "How do you know?"

"Common sense. She's not stupid, Nuke. She doesn't have a death wish. She would have to know what you would do to her. To them."

Nuke grabbed his shake, mulling it over.

"She wouldn't cheat anyway. Wanda is a classy chick."

He leaned over and tapped Nuke's forehead.

"It's all up here. You've just got to relax. Wanda's great. You're a great couple. You're a lucky guy. Enjoy. I know things might be a little bumpy at the moment, but all relationships have their ups and downs. It's just life. Nothing is perfect all the time."

Three grabbed some more fries. "Surprise her. Do something nice for her. Romantic."

"I'm not buying her another Jaguar..."

A bit of chip clogged in Three's throat. "She didn't like the matching Jags?"

"She liked that I gave her a Jag, I think. It was the matching part she wasn't so keen on."

"Really? It's not like they were absolutely identical. Hers had the pink vanity plates."

"I know," Nuke said. "You try telling her that."

Three pulled a surprised face. "I don't mean that anyway," he said. "Do some small things. Show her you love her and everything will go back to being cool."

Nuke chewed on his burger. He wasn't so sure but Three had a way about him that was most reassuring. Maybe he was right. Maybe Nuke was blowing all this out of proportion. Maybe it was his fault and all that was needed was an extra little bit of TLC. Treat Wanda nice. Make her feel a little special. He used to do stuff like that all the time. Why did he stop?

"Thanks, Buddy."

Nuke held out a fist for Three to bump.

21

Nuke's initial instinct was to run off to the jeweller and buy Wanda something super expensive, like a pair of diamond earrings or a fuck off necklace, until he remembered Three had advised him to do something small and that seemed to make sense. He had bought her plenty of pricey things and look where that had got him.

So instead he stopped by the florist on his way home. The plan was to get her some of those flowers like the ones she bought herself the other day. Trouble was he had no idea what they were. He could recognise roses and that was about the extent of his knowledge of flowers.

"Can I help you?" asked a perky florist.

"Yeah. I want a particular type of flower, except I don't know what it is."

"Okay..."

"They were purple if that helps."

The florist showed him a few varieties of purple flowers. Nothing looked right.

"Can you describe them?" she asked with mild exasperation.

"They were purple and the ... whatever you call it ... Flower part kinda looked like a light fitting."

He made a shape with his hand that was intended to be a rough approximation of the petals but was in fact rather useless. Luckily the florist knew her job, returning with a bunch of tulips. That was them. Tulips. Perfect.

THIS WAS GOING to be great. He was home early, all ready to surprise Wanda. Even before he had set foot in the apartment, he knew this was going to work. Three was a smart dude. He knew stuff. Nuke would have to thank him after.

He eased the key into the lock and opened his front door as quietly as possible, wanting to give Wanda a big surprise.

Sneaking up the hall Nuke spied his wife on the phone, pacing in the dark bedroom. She had her back to him, not noticing him come in.

"Baby... Don't you trust me?" Wanda breathed quietly into her phone. She sat on the edge of their bed. "Don't you trust me?"

Nuke watched and listened, edging forward a few steps.

"I love you too. With all my soul."

Her words were white hot, piercing Nuke's skin and scarring his heart. Wanda didn't turn around however she must have noticed him or felt him or something because all of a sudden stiffened.

"I gotta go," she said, hanging up quickly, not making the mess any better.

Nuke waited. Wanda took her time, knowing she was busted and yet in no hurry to face him. Finally, she turned, her expression casual and defiant.

"Who the fuck was that?" Nuke blustered, still carrying the purple tulips like an absolute fool.

Wanda took a moment. He could see it in her eyes. She didn't give a fuck.

"Rocco," she lied.

"Rocco," Nuke repeated. "Your brother?"

Wanda gave no reaction other than the slightest lift of one eyebrow. Something passed between them in that moment. They both knew she was lying and yet... Was she goading him? Daring him to call her on it? To call her a liar? The glare lasted a few more seconds, Wanda insolent, Nuke so furious he could barely see straight.

He turned and stomped out, destroying the flowers in one savage swing as he passed the coffee table.

22

Maybe I've got it all wrong, Nuke pondered as he watched the idiot cyclists ride past. There were always bikes around these days, but Sundays it was like some sort of infestation. So many he was surprised they hadn't closed Ocean Drive off to cars completely.

Nuke didn't get cycling or cyclists. He had a BMX as a kid and loved that. Adults though... He had no idea what would possess a grown man to squeeze into head-to-toe lycra on a Sunday morning and parade around the city streets with his mates. Maybe he should ask them. There were plenty here at Byron's by the Bay with him, their bikes all clogging up the footpath out front.

And yet, what did he know? It's not like his life was firing on all cylinders. Perhaps he should be questioning his disdain for things like cycling. Not be so closed minded. The cyclists all looked happy. Maybe they knew something he didn't.

He sipped his short black and peered over Ocean Drive to the bay beyond. The waves rolled in steadily. He attempted to get his Sunday indulgence to sooth him like it usually did. Striving to step out of himself and not think. Not be Nuke. Just be.

Draining the dregs from the bottom of the mug, he pondered he should have an unprecedented fourth cup of coffee. It seemed somewhat excessive and yet why not? He checked his phone just to make sure it was still on. Nothing.

The decision on a fourth cup was made for him as he glanced up and spotted two cops coming down the road towards him. He recognised them but it took a moment to place where from. Cops were cops, all much the same. Then he remembered.

The two idiots from the surveillance van.

Great.

"You guys must keep this van pretty clean. I'm impressed."

Nuke gazed around. The positions were exactly the same as last time, Nuke at the table, his back to the door. Harris and Hunt opposite. The two tech guys behind them.

"You guys stuck in here all day, sweating and farting and drinking coffee. I'd expect this place to stink, but it smells pretty good."

No one was biting.

"You finished?" Harris asked.

Nuke shrugged. He probably should just keep his mouth shut and let them talk. It was their dance. They were wasting his time and theirs. They had nothing on him.

"I think you and I got off to a wrong start last time, sport," Harris went on.

"You think so, do ya, sport?" He couldn't help himself. He hadn't been called 'sport' since he was eight years old and never by anyone younger than him.

Harris's eyes narrowed. "You want to know what happened, shithead? Your ego got in the way."

Shithead. That was more like it. Nuke raised his eyebrows keeping his mouth shut this time.

"See, we've got this whole big arse investigation going on and you are just one little bit. One tiny piece." Harris indicated something very small with his fingers as though that would help convey his message. "You're a tiny piece of this puzzle. You think we would jeopardise this whole thing just to bring you in?"

Nuke hoped his face accurately conveyed how little of a fuck he gave.

"That doesn't mean we are not watching you. That doesn't mean we don't know all about your cornball stunts."

Without taking his eyes from Nuke, Harris indicated towards the monitor over his shoulder. "We've got you under twenty-four hour surveillance."

The screen crackled to life. It took a moment for Nuke to recognise what he was looking at.

"This is live," Harris stated proudly.

Nuke snorted, beginning to enjoy himself. "Genius. This is fucken genius. What's that? The corridor outside my apartment?" He chuckled. "Well, you'll learn a lot having a camera out there. That's where all the shit goes down, out there in the corridor. I'm sure you have cracked the case wide op ..."

His voice trailed away. The sight of Wanda exiting the apartment quickly wiped the smirk off his face. Nuke stared at the monitor, mouth agape.

It wasn't Wanda so much as the fact she wasn't alone.

"What the fuck...?"

Three exited with her. For a moment it appeared as though Wanda and Three were just talking. Even that was bad enough. Why were they meeting behind his back? How the hell —

Then they began to kiss. Not just a peck or anything. A long and deep kiss.

He stared at the monitor in disbelief. Whether they knew it or not right then those cops were in grave danger. Hell, everyone within a ten-mile radius was in danger.

Nuke was about to go nuclear.

NUKE PARKED his Jag by an industrial estate. He got out and pushed his way through the torn cyclone fence. Weeds were fighting the concrete for control of the block. Fighting and winning. Small piles of junk lay scattered about, crunching beneath Nuke's shoes.

The sun poked its way through the clouds causing Nuke to squint slightly. He should have worn his sunnies, instead of leaving them in the car.

He pulled out his phone. After a few rings Wanda's voice said hello in his ear.

"Hey, honey."

A deafening silence followed. His voice sounded strange to him. He could only imagine how it sounded to her.

"So," he went on eventually. "What have you been up to?"

"Umm, nothing. You know," she replied. There was no cocky defiance in her tone now. She sounded small and scared.

"Oh, yes. I know. I do know."

More silence down the phone line.

A car roared into the street, engine blaring. Twice as loud as it needed to be. Nuke knew the sound well.

"Hey, honey? I gotta go. But I'll be seeing you real soon."

Nuke dropped the phone back in his pocket, watching Three pull up in his Mustang.

IN THE TWELFTH floor apartment the phone went dead in Wanda's ear.

She appeared as though she had been struck by something. A curse maybe. Frozen in terror.

Snapping out of it she placed a call, as fast as her trembling fingers would allow.

"Come on, pick up... Pick up. Shit," Wanda exclaimed as the call went straight to voicemail. "Hey, it's me. He's on to us. Call me."

She hung up, chewing her bottom lip, no idea what to do. Desperately hoping it wasn't too late.

23

See, all of this took place a few weeks after Nuke had his big idea. All that business with the new neighbour and the dinner party. Starting because a new chick moved in downstairs. Pretty hot too, Nuke thought, especially for this building.

A few years earlier when Nuke and Wanda were looking for a place to move Nuke had fallen in love with the building. The location was awesome, close to everything and the building itself was swish and modern and very cool. There was a pool and gym which took up the entire seventh floor. Not that Nuke ever had time to use either, however he thought Wanda might like them.

And it was great to have such a high level of security. Sure, you could have pretty good security in a house too, but you had to take care of it yourself. One more thing to have to worry about. Here the security was all taken care of for you.

There was only one problem. The neighbours. When they moved in Nuke had expected plenty of young couples like him and Wanda. He was wrong. They appeared to be the youngest by a good margin, most of the apartments populated by elderly retired types.

"What did you expect?" Wanda said. "Most people our age don't have your sort of income."

She was probably right. Nuke didn't think about that stuff too much. He didn't care anyway. The apartment was beautiful. What did the neighbours matter?

Then one day there was a new girl in the lift and she was young and sexy and had a bit of fire to her, Nuke could tell, just by how she had responded when he introduced himself. She had a great figure and a cute arse and meeting her gave him an idea.

THE LIFT OPENED and Nuke stepped out into a foyer identical to theirs, yet not. He knocked and waited. He couldn't spot anything different to upstairs and yet it it felt different. The door swung open a little too quickly and there she was. Kelly. The new chick. Wearing nothing but underwear. All right, it was bright and colourful underwear rather than sexy and seductive. Still just underwear though. Nuke certainly wasn't going to complain.

"Hey."

"Hello."

"I'm your neighbour, from upstairs. We met in the lift the other day."

"How could I forget?" Kelly said with a playful smile. Confident and sassy. Nuke liked that. This was the first time he had seen her up close, face-to-face. She was even cuter than he thought. Deep red hair and a smattering of freckles across the bridge of her nose.

"So, my wife and I are having this thing —"

He didn't get any further before the lift door opened and out stepped Wanda, holding a large bunch of flowers.

"Hey, honey," Nuke said, without a second's thought. So curious was he about what she was doing here, it didn't occur to him how it might look, him standing there with an attractive young neighbour in her underwear.

Wanda froze, totally confused.

"What are you doing here, Wan? This is the ninth floor."

"Is it?" Wanda said, in a daze. "I... I must have pressed the wrong button in the lift."

"Nah, it's good you're here. There's someone I want you to meet. This is our new neighbour, Kelly. Kelly, this is my wife, Wanda."

"Hi," beamed Kelly.

Wanda let out a noncommittal grunt, staring daggers at both of them. Before Nuke could stop her she disappeared through the door to the stairs.

Kelly flashed Nuke a conspiratorial grin. "Haven't got you in trouble, have I?" She placed a flirty hand on his arm. "She didn't seem too happy to catch us like this."

"Don't worry about it. I'm always in trouble. That's how she looks about everything these days." It took a moment for him to get his mind back on track. "Oh yeah. Anyway, so we're having this thing..."

ABOUT TEN MINUTES later Nuke meandered back into the apartment. Wanda bustled about in the kitchen. The flowers sat spread out in a large glass vase. Purple flowers of some sort. What were they for? Had Nuke missed something? An anniversary? Or her birthday? He was usually pretty good with that stuff. It was Wanda who never seemed to give a shit. Or maybe she had just decided to get upset about something entirely new, on a whim. It wouldn't be the first time. It was hard to keep up with what upset Wanda these days. Whatever it was Nuke felt confident he would be told he was in the wrong somehow.

"Nice flowers."

Wanda gave a little nod without looking at him.

"What are they for?"

She sighed heavily. "They are not for anything. They're just flowers."

Nuke knew absolutely he should leave it. No question. Yet his mouth kept talking anyway. "Yeah, but why?"

"I don't know," she sighed. "To freshen the place up."

"I can get you flowers if you want. Just every time I get you flowers you don't seem interested."

Wanda had a particular facial expression she used for these exact circumstances. One part tired, one part angry, one part frustrated. Nuke had never seen the expression in the early days of their marriage, now it was almost all he ever saw.

"They're just flowers, Nuke. I was passing a shop and thought they looked nice, that they might be nice in the apartment. There's no subtext to them. It has nothing to do with you or anything you may or may not have done in the past."

An unpleasant silence descended on the kitchen. Nuke crossed to the fridge to grab a beer, timing his run, so not to get in Wanda's way.

Moving back to the stools at their island bench he watched her chop up vegetables for dinner. Her posture was terrible, all hunched and tense through her shoulders. Why couldn't he go over, gently massage her? Help her calm. Initiate physical contact. For no other reason than to be nice. And if that physical contact led to something more, so be it. A man should be able to touch his wife. Experience though told him to keep his hands to himself. Instead, he pulled at the label of his beer.

"So, I invited that girl downstairs, Kelly, I invited her Saturday."

Nuke tried to read Wanda's reaction. There was none.

"That okay?"

Wanda shrugged.

"Thought I would set her up with Three."

"What are you, in high school?" Wanda said with a scoff and an exaggerated roll of her eyes. "Maybe on Saturday you can whisper in her ear '*My friend likes you*'."

Nuke chuckled, not quite sure of Wanda's joke.

"She's a bit young for Three, isn't she? How old is she? Twelve?"

"I don't know. Low twenties? I didn't ask. Three's thirty. Age gaps don't really matter though, do they? Not once you're over twenty."

A good portion of the beer label pulled away cleanly before it ripped.

"Three gets his fair share of women, doesn't he? He doesn't need your pity."

"Usually. He's been in a bit of a dry spell. I haven't seen him with a girl for a while. Be good to see him with someone nice. She seems cool. Doesn't seem like a complete bitch."

Wanda attempted to open a jar without much success.

"Maybe you and her could end up being friends too. Be nice for you to have a friend in the building."

Out of nowhere rage with the jar flared. Wanda slammed it against the bench repeatedly. Unexpected viciousness.

"What's wrong?" said Nuke, taking the jar and opening it with ease.

"Nothing." She folded her arms across her chest. "She seems cool, does she? Little Miss *'It's the afternoon, I think I'll answer my front door in my underwear, hee, hee, hee'*."

Nuke chuckled. "Yeah, that was unexpected. Don't worry she's not my type."

He took a sip of beer. "I do think it's sexy though. She's young. She doesn't give a fuck."

"Who's your type, honey?" said Wanda, giving Nuke a smoking look as she crossed the room with that sexy strut of hers and climbed into his arms...

At least that's what the Wanda in his mind did. The Wanda across the kitchen gave him no reaction at all, going on with cooking dinner.

"You can get around in your underwear more if you want. I won't mind..."

He gave her a playful grin which she wiped off his face with a brutally cold scowl, before stomping out of the room, leaving him all alone as usual. Where had it all gone bad? It was as though the two of them had taken a wrong turn somewhere in the relationship and no matter what he did he couldn't get things back on track.

Nuke sat there wondering if it was him. What had he done to deserve a wife who didn't love him?

LOUD CONVERSATION and laughter filled the twelfth-floor apartment. These people had known each other for years. Well, most of them had.

Wanda had an eye on Three and the young girl sitting to his right. Kelly. The two of them clearly uncomfortable, not knowing where to look or what to say. God, what had

Nuke been thinking? Sure, Three was a few years younger than Wanda and Nuke, but he was nowhere near Kelly's age. The conversation flowed all around them, like two boulders in a stream. Wanda felt sorry for Three. Such a cool guy usually and yet now he couldn't have looked more uncomfortable.

"So," Three offered after an ocean of silence between him and Kelly. "You live downstairs?"

"Uhuh."

"It's a great building."

"Meh, it's okay. Security is a pain in the arse."

"You got a problem feeling secure?" Three asked.

"It's just almost impossible to get back into the place if you forget your pass."

"So, don't forget your pass."

As Wanda watched an awkward pause take hold, the realisation dawned on her that it was worse than she first thought. Far more than a simple lack of chemistry, Three and Kelly actively didn't like each other. She observed them staring off in different directions, drowning in their little pocket of silence.

WANDA FERRIED some plates into the kitchen and checked on the next course. Nuke was busy fixing more drinks.

"Your social experiment's not doing too well..."

"You just wait. The night is young. We'll liquor them both up and see." Nuke shot a glance at the would-be couple and shook his head. "She coulda made a bit more effort though. To dress up."

Kelly wore a simple black button-up shirt and black pants.

"What are you talking about? She looks very pretty."

"Yeah and imagine if she tried. She could look amazing. Speak of the devil..."

Kelly wandered over, away from the main table and the guests.

"Having fun, Kelly? Here, get that into ya," Nuke said, shoving a large drink at her.

"Thanks." She took the drink but placed it straight down again. "Where is your bathroom?"

"Here. This way."

Wanda led Kelly into the hall. "Just down here." She pointed to a doorway.

Momentarily alone and out of view of everyone else Kelly grasped Wanda's hand.

"Sorry," Wanda whispered.

Kelly smiled. Lifting Wanda's hand up she kissed it, drawing out one of Wanda's fingers between her lips, biting it gently.

Heart racing, Wanda held tight onto Kelly, not wanting to ever let her go.

Part 3 - Dangerous Game

24

Wanda had met Kelly a few weeks prior on the supermarket floor, which sounds like an odd way to express it, except that Wanda was literally on the floor of the supermarket in between registers, with very little idea how she had got there. She had not fainted, nor passed out or anything like that. Just one moment she was upright, the next she wasn't.

With her new position came a concerning inability to think or process anything. All she could do was observe, noticing things, like that the floor was cold and hard and sticky.

The checkout chick looked a long way above her, staring, unsure what Wanda was doing down there.

The two customers waiting in the queue behind merely watched on with mild confusion. Nobody had any idea what to do. Why should they? It's not every day the customer in front of you slides to the floor of the checkout.

Wanda had no idea what to do either. Of course, she was supposed to get up, continue with her day, move on with her life and yet she couldn't. She couldn't move. It wasn't fear exactly, but something paralysed her. Rooted her to the spot on the floor.

And then the angel appeared.

She came from the supermarket entrance side, not the aisles, so the large windows to the outside world gave her a soft glow. A little like an angel. Or at least the stereotypical Hollywood portrayal of what an angel might look like if they suddenly appeared, sans wings, to aid a stricken person at a supermarket checkout. An angel in black yoga pants, 2XU singlet and sports bra.

The angel knew exactly what to do. She didn't ask Wanda if she was okay or try to get her to stand. No, she simply squatted beside Wanda and drew her close with a hug. As she did she softly stroked Wanda's hair.

"It's going to be all right," the angel whispered.

Wanda didn't believe her. She wanted to, but how could the angel know? Still Wanda wanted her to be right. So she went with it. Wanda clung to the angel as tightly as she could, never wanting to let go.

After a time the angel stood up and said: "Let's get out of here." She reached a hand down and Wanda realised she was ready. She could move. They got to their feet together. What should she do about her shopping? She glanced furtively at the items, all neatly packed in their bags.

"Just leave it," the angel told her. So she did.

THE ANGEL's name was Kelly and she led Wanda by the hand to a café around the corner, where they grabbed a table. The café had a hippy vibe to it with lots of cushions and fabric hanging from the walls.

Kelly ordered a coffee for Wanda and a juice for herself. It wasn't that she didn't like coffee, Kelly explained. She was on her way to the gym and experience had taught her juice went down better before a workout than coffee. Did Wanda go to the gym? Kelly had just started at this gym around the corner, Slim Gym's, and she really quite liked it so far. Especially at this time of day. There were never many people about. Maybe later in the day it would be too crowded. Like after work.

And this was how it went with Kelly. She liked to talk and talk and talk, about everything and nothing, never leaving too much of a gap in the conversation for awkward pauses or to let Wanda speak. Which was fine with Wanda.

The coffee at the café was surprisingly good. Wanda would have to remember this place. Or maybe it was especially refreshing after the experience in the supermarket. Or maybe it was the company.

Finally, when both the drinks were finished, and Kelly had talked non-stop for about fifteen minutes, without really saying anything, there was the smallest of gaps.

"Thank you," Wanda managed. "God, how embarrassing…"

"What?"

"That business in the supermarket."

"Oh, that?" Kelly said, having clearly forgotten the entire thing already. "Who cares? Don't worry about."

"Easy for you to say. You weren't the one just sitting on the floor in the checkout aisle."

"It wouldn't worry me if I was. There were fuck-all people there. Who cares what a bunch of old women in the supermarket think?"

A handsome barista with a thick beard asked them if they wanted anything else while he whisked away their cups. Wanda decided on a second coffee if only to avoid life for a little longer, while Kelly declined, oversharing with the waiter about not wanting to overfill her bladder before the gym.

"What happened anyway?" Kelly asked once he was gone.

"I'm not sure... I know I was..." What had happened? "There was no money in my account."

"Guess we knew who's paying for coffee then," said Kelly.

A jolt of uncertainty hit Wanda until she realised Kelly was joking and when she did she liked Kelly all the more. "It sounds silly, but I went to pay and... Thank you."

"You said that."

"Yes, but... If you hadn't appeared, I might be still sitting there. You knew just what to do. "

"Not really. It was a human reaction, that's all. That's what I thought I would need if I was sitting in a supermarket checkout. Not that I would ever be caught doing anything quite so stupid or embarrassing," she said with that twinkle in her eyes. After a pause she asked, "Has it happened before?"

"Sitting in a checkout?"

"Panic attack."

This stop Wanda in her tracks. "Is... Is that what you think this was?" It was a pointless question and one Kelly didn't appear compelled to answer.

"You don't really strike me as the type, although I guess anybody could be the type really."

"To have a panic attack?"

"To have no money in your bank account."

Wanda shivered, playing catch up with all this, piecing things together in her mind as she spoke.

"I'm not. We have plenty of money."

"What's the issue then? You go 'Whoops, sorry. Got no money,' and come back some other day."

"It's more what it means. The subtext. It could have been a power-play. He might have deliberately taken out all the money to teach me a lesson."

"Who?"

"Nuke. My husband."

"Really?"

"I don't know. Maybe. Who knows?"

"No, I mean, really, that's his name? Nuke?"

Wanda shook her head. "That's what everyone calls him."

She surreptitiously gave Kelly the once over. She was a pretty young thing, with her dark red hair and deep blue eyes. A bit like Sydney from Melrose Place. Except this girl may not have even been alive when Melrose Place was on. The thought made Wanda feel her age. How old was Kelly? Early 20s? Young enough anyway. Young enough to be free. Not burnt out by life yet.

"Don't let me keep you. Aren't you on your way to the gym?"

Kelly dismissed the notion with a wave of her hand. "Gym, schwimm. I can go to the gym anytime."

"You don't want to stay here listening to my tale of woe."

"Sure I do."

Something about this young woman compelled Wanda to let her guard down. Filled her head with a scorching desire to tell the truth and nothing but the truth. Shatter the foundation of lies her life was built upon. Or perhaps it was the knowledge they would never see each other again. A pretend best friend, just for the day.

"Seeing the account was empty was like getting hit in the face. Sure, we have money, but I have no power. No control.

The money is an illusion. It's his money. He can take it away at any moment."

Kelly pulled a face. "And you think, what? Your husband was reminding you of that?"

"Maybe, maybe not. Whatever, I got the message."

They sat in silence for a spell. The café had a nice ambience to it; the gentle murmur of the smattering of customers mixed with the clinking of crockery.

"He sounds like a prick."

"He's my husband."

"Sorry. Maybe you should leave him."

Wanda laughed. "I should. I should leave him."

Like that was possible.

25

T he next time Wanda saw Kelly, it was completely unexpected. Wanda was on her way home and as she turned into the apartment building's underground car park, she caught a glimpse of someone walking out of the lobby. Someone far too young to be one her neighbours. Kelly?

The timing was all wrong though. Before she could even ponder what the hell Kelly was doing in her apartment building the security gate was on its way down trapping Wanda inside.

She briefly considered abandoning her black Jaguar and chasing Kelly on foot, except she couldn't leave the car just sitting there, blocking the entrance. Instead, she parked in her allocated spot and of course by the time she made it out to the street Kelly had vanished. If it had indeed been Kelly in the first place.

Perhaps it was her mind playing tricks on her. Why would Kelly be coming out of their apartment building? Whoever it was had a yoga mat under her arm and so, Wanda reasoned, they were on the way to the gym, with a strong possibility of coming back. The thought made

Wanda's heart beat a little faster. With nothing better to do she made the decision to stake out the lobby. Sooner or later whoever it was would come back.

While it seemed like a bright idea at first, confusion and indecision plagued Wanda's mind the longer she waited. What was she doing here? Wanda wasn't even sure she had really seen Kelly. What would the angel from the supermarket be doing here? And even if it was her, what interest would she have in seeing Wanda anyway? Then again, why not wait and see? It's not like Wanda had anything better to do. Not just today. Ever.

After two hours Wanda was about ready to give up when she heard the security pad beep.

ENTERING THE BUILDING, Kelly did that thing she sometimes did, her brain not working properly. She let herself in, using her security pass and must have absentmindedly shoved it in her pocket or something because as soon as she got into the lobby she couldn't find it and had that spike of panic that she didn't have her pass with her. That she must've left it somewhere, her brain taking a moment to process that she must have had her pass or else how could she have got into the building? Still, juggling her yoga mat between her arms she engaged in a slightly frantic pat down of her pockets until she located the stupid thing.

She would have loved to blame her scattiness on the exercise, thinking her brain wasn't functioning properly because of the hard work she did in the class. Except she hadn't worked that hard in the class, which pissed her off. Wasn't that the whole point of group classes? To push you harder than you would push yourself? This class had been decidedly soft.

Kelly felt someone sidle up beside her, not taking much notice until they spoke.

"How was the gym?"

The unexpected question gave her a start. Kelly recognised Wanda's voice immediately, not having to turn and look. She had a beautiful voice, deep and husky.

"Uggh, Fuzion." Kelly pulled a face and pressed the button for the lift.

"Fuzion?"

"Yeah, it's a mix of yoga, pilates and aerobics. Why can't they just stick to one thing and do it properly? It's Fusion, except they spell it with a z though because they are so cool."

Kelly pointlessly pressed the button again as they waited for the lift.

"They don't have their own mats at this gym of yours?"

"Sure. You ever see anyone clean a mat after they use it at the gym?"

The lift dinged and the two women stepped in. Kelly pressed the button for the ninth floor, Wanda the twelfth.

"What are you doing now?" Wanda asked once they were safely ensconced.

"Haven't thought too much past a shower."

"Come upstairs with me and have a drink."

"Little early for a drink, isn't it?"

"Depends what we're having."

KELLY STOOD ADMIRINGLY on the balcony, drinking in the view. The panorama stretching from the Melbourne city skyline unfolding out in front of her, all the way to the bay if she followed the balcony around to the left.

"Wow. This is some view..."

"Be careful out there."

Careful? She was standing on a balcony. What was there to be careful of? Kelly walked back in.

"Doesn't your apartment have a balcony?"

"Not like this one. Mine is a regular two person balcony. You could have a party on that thing. Plus, I'm several storeys down and facing the other direction. My view is good, but it's not... That. That is amazing."

"I guess so. You stop noticing after a while."

"The balcony is so good you forget about it? I wouldn't. If it were me I'd live out here, especially in summer."

"The only time I ever think about the balcony is to wonder what it would be like to go over the edge. What it would feel like."

"What it would feel like falling to your death?"

"Umm, I guess. Not so much the slamming into the cold, hard ground side of things. More the sensation of flying through the air."

Kelly stared at her. "Are these the sort of things that occupy your mind? Throwing yourself off your balcony?"

"Sometimes. Not in a suicidal way. More in an abstract, what would it be like kind of way."

"I think the fear of hitting the ground would override any even remotely pleasant feeling the falling might have."

Wanda nodded. "Yes, you are probably right."

"Whatcha making?" she asked, approaching Wanda.

"Fruit smoothie. It's what I like after exercise. I considered making you a coffee, but this will be far more refreshing."

"Sounds good. Can I have a look around?"

"Help yourself," Wanda replied, busying herself with the juicer. The machine hummed loudly.

Kelly strolled about, doing her best to remain cool.

She felt like her eyes were on stalks. If she didn't control them they may well pop right out of her head. It wasn't just the view that was amazing. The entire apartment was breathtaking. Kelly had thought her ninth floor place was nice, but this, this was something else. Luxury. There was no other way to describe it. Enormous open plan layout. The kitchen flowing to the lounge and dining area. Everything seemed utterly perfect. Nothing out of place.

"So, we're neighbours..." Wanda asked.

"Guess so," Kelly replied making her way into the bedroom. She resisted the urge to flop down on the bed. It looked so soft and inviting. "Wow, that is a lot of pillows."

"That's the modern style, apparently."

"Maybe, but surely that's too many. I don't know how you find the bed."

Being a little naughty Kelly snuck a quick look inside the built-in robes. They were like another whole room. A sea of elegant designer clothes.

When Kelly emerged, Wanda poured a large glass from the juicer and handed it to her.

"Hey, let's have them out there." Kelly pointed to the balcony. "In the sun."

"You can if you like."

It made no sense to Kelly why someone with a fear of heights would buy a twelfth-floor apartment. It seemed like a waste of such an amazing balcony. She held her tongue though.

Instead, the two of them adjourned to the couches.

"Well, I'm glad I ran into you. I wanted to say thanks."

"For what?"

"The other day, in the supermarket."

"You already said thank you. Twice."

"Well, I mean it. If you hadn't come along, I might still be stuck there."

Kelly took a sip of the drink. "Wow, that's delicious. What is in it?"

"Just juice stuff. Frozen berries. Oats."

"God. You could sell this. Open a juice shop or something." She downed a big swig. Wanda chuckled.

"What's funny?"

"You. Your youthful enthusiasm. I'm trying to recall if I was ever like you. So young and full of energy and life."

"So, did you get it all sorted?" Kelly asked, wiping her lips with the back of her hand.

"What?"

"Your money concerns."

"Yes and no. There is money in the account now, if that's what you mean. The underlying issue is still there though."

"Your husband?"

"My lack of control."

A small silence took over the room, but it was nice. Not awkward or uncomfortable.

"No work today?" Wanda asked after a time.

"No work any day. How about you?"

"No, I don't work either. What does your husband do?"

Kelly twiddled her fingers. "Do you see a ring?"

"I just assumed..." She narrowed her eyes. "So, if you don't mind me asking, you don't work, you're not married. How do you afford a place like this?"

"Daddy. He thought it was important I have somewhere nice to live."

"Lucky you."

"How about you?"

"This is all Nuke. I mean, my design. His money."

"So, what does he do? This controlling husband of

yours."

The expression on Wanda's face was difficult to read. Like she was considering whether to lie or not.

"Take a guess."

"Apartment like this. All this money. Stockbroker?"

"Drug dealer."

"Oh. Are you supposed to admit that? Shouldn't you lie or something?"

"Would you prefer me to lie? I'm not sure it matters. Unless you are planning to dob us in. Even then." Wanda stretched, loosening her shoulders and neck. There was something terribly elegant in the way she moved, Kelly decided. Lithe. Almost cat-like.

"Well, not exactly a dealer, I guess. Strictly speaking, he works as muscle for some drug dealers. Organising and making sure everything goes to plan."

"So, you could have said in logistics?"

"I guess, if I wanted to be euphemistic."

"A scary dude then."

"Most definitely."

"Hence why you can't simply leave him."

"Hence why."

Kelly stuck her tongue in the glass, trying to lick the last little bits from the side. Wanda smirked. She handed the remains of her glass to Kelly.

"Here you can finish mine."

"You don't like it?"

"It's fine. Nothing special."

Kelly snatched the glass enthusiastically. "Nope. You're wrong."

"You're fun," Wanda told her. "Well, since we both don't work, you're welcome to pop around for a juice whenever you want."

26

A nd so it was that Kelly and Wanda became friends. Although in a strange way it was like they had always been friends and this was merely a continuation. It was nice. Wanda didn't have any friends. Not of her own, not for a while. The friends she had were hers and Nuke's and that was different. She hadn't been in a position to make friends for a long time. Either that or she had actively shied away from it, unwilling to draw people into her world.

Kelly felt like a breath of fresh air in her increasingly stale and unfulfilled life. Something new and exciting, brimming with youth and enthusiasm. As neither of them were employed the days were theirs to wile away however they saw fit. Going to the movies or watching the crappiest of crappy daytime television together. It wasn't a lot different from how Wanda had been spending the past few years, but it sure felt better having a person to experience it with.

Things evolved to the point where the thought of Kelly would spark a little excitement in Wanda, a small flutter in her belly. The knowledge they were going to see each other enough to make that day a bit brighter.

Kelly didn't appear to have many friends either. They were kindred spirits. Kept women enjoying one another's company. At least that's how Wanda saw things. She never asked Kelly in case she felt differently about all.

"Can I ask you about Nuke?" Kelly asked one day out of the blue.

They were half watching an old 80s movie about killer robot sent back from the future to kill everyone. It seemed like a good film, they just weren't really into it.

"If you have to."

"Is he abusive?"

"Why do you ask?"

"I don't know. I'm worried about you."

Wanda smiled. "That's nice." She had to think about it. "Define abusive."

"Does he hit you?"

"No."

"Is he verbal abusive?"

"No."

"So he's abusive by loving you and giving you money to buy lots of nice things?"

"He's a violent man."

"But not to you."

"The spectre is always there."

They half-heartedly watched a little more of the film.

"What about you?" Wanda asked.

"No, Nuke isn't abusive to me."

Wanda hit her gently. "Smartarse. No, I mean tell me about the man in your life."

"Who says there's a man in my life?"

"Pretty young girl like you would be beating them off with a stick."

"A stick. That's a good idea. I'll have to try a stick." She gave Wanda a crooked smile. "No man at the moment. Although I could have used to stick with my last man. He was more a boy actually."

"What happened?"

"Nothing really. He loved me. He was nice."

"Sounds good."

"Maybe. If nice and love is what you feel like. I don't know. We began in one place but quickly moved in opposite directions. He was starting to annoy me and so I was mean to him. And the meaner I was, the harder he would try in return like he was so desperate to cling to whatever we had. It got to the point where I just wanted to shake him, make him see that what we had wasn't that great in the first place."

"What did you do?"

"I did what I had to do, you know? I hurt him. In a way that was clear I couldn't mean anything else."

"Pretty dangerous... He could have ended up proposing."

"Ha, ha. Yeah. Exactly."

Kelly stretched and stood and began to explore the room again. She tried to play it cool, but Wanda could see her gaping at all the stuff, like a wide-eyed child.

A single solitary photo sat in a silver frame on the coffee table. Kelly picked it up and examined it. The picture was a black-and-white image of Nuke and Wanda on their wedding day. Wanda stunning in her long flowing dress. Nuke dashing in his suit. Both of them young and happy and ready to take on the world.

"How'd you guys end up together?"

"I don't know."

"How can you not know?"

"We all make mistakes," Wanda told her.

"I don't know. A mistake is like... Forgetting where you've parked the car when you go shopping. Or accidentally locking yourself out of your apartment. How long has it been? That you've been married?"

"A bit over fifteen years."

"Exactly. It's not like you woke up married to him yesterday."

"We do stupid things when we are young. Make mistakes. If we're lucky they are mistakes that don't matter."

"You must have had some idea what he was like."

"I knew exactly who he was. I didn't know who I was. I thought I wanted different things." Wanda let out a loud sigh. How could she explain what she was feeling? That it had become far too much. Too hard to face the awful reality of her life. As though she had been sleeping these past few years, floating along, not really there. Like Snow White or something. Although she was no princess. More like a hibernating bear. Shutting down for the long, cold, seemingly endless winter. And for the first time for a long time, in the presence of this young lady, she felt like she was waking up.

"Do you ever find it hard to reconcile your past actions and make any sense of them? There's shit I did when I was twenty that I remember doing but I can't for the life of me understand why I did them. It seems like an entirely different person."

She gazed at her new friend. "You're probably too young to understand."

Kelly replaced the photo and sat back down. "Gee, thanks, Grandma."

"I just mean you're young enough not to have made any real mistakes yet. Not to have fucked everything up.

Sometimes you just make a mistake. Get yourself into a bad situation. Most mistakes wash away, forgotten with time. Others leave a permanent stain. They linger, like a poison rotting you slowly until you're dead on the inside. Just an empty shell, going through the motions. Nuke was a mistake."

Silence descended on them, sucking the air from the room.

"Jesus, Wan, I was expecting 'Oh, we met through friends' or something. Is that you? Rotting from the inside?"

"I don't know. Maybe."

In fact, that is precisely how Wanda felt. Or more how she felt now in Kelly's company. There had been something wrong for a very long time. It was only now in Kelly's youthful vibrancy that Wanda grasped that.

Kelly slipped off her shoes and swung her legs up on the couch, her feet resting softly against Wanda's thigh. What did Kelly see when she looked at Wanda? An old woman, as tired and spent as she felt? She never understood how could she be so tired when she never really did anything. Tired from life.

"Should I be worried about you?"

"Worried about me?"

"Yeah," Kelly said. "Every time I speak to you, you seem verging on suicidal."

"Really? Maybe it's you."

"Thanks a lot."

"No, not that you're the cause. That you're bringing it out, to the surface."

"So should I be worried?"

"About what?"

"That you might decide to stick your head in the oven?"

"The oven is electric, wouldn't do me much good."

Kelly pushed her foot gently into Wanda side with a smile. "Ha, ha."

In return, Wanda rested her hand on Kelly's foot. She liked having it there. Not ready to move it just yet.

"You know what I mean. Throw yourself off the balcony then."

"Can't happen if I don't go out there." She smiled. "No. Not really my style. Happiness is just one of those things. Maybe we don't all get to be happy."

Kelly nodded. "If you were happy every day of your life, you wouldn't be a human. You'd be a game show host."

Wanda smiled, appreciating the quote. It was from an obscure Winona Ryder film they'd watched the other day.

"You should be happy some of the time though," Kelly went on.

LATER, when Kelly decided it was time to leave, she surprised Wanda with a goodbye hug.

"Don't forget what I said. No jumping off the balcony. If I see you go flying past my window, I'll be pissed."

"Don't worry about it. You won't see. Your apartment is on the wrong side." She smiled. "I'll tell you what, if I decide to, I'll let you know first."

Wanda held onto the hug for a moment or two longer than she should have. She hadn't hugged anyone for a very long time. Not a warm embrace from someone who she cared about and genuinely seemed to care about her. And Kelly felt so soft. Wanda didn't ever want to let go.

Kelly didn't seem surprised but she certainly did notice.

FROM THAT MOMENT on Wanda knew she was in trouble.

The flutter in her chest became more pronounced every time she thought of Kelly, which was increasingly frequently throughout her day. Thoughts of the softness of Kelly's touch, the red of her lips, the smattering of freckles running down her neck, down her chest.

Wanda found herself curious to discover if there were any more freckles elsewhere on Kelly's body. Similarly to how they never really discussed their friendship, slowly their relationship became physical, just kind of happening. Incidental contact as they talked. Legs touching on the couch. Wanda's head on Kelly's lap. Kelly running her fingers through Wanda's hair, every nerve ending in Wanda's scalp roaring with pleasure. Wanda taking Kelly's hand and tracing tiny circles around her palm, like a child's game of Round and Round the Garden.

One afternoon Kelly simply took Wanda by the hand and led her to the bedroom. No words necessary as they lay, hugging and kissing and stroking and slowly removing each other's clothes one by one and gently exploring each other's bodies.

The sex, if that's what you call it, was nothing like any sex Wanda had ever experienced. Vastly different to the rough performance of Nuke, which was why Wanda wasn't even sure she would classify her sex. More exploration and enjoyment. That's not to say there weren't moments of extreme heat and dizzying passion and excitement, moments where they stole each other's breath and caused weakness of the knees. It simply didn't have that same race-like feel that sex had with Nuke. None of that eye on the prize, speeding towards a very specific, preordained endpoint mentality.

To Wanda Nuke seemed like a foreign invader in their lovemaking and exciting as that may have once been it had long since grown tiresome and unpleasant. By contrast, Kelly seemed like an extension of herself. A part of her soul who understood what Wanda wanted even before she did. Kelly's touch taking her to the brink of somewhere she had never been before.

The sex didn't really start or stop, but it slowed at times, leaving them lying naked beside each other, Wanda caressing Kelly's soft stomach. Wanda was surprised not to feel more self-conscious and yet being with Kelly like this was so natural, an extension of the truth Kelly seemed to bring about. No pretence or hiding.

"These sheets sure are soft. I've never felt anything like them," said Kelly, sashaying around on her back, making Wanda smile.

"I was just thinking that the longest we've been together without you saying anything."

"Are you saying I talk too much?" said Kelly.

"Too much, no, but a lot. All the time in fact."

Kelly made a show of deliberately closing her mouth. As though she intended to never talk again. It didn't last.

"So, are you a lesbian?" Kelly enquired in her usual, matter-of-fact fashion.

"No. Not that I know of."

"I'm the first girl you've kissed?" Kelly propped herself up on her elbow.

"No, I've kissed girls before."

"But not a lesbian..."

Wanda shook her head. "It was all show, when I was much younger. Younger than you are now. Nothing to do with passion."

Kelly reached a hand behind the older woman's head, lightly tickling her skull. "Anything more than a kiss?"

"No. Fumbling hands over clothes maybe. But none of it was real. It was all a kind of performance."

A lazy smile stretched across Wanda's lips. It was the closest to content Kelly had ever seen her. "Why? Are you jealous?"

"No. Curious."

The two women fell back into silence, laying there, no need to talk. Eyes drinking each other in, hands gently feeling and exploring and caressing. The silence stretched on. Maybe the hands would get them all worked up again, back into the throes of passion, maybe they wouldn't. It didn't matter.

IN THE AFTERMATH, Wanda felt like a giddy schoolgirl who had just experienced her first kiss and was itching to do it again. Kelly was all she could think about. All she could focus on. She worried Nuke would notice. How could he not? She was a different woman all of a sudden, radiant and glowing and alive. At least that is how she felt.

For the first time in a very long time, she experienced the warmth of happiness and desperately wanted to hold onto it while she could.

It didn't occur to her until sometime later that she had cheated on Nuke, something she had never done before. Something she would never have even considered doing. She didn't feel bad about it or feel anything about it really, it just was.

What she did feel was the desire to get physical with Kelly again. To curl up into her soft, warm embrace. To feel Kelly's fingers up and down her spine. She had no idea how Kelly felt though. Would it just be a one-off aberration never to happen again? Would Kelly awkwardly address it, claiming the sex was a mistake? Or would she ignore it altogether, the spectre of their intimacy creating a blight on their burgeoning friendship, making things uncomfortable and slowly killing it?

WANDA NEED NOT HAVE WORRIED. Kelly arrived the next day just as determined as Wanda to do it all over. The contact was different this time though. The first time had taken them both by surprise. This time they were both ready. Prepared.

Kelly bided her time. She enjoyed the power she appeared to have over this older woman, learning how to get her to catch her breath. There were new things she was keen to try. Experimenting with words like touch. She waited until she sensed Wanda was nearing the edge.

"Do you think about me when I'm not here?"

"Yes," Wanda said, starting to breath hard.

"How much?"

"All the time."

Kelly's fingers etched their way around the older woman's body, playing her like an instrument.

"What about when you are with Nuke? Do you think of me when you're fucking him?"

"I haven't been with Nuke since I met you."

Oh. Kelly had intended the question to be flirty and sensual and cheeky. The response felt a little sad. The whole thing was complicated. Kelly hadn't begun to process how she thought about all of this, let alone whether it was a good or a bad thing Wanda and Nuke weren't sexually active anymore.

"I think I would now though," Wanda went on. "If the situation arose."

Best not to think, Kelly told herself. "Who knows? You both might end up thinking of me."

"You haven't met Nuke yet, have you?"

"No, I met him the other day."

"Where?"

"Here. In the lift. He is very handsome."

Wanda let out a noncommittal grunt, ignoring the teasing in Kelly's voice. Kelly pressed on anyway.

"He said hello, introducing himself. Very confident."

She grabbed Wanda's hand, pressing her fingernails into Wanda's palm enough to hurt.

"We rode up in the lift together," she continued, breathily in her ear. "He had his eyes on me the whole time, you know, that way that guys do when they think they are being subtle? But really they're just staring. He watched my arse the whole way out of the elevator."

The nerve endings in Wanda's palm tingled, driving her nuts.

"He was completely under my spell, just like you."

"Do... do you want him under your spell?"

"I couldn't care about having him under my spell. But I want control of you."

"You've got it," Wanda managed to blurt out. Although any control Kelly had was immediately curtailed by the sound of the apartment's front door slamming.

Nuke had unexpectedly arrived home.

27

Gripped by panic Wanda and Kelly momentarily froze. Could Kelly make it to the ensuite? Or the built-in robes? Maybe, although it was likely Nuke would notice a naked woman sprinting across the bedroom.

"Wanda?" came his enquiring voice from the other room.

"Quick," Wanda hissed, pulling Kelly close with one hand and throwing the sheet over her with the other. Kelly clung to Wanda's waist, holding her breath.

Wanda grabbed a few of the pillows from the floor, tossing them about the bed. It wasn't much of a ruse but it was the best she could manage at short notice.

"I forgot to bring..." Nuke strolled in and stopped dead in his tracks. "Well, well. All right for some. You back in bed or do you never get up?"

Wanda didn't respond. The additional human-shaped lump under the covers had to be blindingly obvious, didn't it? Yet Nuke said nothing. Tempting as it was to turn and look for herself, the last thing Wanda wanted to do was unnecessarily draw his attention to it.

A grin smudged Nuke's face, totally distracted by the sight of Wanda in bed to notice anything else. "What 'cha wearing under there?"

He reached for the sheet.

"Nuke." She pushed him away.

He tried a second time and Wanda slapped his hand with such venom the sound reverberated through the apartment. Not to be so easily waylaid, Nuke sat on the edge of the bed and ran his hand along what he assumed to be Wanda's leg, which was, in fact, Kelly's.

"Come on, Wan I'm home, you're already in bed. Why don't we...?"

"Nuke..." scolded Wanda with that well-practised mix of disinterest and impatience and exhaustion. "Please, just..."

She didn't need to finish. Her face said enough. Nuke's grin turned into a stony look of disappointment then anger.

"Fine." He stomped out of the room.

A few moments later the front door slammed shut, shaking the entire apartment.

Kelly and Wanda lay there for several minutes more. Not daring or wanting to move.

FROM THEN ON Wanda and Kelly continued with their affair in a much more cautious manner. There may have been an extra bit of spice and excitement in the idea of getting caught, however it was an excitement Wanda could do without. Besides the tryst with Kelly alone was enough excitement for her.

For Wanda, Kelly felt like something of a lifeboat in a raging sea of uncertainty. The hope of rescue, when you had long since resigned yourself to drowning. She yearned for her when she wasn't there and detested Nuke all the more when he was.

Despite herself, she found her mind fantasising about a possible next step. Kelly was from money, her father wealthy enough to not think twice about buying his daughter a ridiculously expensive apartment. Enough that Kelly didn't have to work, nor did she seem to consider the possibility. When Wanda had these thoughts, she immediately attempted to shut them down. She had no idea what this was with Kelly. Maybe to Kelly it was nothing. A momentary fling. A youthful indulgence. Wanda had no desire to heap pressure on her. Turn her into some kind of saviour. Yet every now and then she couldn't stop her mind indulging in the fantasy.

At the same time, Kelly was having profound effects on Wanda's sense of self. She felt younger. More attractive. Desirable. It was clear Nuke still found her desirable and yet that was something else entirely. The way one might look at an object or possession.

Wanda had felt stained for the longest time and Kelly seemed to be washing some of that stain away.

FEELING frisky one morning Wanda decided to surprise Kelly. They usually saw each other at Wanda's place because Kelly liked it so much. Wanda teased her that Kelly didn't like her at all, she just liked her apartment. However, on this occasion, Wanda decided to switch things up.

She knocked on Kelly's door, marching straight in when Kelly opened up, trying to be bossy and assertive but in a sexy way, while also doing that thing they did of starting the conversation halfway through.

"Oh, this is nice," Wanda said, strutting through the apartment as though she had been invited.

"I didn't say you could come in," Kelly scolded.

"Too bad."

After a cursory look around Wanda crossed to the balcony. "You're right about this view though."

She stared at the roads and buildings below.

"What are you doing?" Kelly asked, joining her outside.

Wanda said nothing.

"I was just on my way out."

"Let me guess, the gym? You'll have to go later." And with that Wanda grabbed Kelly and forced her into the bedroom.

"Can I ask you something?" Kelly asked while they were intertwined on the bed a short time later.

"Sure."

"You're scared of heights and yet the first thing you do when you come over is go out on the balcony."

"I'm not scared of heights…"

"I thought… You never want to go out on your own balcony."

Wanda rolled onto her front hoping Kelly would take the hint and stroke her bare back.

"I'm not scared of heights. I'm scared of my balcony. There's a difference."

"Okay…"

There was something immensely pleasurable about lying here chatting, with no clothes on. Not as exciting as the sex, yet still extremely pleasant.

"There used to be this hill when I was at school, down to the oval," Wanda said. "Anyway, one day this year seven got thrown down it. Broke her arm. When the principal told us about it at assembly, he said she was 'inadvertently propelled' down the hill. Inadvertently propelled. I've always remembered that."

She picked up Kelly's hand, holding it flat against hers.

"That's what scares me about my balcony. That one way or another I'll end up going over, whether of my own volition or not."

"Nuke?" Kelly asked.

"Maybe. It's not like he doesn't have it in him. With that temper."

She pressed the palms harder together.

"He threw a table off there once."

"As in, an actual table?"

"Yep. Not like a dining table or anything but not small either."

Kelly waited, giving Wanda the space to go on.

"I had made him mad about something and he was throwing things at me. He threw a vase and completely smashed the glass door out onto the balcony."

Wanda's voice was emotionless. Matter of fact.

"Then he grabbed the table and threw that at me. He kind of launched it in an arc, like a hammer thrower or discus or something. It missed me, just, although I felt the wind as it went past. Anyway, without the door being there as resistance, the table flew straight out."

She acted it out with hand gestures.

"The legs clipped the rail and the thing flipped and fell all the way to the street below. Made a hell of a noise hitting the ground. Four in the morning. Everything else was quiet."

Kelly waited for her to go on except Wanda appeared to be finished.

"What happened?"

"Oh, nothing. That was the terrifying part. When the table went over, I was scared and yet also elated, you know? This was it. Something would have to happen now. You can't just throw tables out twelfth storey windows. The police would do something. But I don't know. He called police he knew or something and they sorted it out. The table somehow didn't hit anyone or anything. It just smashed on the footpath. It was four in the morning, so only a couple of people saw it. The police pretended they were taking care of it. In reality they didn't even give him a warning. It was more like a blokey backslap and a laugh. You can't do that, mate. That type of thing. Like it was a bit of fun."

Wanda traced her finger along the lines of Kelly's palm.

"The police didn't even look at me, let alone ask if I was okay. That's when I knew just how much trouble I was in. I may as well have not been there as far as they were concerned. Ever since I haven't liked the balcony."

Kelly watched Wanda for a few moments before pulling her in for a tight hug. It wasn't that Wanda was upset or looked as though she needed a hug, it was all Kelly could think of to respond.

"Right. I'm off."

"I don't get it," Wanda said, staring up from the bed. "You hate Fuzion. But you keep going."

"Hey, you don't get this sexy by accident," said Kelly, giving a little shimmy in her lycra pants. It was the same outfit she had been wearing when they first met in the supermarket. Wanda agreed. She looked great.

"All right if I hang about here?"

"Why?" Kelly blurted out, unable to hide a shadow of

uncertainty sliding across her face. "I mean, of course, sure. Why would you want to? Your place is so much nicer."

"My place is a prison. I promise I won't steal anything."

"Why would you? You have better, more expensive versions of everything at your place anyway."

Kelly hustled over and kissed Wanda on the lips. "See you in an hour."

HAVING the place to herself Wanda didn't bother to get dressed. Why not? With luck, they would head straight back to bed when Kelly returned. Instead, Wanda dragged the sheet from the bed and wrapped it around herself. It was the sort of thing they did in movies. It would be kind of sexy, wouldn't it? Wearing just the sheet when Kelly returned? Kelly comes in, they kiss, the sheet falls. It had been a long time since Wanda had actively tried to be sexy. In reality, the sheet wasn't terribly practical. Wanda persisted anyway, hoping Kelly would appreciate the effort.

She moved into the kitchen, deciding Kelly was quite right - her sheets were nearly as nice as the ones upstairs.

Wanda glanced about, not to be nosy, simply to have a look. The apartment was cozy and yet... There was something indefinably ... What? Out of place? Something didn't quite fit. Something she couldn't quite put her finger on.

And then the front door swung open.

An elderly woman bustled in. At first, she didn't see Wanda and when she did she let out as loud a scream as Wanda had ever heard.

28

"What are you trying to do? Kill me?" the woman screeched, clutching her chest. "I nearly had a heart attack."

Wanda wasn't feeling so hot either, standing naked in the middle of the apartment, draped in only a sheet.

"Who are you?" the old woman asked briskly.

"I might ask you the same question."

"I'm Ita. I live next door." This seemed plausible to Wanda. She vaguely recognised Ita's face as someone she had seen around the building.

Wanda hoped desperately Ita didn't recognise her. She somewhat pointlessly wrapped more and more of the sheet around herself. The impression she had was that Ita was somewhat of a gossip. Competing instincts tore through her. The desire to question Ita about why she felt she had the right to barge into Kelly's place versus the desire to get her out of the apartment as swiftly as possible.

"I heard her go out. What's her name."

"Kelly."

"Yeah. Her. I didn't know you were here."

"Well, I am," stated Wanda, somewhat redundantly.

"Hmm," Ita said, looking Wanda up and down with a stern eye.

"What... what are you doing here?"

"The Pecks asked me to keep an eye on the place. Make sure she isn't destroying it."

"The Pecks?"

"Yes, the Pecks," Ita said, an underlying impatience in her tone. "This is their apartment. They're in Europe for twelve weeks."

"No, this is Kelly's apartment," Wanda tried, the words sounding as stupid as she was feeling.

"The girl? How would a girl that age afford an apartment like this?"

"Her... Dad bought it for her?"

"No. Ridiculous. This is the Peck's place. The girl is just house-sitting. Apartment sitting. Whatever you call it. I don't know. I had never heard of such a thing before. They got her from some agency. She had good references and whatever but they were still a little unsure, having a stranger living in their apartment. Fair enough too. So they asked me to nip in every now and then, just to make certain she wasn't destroying the place."

Once Ita left, Wanda had absolutely no idea what to do. About all she managed to decide was that the sheet was a bad idea.

WANDA WAITED ON THE COUCH, wondering how she ever believed this could be a 23-year-old's apartment. The decor, the furnishings. Everything about it was all wrong.

Kelly returned with that usual slightly pinkish hue, having worked hard yet not too hard. The part of Wanda that wanted answers was stronger than the part that wanted to run and hide.

"I like your apartment," Wanda told her.

"Thanks. Daddy has good taste." Kelly moved to the kitchen and poured a large glass of water.

"It must have cost him a lot, buying somewhere like this for you." Wanda giving her a chance to back out now. To come clean. Except Kelly didn't. Instead, she doubled down on the lie. "Oh, yeah. You know fathers. Nothing is too good for their little girls."

Wanda fixed her with a serious glare. "Are you sure about this? You sure you want to play like this?"

"What? This is my apartment. Daddy bought it for me."

Wanda looked deep into her eyes before walking for the door.

"Wanda, wait..."

"Is your name even Kelly? Maybe I should ask Ita next door. She told me all about the Pecks being in Europe and you housesitting. I would watch out for her if I were you. She has own set of keys and I'm pretty sure she has been spying on you."

Kelly's face fell, no idea what expression it was searching for. "Wanda, stop." She grabbed the older woman by the shoulder. "I was just... mucking about."

"Oh, yeah? Which part?"

Kelly couldn't come up with an answer quick enough to prevent Wanda from leaving.

KELLY HAD no idea what she should do. She wanted to at least talk to Wanda. Explain herself. Something. Except Wanda refused to give her the chance.

What options did she have? She rang but Wanda didn't

pick up. Much as she wanted to speak to Wanda, she didn't want to turn into a stalker. She knocked on Wanda's door a few times, almost certain Wanda was home, simply not answering. It wasn't as though she could hang around there and wait or make a scene. Plus Kelly had no desire to run into Nuke.

And so she decided fuck Wanda, if that's how she wanted to act. If she wasn't going to listen, what could Kelly do? She set about getting on with her life.

That tough 'screw you' attitude lasted about a day until she started to process how much she missed Wanda and how much she enjoyed being with her. The rejection hurt. Idly it occurred to her this is possibly similar to how her ex Jonathan must have felt. The realisation didn't sway her in any way or make her feel any more sympathetic towards Jonathan. It merely occurred to her.

When Kelly did finally come across Wanda, it was a chance meeting in the lift. Kelly was waiting at the ninth floor when the doors opened, revealing Wanda and fortunately no one else. It was perfect. Wanda couldn't hide or run away which Kelly assumed she would have if she could.

"Hi."

Wanda said nothing.

"Can we... We need to talk."

A cold, stony look was all Kelly got in return. Wanda eyeing Kelly like she was nothing. She didn't say no though.

They went to the café across the street. That same place they had gone after the supermarket incident. Their place.

Except it didn't feel like their place. Kelly knew Wanda well enough. Going to the café instead of the twelfth-floor apartment was a sign. Wanda not inviting her up. Keeping Kelly at arm's length. No more asking her in, literally or figuratively.

Wanda stared across her coffee at Kelly, with eyes of marble.

"So, this is it? This is how it's going to be?"

"What would you like me to say?"

The chills coming from Wanda were pissing Kelly off. "Look, I fucked up, alright? But I don't see what the big deal is. This..." She gestured to the two of them. "What you're doing now is far worse."

A barely perceptible raise of one eyebrow was Wanda's only response.

"So, I lied about the apartment. So what? What does a matter?"

Wanda blew the steam off her coffee.

"Look, I'm a liar, okay? It's a skill I have. I'm good at it."

"Clearly."

"Hardly something I can put on my resume. That doesn't mean what we had... It doesn't mean that was..."

"How am I supposed to know where the line is?" Wanda asked. "Maybe it is all lies. How would I know?"

"I don't know. You're supposed to trust me."

"Trust you when you are lying to me?"

"Yes. You're supposed to see..." Kelly's voice trailed off. She did really have an end to the sentence.

Wanda waited. Nothing more came.

"There was something about you, Kelly, from that first day in the supermarket. You were an x-ray, staring straight into me, into my soul. A truth detector. I couldn't help but be honest with you."

"That's part of the problem. You were so intense. Telling me all these things, a stunning woman in this gorgeous apartment, with so many expensive things, talking about jumping off the balcony and drug deals and your violent gangster husband. I was merely trying to keep up."

"I'm not sure what that means."

Kelly closed her eyes. The conversation was making her head hurt. "At first I was just mucking around. Playing a game. Then it all became something else. And when it did, I was stuck. There was no chance to say 'Oh, by the way, all that other stuff I told you? That was all bullshit'."

The folly of youth, Wanda thought. How could she not realise she would get caught out at some point? Or did she not think that far ahead?

"I let you in, Kelly. I haven't let anyone in for a long time."

"I know. Look, this whole thing took me by surprise. I'm not in the habit of jumping into bed with beautiful, older women."

"And your rich dad?"

"Just a dad. I'm sure he loves me, but he's not buying anyone apartments."

"Where's all your money come from?"

"Money? I don't have any money."

The fabric of who she thought Kelly was seemed to be being ripped apart before Wanda's eyes.

"How can you afford not to work?"

"I can't. I mean I can for a couple of months." Kelly sighed. "I had a job. I was working at this company, doing some office work. Nice place, nice people. Or so I thought. I'd been there a little over a year, just casual, but I saved up a bit. I thought they were going to put me on full-time. Except they got rid of me instead. I was pissed. I dumped my ex and my life was a bit of an echo chamber, you know? I wanted to step out of it for a while. The opportunity to apartment sit came up, the chance to be someone else for a while. Or at least pretend. And then I met you and you were kind of an extension of that pretend new life. If I had known... I had no idea how it would develop. I never intended to lie to you."

Wanda nodded. It was about all she could do. What Kelly was saying made sense and sounded fine.

Yet so had all the lies.

29

The following days Wanda descended into darkness. An unpleasant black fog. At first, she blamed Kelly for lying to her. It is never pleasant being deceived. She felt stupid, which she hated.

Slowly though she came to the conclusion she was being silly. Wanda felt crappy now, but the crappiness was caused by Kelly's absence all of a sudden, not her duplicity. Besides, didn't she tell a lot of lies when she was Kelly's age? Probably a whole lot more than Kelly had. Maybe it was all bullshit with Kelly, but it was exciting bullshit. Kelly was something in a life that desperately needed something. Was she a risk? Sure. What hadn't been a risk with Kelly?

Wanda felt foolish and wanted nothing more than to apologise immediately. She decided to buy Kelly something to make up. Shopping was something she was good at. But what to get. Should she buy Kelly a juicer so she could make juices of her own? Although a juicer was a little extreme. Buying Kelly off with expensive gifts wasn't really what she wanted to do.

Instead, she went to the florist across the road, intending

to return with the biggest bouquet of flowers they had, all ready to surprise Kelly. Except the moment she was in the florist she had second thoughts. A big bunch of flowers? Isn't that what a man would do? It's how Nuke would apologise.

She still liked the idea of flowers, searching the florist for something more original than a pointlessly enormous bunch. Something intimate that spoke of the two of them and what they had. She settled on a stunning bunch of purple tulips. Kind of an in-joke. Kelly had a pair of purple underpants the exact same colour.

The mere thought of Kelly excited Wanda once again. The chance to hold her in her arms, to dance her fingers across Kelly's soft skin. It was ridiculous to think she wanted anything else.

The lift dinged and Wanda stepped out, lost in thought. She planned to hold the flowers in front of her face, so that is all Kelly would see when she first opened the door. Kind of a corny idea and yet she was going to do it anyway. And if Kelly wasn't home maybe she could go next door and borrow the key from Ita.

The tantalising excitement of the seeing Kelly again had Wanda so wrapped up for a moment she couldn't make sense of what she saw when she stepped out of the lift.

Kelly standing there in just her underwear, talking to Nuke.

Wanda did her best to back away, return to the lift, except she wasn't fast enough. The lift doors shut without her and Kelly and Nuke looked around. Caught.

"Hey, honey," Nuke said, like talking to a semi-naked neighbour was the most natural thing in the world. "What are you doing here? This is the ninth floor."

"It is? I... I must have pressed the wrong button."

Reaching back she mashed the lift button. She had just been in the lift, it couldn't have gone away already. But it had. She had to get out of there. Now.

"Nah, it's good you're here. There's someone I want you to meet. This is our new neighbour, Kelly. Kelly, this is my wife, Wanda."

"Hi," Kelly beamed brightly.

Wanda let out a noncommittal grunt, staring daggers at both of them. Without another word she pushed her way into the stairwell.

As the door sprung slowly closed, Wanda caught one last glimpse of Nuke and Kelly and saw Kelly place a flirty hand on Nuke's arm. Kelly standing there, virtually naked. Well, not really. She was overreacting. It was no worse than a bikini, she supposed. Still, what would possess a person to answer the door looking like that? Unless she assumed it had been Wanda. That would make some sense. A knock at the front door meant an internal visitor. Visitors from the outside needed to be buzzed up with the security intercom. Except it could have been Ita coming to visit. Or maybe Kelly was just Kelly and it didn't occur to her to put more clothes on. Why not? She was young and beautiful. What did she care? Or maybe she wanted to be scantily clad and flirty with Nuke? Who knew?

And as the door slowly closed, a firm realisation lodged in Wanda's brain. Kelly's motivations were immaterial because Wanda was stricken with her. She loved Kelly and trusted her and was all in, no matter what.

Turning, Wanda hurried up the three flights of stairs to her floor, flowers and all.

. . .

A FEW NIGHTS later Nuke and Wanda's dinner party dragged on into the early hours.

Kelly was the first to leave, politely excusing herself and thanking her hosts for having her. Nuke wasn't exactly hostile, nor was he especially polite, half drunk and convinced the lack of chemistry with Three was entirely her fault.

The combination of the other guests hanging about and Nuke's inebriated state allowed Wanda to slip off to bed early, feigning deep sleep by the time Nuke finally stumbled in. When they were younger he would have woken her for sex. Sex Wanda would have quite willingly engaged in. However, he knew better now. Within minutes he was snoring heavily beside her.

The fleeting moment en route to the bathroom was the only second Wanda and Kelly had managed to find alone at the dinner party and yet Wanda knew Kelly wouldn't be asleep. That she would be waiting for her.

Confident Nuke was down for the night Wanda slipped out of bed and out of the apartment.

The corridor remained lit, no discernible difference between day and night. Wanda snuck down to the ninth floor where she knocked softly on Kelly's door. It opened almost immediately, Kelly still in the black outfit she had worn to the party. Nuke was an idiot. She looked great. Good enough to eat.

"Not answering in your underwear this time?"

"I assumed that was you at my door the other day. Good thing I didn't answer naked."

Kelly ran a hand through Wanda's hair, sending sent chills down the older woman's spine. She had missed her. Missed being close to her. Missed her touch. To her surprise Kelly shut the door, locking them outside her apartment.

"Come with me," Kelly breathed.

She led Wanda downstairs to the seventh floor. Past the dormant treadmills, elliptical trainers and weights to the deserted pool. Wanda had forgotten how luxurious the pool was. She didn't tend to swim terribly often because the pool was almost always in use. Clearly three A.M. was the time to come.

Condensation drifted in the air, fogging the windows. The shimmering green of the water looked most inviting.

Letting go of Wanda's hand, Kelly stripped off her clothes. Naked, she turned and kissed Wanda firmly on the lips.

"Coming with me," she breathed again, backing her way into the water.

A slight sense of hesitation held Wanda back. This wasn't a good idea, surely. No matter what time it was, there was still a chance someone might see. Someone might be around. Besides, Wanda had nothing to swim in. Until she remembered she was wearing her bathers.

Wanda hurried into the water, struggling to keep up. Kelly moved quickly. The steam from the water made it difficult to see even the far end of the pool. Was it always this warm in here? The water, more like a bath than a pool, caressed Wanda's body, drawing her in deeper.

"Come on," Kelly called. Wanda wanted to, except she had difficulty keeping up. She lost sight of Kelly for a moment.

"Kelly?"

"I'm here," came Kelly's sultry reply. "Come on."

She paused. Wanda hurried to catch up.

The water felt thick, clinging to her. More like moving through jelly.

"Kelly?"

It was getting too deep. She glanced about. Deep and unaccountably choppy. As though a dozen fat kids were doing bombs in the deep end. Except there were no fat kids. Just Wanda and Kelly and the pool.

Wanda felt a frazzle of nerves as she lost sight of Kelly again, obscured by the undulating water. She glanced about, the waves getting bigger and bigger.

The sides of the pool disappeared altogether. All Wanda could see was water. Water that was becoming increasingly choppy.

"Kelly?"

She was gone now, Wanda all alone. Not in the pool anymore, she was outside. Lost at sea somewhere. The waves towered way above her head. Wanda thrashed about, desperate to stay afloat...

WANDA OPENED HER EYES, taking a moment or two to regain her bearings. Nuke's snores drifted across from beside her. The dream stayed with her, leaving an unsettled mark. The problem was being awake and back in reality didn't feel a whole lot better.

She lay there, pulse hammering, trying to find sleep she knew was never going to return.

As the night slowly disappeared, the thoughts in her mind crystallised. In a sense, despite all the problems and complications, everything suddenly seemed quite simple. Wanda sure of one thing. Life could not continue like this.

KELLY LAY across the expansive couch with her head in Wanda's lap, gently playing with Wanda's fingers. She wondered what a couch like this would set you back. Probably more than her car.

She couldn't quite believe what Wanda was telling her. And yet that was not unusual with Wanda. The most extraordinary things seem to drop out of her mouth, with no filter at all. Wanda had started by saying she couldn't do this anymore and Kelly had assumed she meant with her, their relationship or affair or whatever you wanted to call it, except she didn't. She meant Nuke.

"You want to run away?" Kelly asked.

"I want us to run away," Wanda clarified. "Together."

"This isn't another attempt to kill yourself, is it? Not death by cop. Death by psycho husband."

"Another attempt? I haven't been suicidal."

"You haven't had my view."

"I just need out, Kel," Wanda said. "Normal person, normal situation, I would walk away. There is no walking away from this."

"That's my point. You can't just walk away. I don't think you've thought this through."

Kelly saw the slightest hint of hurt in her eyes before she managed to disguise it.

"Think about it," Kelly went on gently. "We —"

"I have been thinking about it. There has been no possibility to think about anything else."

"I'm just saying it is not that simple. We couldn't do it. We would need some serious cash. Start-up money."

"I could get a job."

Kelly laughed.

"Why is that funny?"

"Have you ever had a job?"

"I'm sure I'd manage. I think I would quite enjoy a job.

Something to do. Another world to be involved in and think about."

"It's more the lifestyle you would have trouble with." She indicated to the apartment. "Leaving all of your things."

"The things don't matter. For a long time I thought I could fill the hole in my life with beautiful possessions. It doesn't work. All of this doesn't make me happy. I thought it would once, but it's only a weak substitute. I don't see beautiful things when I look around my apartment, I just see ugly. All this stuff, it's tainted by how it was acquired. Purchased with money made from the misery and suffering of others."

"It's easy to say you wouldn't miss your stuff with your four thousand dollar toaster sitting right there. If you were living in a roach-infested shithole with no heat, you would miss your things pretty quickly."

"I wouldn't care. Not if I was with you."

There she was again, with her overbearing intensity. Kelly quite liked it, although it wasn't difficult to imagine it becoming smothering.

"We would still need money," Kelly told her.

Wanda jabbed Kelly playfully in the ribs. "You don't think I'll be able to get a job, do you?"

"I think it's a nice fantasy."

Another look of disappointment spoiled Wanda's face. A look she couldn't quite hide quickly enough. Like a little girl, lost and in over her head. Silence weighed down on them.

Kelly went on, mainly because she thought she should say something. "If you did run... Would Nuke come after you?"

"Only to kill me."

The sound of keys in the front door alerted them to

Nuke's imminent arrival. Kelly casually removed her head from Wanda's lap, while Wanda unmuted the TV.

"Hey, girls."

"Hi," Kelly said with a smile and a wave. The women pretended to be engrossed in their viewing. Nuke squatted behind the couch, between them.

"Whatcha watching?"

Wanda put a finger to her mouth and pointed at the TV. Nuke loitered awkwardly, unwanted in his own home.

After a few moments, he walked out.

Kelly curled her toes up onto the couch, so her feet touched Wanda's. Her big toe caressed Wanda's foot. Wanda didn't react. The best Kelly could get out of her was a weak smile stretched thinly across her lips, with a hint of lingering hurt in her eyes.

30

The large abstract painting on the wall commanded the attention of the room. Commanded it. That was why she purchased it in the first place, wasn't it? Or was it because the painting was modern and enormous, its size only matched by its fiendish price tag and she thought buying it would piss Nuke off forever more?

Was Wanda staring at the painting or was the painting staring at her? Funny how you stop noticing things after a while. She saw this painting every day, yet how often did she actually look at it? Wait, was that right? She looked at it but she didn't see it? Or she saw it but didn't look at it? Whatever, she was both looking at it and seeing it now. And the painting was better than TV. The complex splatters of brightly coloured paint danced and rearrange themselves, striving to form some sort of cohesive pattern.

"Keep trying," she muttered, encouraging the painting. They were getting closer to a resolution, the splatters. Making order from the chaos.

"What did you say?" Three's voice swam to her from far away.

"I was talking to the painting." The most natural thing in the world. The colours continue to move. An excitement boiled in Wanda.

It was odd to think she would usually be here with Kelly at this time of the day. The circumstances about as different as you could get.

"I can't see you Friday," Wanda had informed her.

"Oh, yeah?"

"Yeah. Friday is taste testing."

"Taste testing?" Kelly asked.

"There's a new shipment coming in. Whenever a new shipment comes in if it's something we would like, we do a taste test. Spend the day getting fucked up."

Kelly pulled the face. "Really? Don't get high on your own supply. Isn't that a thing?"

"Sure. This is a variation on that, I guess. We do this once every other month. It's an outlet. It helps keep the temptation away the rest of the time."

"So, you take drugs to stop yourself taking drugs?"

"Rules are generally a good thing. Rules are how you keep order."

"Hey, I'm not judging," Kelly said.

"Wan," Nuke giggled, interrupting her thoughts and drawing Wanda back to reality. Or given their current state, perhaps not reality. Whatever this was. "You've been staring at a painting for hours."

Had she? No, she hadn't. Not hours. What did it matter if she had? She'd happily stare at it for ever more. Except maybe she would have one more line first. She dragged herself away, separating a line from the remaining mound of powder on the coffee table.

Vrrooomm!!!

The powder tickled then burned as it shot its way up her

nostrils and dripped down the back of her throat, into her bloodstream. She slumped back into the couch, the painting long since forgotten.

Where was the pesky dot? The tiny black dot Three had given her first thing. He had instructed her to stow the dot under her tongue and she had been so careful to do that except now it had vanished. Why was keeping track of a little dot in your mouth so difficult to do? Oh well, the dot had completed its mission. Godspeed little microdot. Your duty is done.

As the line enforced its additional layer of bliss upon her, Wanda glanced up. Nuke and Three were on the couch opposite. Nuke was saying something. Saying something to her. And yet no sound was coming from his mouth. It wasn't until Wanda glanced away that Nuke's words decided to catch up. Lazy words.

"What do you think?"

Wanda glanced back. Both Nuke and Three were staring expectantly at her. A smile and a nod is about the best Wanda could muster. They laughed.

"It's good shit," Three said, all of them captive to the drug's powers.

Of course, she would love to have Kelly here. Just Kelly. She could only imagine Kelly's magical hands on her while she was feeling this good. It might be too much. She may well explode into a million blobs, not unlike the painting. They had talked about it. Briefly. Not the exploding. The taste testing.

"Sounds fun," Kelly had said. "Can I come?"

Wanda thought for a sec. "I can't decide if that would be the most exciting or most terrifying thing ever."

Was she serious? Like with most things Kelly said Wanda could not be entirely certain. They had to be careful.

Fun as their clandestine affair was, one slip could be deadly and locking themselves in the apartment together with Nuke while smashed out of their minds was almost certainly asking for trouble.

Even without Kelly there Wanda hadn't been sure she trusted herself not to do or say something completely stupid that would somehow alert Nuke to what was going on with Kelly. However, as soon as the drugs kicked in any worries like that were long gone.

The drugs smothered her with calm contentment and bliss. She had this.

Nuke's voice swam through the thick fog and into Wanda's brain. "So, what's happening with the shipment?"

The word, shipment, lodged inside her, bouncing off the walls of Wanda's mind.

Shipment. Shipment. Shipment.

A razor-sharp silence took over the room. Wanda glanced up to see Three staring right through her.

Nuke and Three never discussed business in front of her. Never. It was an unwritten rule. A game they played. The façade of never explicitly involving her in precisely what they did. It was how things worked and messy as they were right at this precise moment Three wasn't about to break that.

Wanda got the message. She pushed herself off the couch with tremendous effort.

"I'm gonna... with the... Yeah..." She stood, almost toppling forward and for a moment she wondered whether her toothpick-like legs could support her or if they might snap under her body weight. No problems. Once she started to move her legs worked fine. Wanda could feel Three's eyes. Lasers burning into her, waiting until she was gone.

In the hallway, she stopped just out of view and listened.

"Sunday," Three said once he was confident she was out of earshot.

"Someday what?"

"Sunday. Not someday. You asked what was happening with the shipment."

"I did?" Nuke had definitely had too much. He was never this messy.

"Sunday Van Damme is doing the run to the Buyer."

And to Wanda listening from the corridor, the words were like magic. Words she had been desperately longing to hear, even though she had no idea she been waiting to hear anything.

"Right. Whose turn to babysit?" Nuke asked.

"I'll flip you for it..."

Angelic voices serenaded Wanda's soul as an epiphany hit her like an orgasm.

"If it's your turn, then take your fucken turn," Nuke said from the other room.

"I should have just said it was you," said Three. "Actually, you probably won't even remember we had this conversation. When you ask again tomorrow, I'll just say it's you.

"Ha, ha," Nuke said giving him a playful punch. "Never going to happen. My head is like a steel trap."

In Wanda's mind she walked through a dark room, the room she'd been trapped in forever. Except now for the first time, there was a door. A door with a big fucken exit sign over it. Kelly stood by the door. She pushed down on the bar and the door swung open to reveal an impossibly blue sky and greener than green grass and happiness.

Oh my God. Kelly. She had to let Kelly know.

Resisting the urge to go running from the apartment Wanda extracted her phone from her pocket with some difficulty. Wanda's fat fingers and drug-addled mind ganged up to make texting far more challenging than it should have been. Somehow she managed the three letters she was trying for.

Y - E - S

She followed this with an ever increasing number of exclamation marks.

!!!!!!!!!!!!!!!!!!!!!!!!!!!!!!!!!!

Send.

The exclamation marks exploded out of her phone and into the air all around her.

"WHAT DOES Y E N MEAN?"

Wanda was confused until Kelly her showed her the text she had sent.

"Oops. It was supposed to say Y E S. I wasn't quite with it at that point."

"Okay, what does Y E S mean?"

"My husband is a bad man. He works as muscle for The Sharks. Have you heard of The Sharks?"

Kelly shook her head.

"Bad people. Scary. They import and deal drugs. There is a big shipment coming in. That's our in. The phone. The phone is key."

THAT AFTERNOON with drugs still coursing through Wanda's body mixed with the elation of her plan she bumbled about, waiting for Three to leave.

As the two boys said their goodbyes at the front door she stole away back into the apartment. Wanda's breath caught in her throat, nerves tingling her fingertips.

Near the smeary mess of leftover powder on the glass coffee table sat Nuke's phone. Wanda scooped it up and examined it. Just an ordinary phone. Nothing special.

"What are you doing?"

Nuke's stern voice sliced into her. She had been so focused that she hadn't heard her husband come back in. Busted. She froze, like an animal in headlights, clutching Nuke's phone in one hand.

Nuke chuckled. "You're so fucked."

Placing the phone back down where it was, she nodded and smiled.

"Three's going. Come and say goodbye."

THE MESSY TRIO spilled out of the apartment into the corridor.

A repairman stood up a ladder, attending to a light globe. The repairman's face turned red with a nervous embarrassment. Wanda wondered what he had to be embarrassed about. But as she looked at him his face continue to redden until he resembled a cartoon devil.

The devil repairman turned and leered at Wanda, teeth bared, flames rising up behind him. She considered asking Nuke and Three if the repairman had turned into a devil surrounded by fire for them too except if they were seeing that they probably would have mentioned it. Instead, Wanda blinked a few times. When she looked again, he had returned to being a plain old repairman.

"All right," Three stated, as though ready to leave, as though his mind was free and clear and not entirely muddied by the drugs.

Nothing happened. No progress was made. And so after a while he said it again.

"All right."

The repairman ignored them, focused on the light.

Eventually, Three reached a lazy hand up and he and Nuke bumped fists.

"Seeya, Wan," Three said. They pecked on the lips. Perhaps a little overly affectionate thanks to their altered states but still just a peck between friends.

"All right." Nothing. "All right."

Finally, Three shuffled away. He stopped at the ladder and stared up at the repairman for a second, then gave Wanda and Nuke a little nod, before ambling towards the lift.

Wanda and Nuke disappeared back into the apartment, leaving the repairman to his work.

FOR THE NEXT few hours Wanda couldn't sit still. Sure, that wasn't unusual after a taste testing, however this was more. It was the choirs serenading her mind, telling her that after all these years she may well have discovered a way out.

Part 3a - Kill Us Now

31

The day was so lovely Wanda and Kelly chose an outside table at the café for once. The two of them made an attractive couple. They could have had this conversation at her apartment, except Wanda didn't want to risk it. What if Nuke had the place bugged? She was almost positive he didn't and yet there was a little lingering paranoia, presumably not helped by coming down from the taste testing. Whatever, it didn't hurt to talk here instead.

Kelly studied the older woman, hearing her out but not saying anything.

"What?"

"I am never sure how serious you are."

"Funny, I have the same problem with you. You think I'm not serious?"

"You seem serious. Although it is possible your little drug adventure has melted your brain."

Wanda ignored her and kept talking. "Part of the issue is getting the drugs from A to B, yeah? From the supplier to the dealer. That's where Van Damme comes in."

"Van Damme?"

"Nickname. He is the courier. He's the only one who physically handles the drugs. That way everybody else has plausible deniability if anything goes wrong. Yet they can't just let him take the drugs by himself. He needs some sort of protection," Wanda explained.

"Protection from being attacked or protection from himself?"

"Both. To stop him or anyone else doing anything stupid. Nuke and Three are both supposed to be there with him at all times, but these days they've got a little complacent. They take turns. They call it babysitting."

"Okay. But this time you're going to somehow make it that neither Nuke or Three are there."

"That's where this comes in."

She slid a mobile phone across the table to Kelly. "This is the same as Nuke's phone. All I have to do is copy the information across from his phone onto this new phone and then I'll switch them last possible moment."

Kelly turned the decoy phone over in her hands a few times and shook her head.

"Won't work."

"Why not?"

"This one will have a different number."

"Won't matter. Nuke is not a phone person. He will just think no one is ringing in."

"Yeah, but what if he tries to ring someone?"

Wanda adjusted her sunglasses, stretching her neck. "Chances are he won't. And if he does somehow realise this isn't his phone, chances are it will be too late."

"Chances are?"

Wanda shrugged. Kelly gave her that look again, handing back the phone.

"So, this guy... Steven Segal."

"Van Damme."

"Van Damme. It's his job to deliver the bag of drugs to the buyer."

"Yep."

"You think we can somehow steal the drugs ourselves and sell them to the same buyer."

That is precisely what had been playing out in Wanda's mind, except in an over-exaggerated manner. For some reason, she saw them driving off in a convertible with loose bills flying out the back as they went. Of course, it was unlikely to play out that way. Where would they get a convertible?

Kelly didn't need to say anything. The look on her face made it quite clear what she thought of this plan.

Wanda pressed on. "Van Damme. He's just a mule. The Buyer doesn't give a shit who hands him the bag, he just wants the shipment."

"How do you know?"

"What can we know in this world? I mean truly know? You can't know anything with one hundred percent certainty in life. There are always variables. Let's say you go to the shops to buy some milk. There may not be any milk at the shops. They may have run out. Or the shops might not be open."

"Or you might find you have no money in your account."

"True, although you would probably buy milk with cash if that's all you are getting. But there are always unforeseens. There are just more of them with crime. Like if you wanted to rob a bank. You're always going to have to make assumptions. Take some risks."

Kelly's expression wasn't improving. "What's the jail time if we get caught?"

"It's not the police we have to worry about."

The women stared deeply into each other's eyes, each trying to get a read.

"What do you think?"

"I think I can save some time and just kill us both now."

"You're focusing on the negatives."

"There seems to be a lot of them."

"Like I said, all plans have an element of risk. What are our options?"

"Not doing it?"

Wanda shook her head.

"You'd rather die?"

"I'm dead now. At least this way there is a chance."

A fly landed in the vicinity of their food, pesky and persistently trying to settle. Kelly waved it away.

"What are you thinking?" Wanda asked finally when she couldn't stand the silence any more.

Kelly didn't respond, her mind presumably overrun with thoughts. She excused herself and went to the bathroom.

To her credit, Kelly did go to the toilet. She didn't merely get up and leave. Walk away and never come back. I mean, Wanda got it. She really did. Kelly was young with her whole life ahead of her. She didn't sign up for any of this. She didn't sign up for anything. She was just having fun. That's what 23-year-olds did and suddenly Wanda was piling all of this on her, asking Kelly to risk her life to save Wanda's. It was too much.

Wanda wanted to say all this to Kelly and to tell her it was all right. That she didn't have to do this. Any of it. Except she couldn't. What if Kelly said no? What would that mean for Wanda's life? Where could she possibly go from here without Kelly?

Wanda spent a nervous few minutes waiting for Kelly to return. It was a little like after they'd had sex that first time.

What if she had pushed things too far? What if she had pushed Kelly away?

So, she was thrilled when Kelly returned and said: "The phone. I don't get the phone."

Wanda tried to quell the excitement bursting inside her. Just because Kelly had said no yet, it didn't mean it was a yes.

"It'll take a while, won't it?" Kelly went on. "Transferring all the information across."

"Don't get hung up on that. That's my problem."

"When will you do it?"

"I don't know. It's not a big thing. He just has to think the replica is his phone for a while."

"Yeah, but if he looks closely..."

"If he looks closely, we're screwed. I can't give you an absolute guarantee on any of this. Like I said, it is full of variables. We can do our best to make sure as many of them go our way as possible, but it's a risky plan. Any part could go wrong for any reason, at any time."

"And you want to do all of this with me, because you love me and because you're going to die if we don't?"

"Can you think of a better reason?"

As it turned out, the phone was a bigger deal than Wanda though. At least, trickier to get her hands on it. If Nuke was out he had his phone with him. And there weren't many opportunities when Nuke was home that she could grab it, only when he was out of the room, in the toilet or the shower or whatever and those times were limited.

Wanda was ashamed at how flustered she became. In her head she had nerves of steel, simply plucking up his phone whenever she needed to and subtly replacing it whenever Nuke returned. In reality, she could barely hold the thing with her shaking hands and fast beating heart. She felt sure she was being too obvious, leaving some tell-tale sign behind of her duplicity.

She decided night was the only realistic option, while Nuke was asleep. She lay in their enormous bed, listening to his rhythmic breathing. She knew he was asleep, and yet what if he wasn't? What if he was merely waiting to catch her out?

Finally, she worked up enough courage to ease herself off the bed.

Nuke stirred but didn't wake.

Tiptoeing as quietly as possible she edged around the bed and over to his dressing table where the phone sat waiting. A scenario danced through her mind. Her reaching for the phone and just before she picked it up his powerful hand grabbing hers.

"Wanda... What are you doing?"

What would she say? What could she say? He didn't move though, continuing his light snores.

She emerged from the bedroom without a problem. Wanda took a deep breath. See? It was fine. What had she been worried about? Her breathing calmed and her heart returned to normal.

His code was easy. Six Eight Five Three. Nuke in numbers.

The home screen sprung to life as she sat at the dining room table. What would she need that was here? Same access code. Same home screen. She turned the phone over in her hand committing all the bumps and scratches to memory. There was no way to replicate all of his text messages. What about his texting style? If she was going to send as a text as Nuke, it had to appear authentic, at least initially. How —

"Wanda?"

Nuke's voice startled Wanda to the point she fumbled the phone completely from her hands.

In the otherwise silent apartment the clattering noise the phone made hitting the table was substantial. There was no way to come back from that. No way to hide what she was doing.

Wanda turned. Nuke glared at her, bristling with barely restrained fury.

32

One afternoon Kelly surprised Wanda with a knock on her door.

"Can I borrow a dress?"

"Sure. What do you need?"

"Something sexy and amazing. You've got so many great clothes."

The two of them were a similar height, Kelly with a slightly fuller body than Wanda.

The older woman led them to the built-in robes in the bedroom. She showed Kelly a few different things, however Kelly knew exactly what she wanted. She pulled out a striking red dress.

"What's this for?" Wanda asked as Kelly tried the dress on.

"Slight change of plan."

"Oh yeah?"

"I don't think you and I can rob Van Damme. Specifically you."

"Why not?"

"Van Damme knows you, yeah?"

"Not well, but by sight, yeah."

"He might recognise you. We can't take that risk. This plan is all to do with timing, and if he recognises you, it will muck the entire thing all up. It could come down to seconds."

"Muck it up how?"

"What is the first thing Van Damme will do once he's been robbed?"

"Tell someone."

"Exactly. Whoever he tells, their reaction will be very different if he says a random person robbed him versus if he says Nuke's wife robbed him."

She had a point.

"So, what are you suggesting?"

"To give us the best possible shot, he needs to be robbed by somebody he doesn't know."

"I can't ask you to do this by yourself."

"You're not. I've got someone I can do it with. That's where the dress comes in."

A sinking feeling descended to the pit of Wanda's stomach. Kelly looked amazing. Stop traffic sexy.

"When?"

Kelly grabbed one of Wanda's lipsticks. A perfect shade to match the dress.

"Tonight."

Wanda watched Kelly trace the lipstick along the curve of her already juicy lips. In no hurry.

"Was the plan to spring this on me, so I had no time to say no or talk you out of it?"

"Something like that. How do I look?" Kelly asked, smacking her lips and studying her made-up face.

"Too good. Amazing." Wanda's dress clung to Kelly's body, accentuating her exquisite figure.

"Who is this guy?"

"Just some guy."

It didn't seem possible, however crossing her arms over her chest Wanda managed to pout that little bit more.

Kelly shifted close to her, in her personal space. "This is a much smarter way to do things, Wanda. It is safer if somebody else steals the shipment."

"Safer or you don't want me there?"

"I don't want you there," Kelly said, moving even closer to Wanda. "I don't want to risk you getting hurt."

"I don't want you there either."

"Well, unless you can come up with a way for the bag to steal itself one of us will have to be." She gave Wanda a soft kiss on the lips. The kiss hurt. It tore Wanda apart that the next lips on Kelly wouldn't be hers.

"What are you going to do?" she asked, surprised by her own raging jealousy.

"Whatever we need..."

"Yeah, but..."

Kelly put a finger to Wanda's lip. "I like your jealousy. It's cute. Just not now, okay?"

Wanda said nothing.

"You trust me, don't you, Wanda?"

Wanda nodded, her mind swimming in unpleasant thoughts.

"We need a story," Kelly told her. "Jonathan won't steal this if he thinks it's drugs. It needs to be money."

WANDA FOLLOWED Kelly out of the apartment. God, the

dress looked sprayed on. Wanda stared at the fabric barely stretched over Kelly's thighs. She understood the plan, but did it have to be this dress? She hated the idea of Kelly made up like this for somebody else. Surely the plan could have worked with a less provocative outfit?

"Big night, Kel?"

Wanda hadn't even noticed Nuke in the hallway.

"Just going out," Kelly said breezily with a flick of her hair. "Your lovely wife was kind enough to lend me a dress."

"I can see," Nuke said, making no attempt to disguise giving Kelly the once over. As she went he turned, watching Kelly sashay her way down the corridor.

"She looks amazing."

"Hmmm," Wanda responded noncommittally, doing her best to appear disinterested.

Nuke's eyes remained glued to Kelly as she disappeared into the lift. "Fucken cunt."

Wanda glared at him as she opened the door to their apartment.

"If she had worn that to the dinner party, Three might have been interested."

Wanda rolled her eyes and stomped inside.

"What?"

THIS WAS GOING to be fun. It was a challenge. Something exciting. A game. Kelly liked games. She always had. She was good at them. The dress emboldened her.

She could feel The Drake almost before she stepped through the door. The muggy air, just that bit warm to be comfortable. The stink of stale beer and sweat and disinfectant. The slap of pool balls, competing with the voices and the same music, again and again, as though stuck in some kind of unfortunate, unforgiving time loop. Did the crap eighties bands know their place in history when making this trash? Understand that a certain proportion of the population would never let them go? Belinda Carlisle? A-ha? Queen? Perfect. That will do us forever more.

The Drake was Jonathan's favourite place in the whole world. He was going to grow old here. Become one of the locals everyone knew. Typical Jonathan. No scope or ambition or imagination. He had found somewhere he liked so fuck the rest of the world, he was staying put. No sense there could be bigger and better.

The place was fairly full with the after-work crowd. Not pumping yet but on its way.

Lots of eyes followed Kelly as she walked in, just as Nuke's had, the allure of Wanda's red dress, impossible to resist.

Kelly picked out the table she wanted - a perfect view of the pool tables, ignoring the previous occupant's empties.

After a while George the bitchy bartender appeared, clearing away the glasses and bottles.

"Bit overdressed for the pub, aren't you?"

"Of course. That's the point," Kelly purred, her eyes trained on the door. "I'll have a beer, please."

George began to tell her that there was no table service, except Kelly knew that and George knew that Kelly knew and put it together Kelly wasn't serious, that she was just fucking with her, so she didn't bother telling her after all.

Kelly couldn't have cared, she was already on to other things, watching closely as Jonathan and his useless posse walked in, right on time. Regular as clockwork. The group chatted and laughed loudly, looking happy. None more so than Jonathan, at least for now.

George followed Kelly's eyes.

"Just leave, Kelly. No one wants you here."

Whatever. Kelly watched and waited. Jonathan hadn't noticed her yet, too focused on snaring a pool table and figuring out whose shout it was. Kelly didn't mind. She was in no hurry. He would notice her soon enough.

As she watched her prey, Wanda's cute, pouting face sprang into her mind.

"Why him? Why Jonathan?"

"Cos he's an idiot. I can use him."

"Can you trust him?"

"Sure."

"How do you know?"

"Because he loves me."

Jonathan grabbed a pool cue, swinging it around without a care in the world.

"Maybe I'm in the same boat," Wanda had said.

"Maybe," Kelly agreed. She liked Wanda's jealousy. It was cute. The older woman acting like a little girl. Jealousy was a Kelly speciality. She always seemed to be able to conjure it in others. In boys. In her school friends. When she was younger, she used to take great pleasure in making people jealous. Just for fun. Not jealous of her, of each other, with Kelly positioning herself happily in the middle, right where she wanted to be. Drama for drama's sake.

It took longer than expected but finally one of Jonathan's mates noticed her on his way to the bar. Good. It wouldn't be long now.

KELLY SLID herself onto the very edge of the bed, doing her best to touch as little as possible. She could still feel him all over her. A sticky stain might never wash off.

The ensuite door was wide open. Jonathan sang loudly in the shower.

"I know you didn't come home last night," Wanda whispered in her ear.

In Kelly's mind, the game was all meant to be easy. Kind of fun too. Snaring Jonathan, manipulating him into doing exactly what she wanted, because she could. And it was fun and easy, right up until the moment the two of them left the pub. From that point on though it became uncomfortably real.

As an abstract concept seducing Jonathan was fine. As a real living, breathing entity, it was horrible. She had forgotten all the things she loathed about him. The way he tasted of curry and cheap beer. His slobbery kisses like he was trying to digest her. His fumbling hands that seemed to think her body consisted of breasts and crotch and nothing more. His endlessly whiny voice. His plaintive gaze during sex, begging for her soul. They hadn't separated by chance. Kelly detested everything about Jonathan.

And here now, in his bedroom, with his voice ringing out from the shower, like some sort of victory anthem Kelly felt herself gag.

What was worse than just him was having to pretend she was into him to help sell the illusion. Hide the utter contempt radiating through her body.

"Kelly?"

Kelly chewed on her bottom lip. "I can't do this, Wanda. I can't do the whole jealousy thing. Not right now."

Where was Wanda? Kelly tried to picture her. In the lounge? On the edge of the bed like her? Or out on the balcony, reclining in the sun?

Kelly switched her phone to her other ear. "Although, let's be frank. If either of us is being played, it's me."

Because if Wanda was on the balcony, perhaps it was all lies.

Everything had rearranged itself in her head last night as she lay awake, staring up at peeling paint on Jonathan's ceiling. Kelly had believed involving Jonathan was all her idea but was it? Had Wanda planted the idea somehow?

The more she thought about it and didn't sleep, the more she fretted about the entire thing. Wasn't there a chance this was all just one big con? More than a chance? The beautiful woman with everything she could possibly desire deciding she didn't want any of that, she wanted Kelly. Kelly couldn't see what the con was exactly, except the person being conned never should.

Was Wanda real or some sort of act? The mysterious suicidal older woman. The supermarket. The gangster husband. Wanda the one who wanted to get away, and yet here Kelly was, the one with Jonathan doing all the heavy lifting.

She may have been thinking it, but Kelly hadn't realised she would say it to Wanda, sitting here, the vulnerability and discomfort swelling inside her.

"You think I'm fucking you?" Wanda asked.

"I would know you were fucking me if I could just see the angle."

"Baby... Don't you trust me?" came Wanda's breathy voice in her ear. The shoe was on the other foot now. Kelly recalled asking Wanda this exact question not eighteen hours earlier.

Jonathan had finished in the shower and he continued to sing as he dried himself. Kelly caught a glimpse of his naked body and looked away with contempt. If he tried to go to the toilet with the door open again, that was it. She was out of there.

. . .

KELLY NEED NOT HAVE WORRIED. Wanda wasn't on the balcony, she was striding about her still dark bedroom. She hadn't bothered to open the blinds yet, hiding from the day.

"Don't you trust me?" Wanda asked again. Where was all this coming from? Kelly like a different person suddenly from the confident sex kitten that strode out of here in the red dress yesterday. Wanda wondered what had changed. It was tiring trying to keep up. Tiring and slightly frustrating. God, she was becoming a cliché. Isn't that what men did? Always complained about women being irrational?

She sat on the edge of the bed. "Don't you trust me?"

"I love you," came Kelly's reply finally.

"I love you too, babe, with all my soul."

As she said the words, a chill crept through Wanda. She felt him before she saw him, felt Nuke's hulking presence and knew she had just made a horrific mistake. Knew that moment too late. No way to suck the words back up. What if she simply didn't turn around? Didn't acknowledge him at all? No, it was better to face him. To get it over with.

"I gotta go." She hung up on Kelly and turned impartially towards her husband, who was standing there, clutching a bunch of flowers. Purple tulips.

"Who the fuck was that?" Nuke's voice relatively soft and calm but the vein in his forehead appearing about ready to rupture.

Wanda ignored him, walking out into the lounge room.

"Wanda, who the fuck was that on the phone?"

"Rocco," Wanda stated, as offhand as she could manage. "Rocco. Your brother."

There was a moment or two of sweet nothing before

Nuke smashed the tulips decisively against the table. Purple petals scattered in all directions.

Wanda just sat there, determined not to react as Nuke stormed out of the room. Nor did she react when he returned moments later, clutching his trusty revolver so tightly his knuckles turned white.

And with the gun in play, time seemed to stop.

33

W anda did her utmost to maintain her tough façade. Not reveal even a glimmer of the terror surging through her body.

While Nuke wasn't pointing the revolver at her, he wasn't not pointing it at her either, waving the thing around erratically, as though trying to make up his mind. His brain looked ready to burst.

Wanda remained very still, her resolve draining. Should she run? That could easily rile him up even more. The moment needed to pass. No matter how angry he was, he didn't want to kill her. Did he? Should she say something? Try and talk him down?

With a wild swing of his arm Nuke smashed the decanter of wine sitting at the side table. Deep red stained their pristine white walls. Oh great, she thought, who is going to clean that up? Wanda had to fight the urge to burst into laughter. He would have much worse than a wine stain to clean up if he went through with this.

Eyes blazing, Nuke stalked up. He raised the gun to his

wife's forehead. Wanda did all she could to remain still, to hold it together.

Nuke tapped her forehead surprisingly lightly with the gun barrel.

"Be careful," he muttered, through gritted teeth.

With that, Nuke turned on his heel and marched out of the room.

Wanda finally allowed herself to let go. Her knees went out from under her. Her arms shook. Her chest felt as though it was trapped under a massive boulder. She dissolved into tears, wondering how much worse she would feel when the adrenaline wore off. She took herself to the bathroom on shaky legs, ready to throw up.

MORNING SUN FILLED THE APARTMENT. Wanda loitered around the kitchen, willing Nuke to leave. For the longest time, she tried to sleep through until he had gone to work so she wouldn't have to face him. With the task at hand, she had been getting up earlier and memorising his routine.

His little pile was the object of her focus. Keys, wallet, phone. The phone was always going to be a significant risk. Best to swap it at the last possible second. At first, it had seemed smart to swap the phones in the night while he slept, except she had noticed occasionally Nuke used the phone first thing. Not so much Sundays, but who knew? The last thing she needed was to blow the whole endeavour before it even started because she switched the phones too early.

She had scuffed up her replica and was pretty happy with the results, confident the two phones were indistinguishable.

Nuke finished his cereal, babbling on about something. She had no idea what. There was no way of listening to him, not right now. What if he didn't go to the toilet? He almost always went before he left, but not absolutely always. What if he didn't today? Or what if he took the phone in with him? She hadn't thought of that. Regret swirled inside her, spiked by the fear. Why hadn't she just switched them last night while she had the chance?

"Wanda?"

She glanced up, snapping out of her daze.

"I said, it's been nice. Having you up in the mornings."

She did her best to give a little grunt and nothing more. She had the urge to smile and pretend and play nice, except if she was too nice it would seem out of place and he might twig something was up.

Go to the fucken toilet, she willed him as hard as she could.

Finally, he left the room. Wanda dashed over to his pile. She whipped the replica phone from her pocket all ready to make the switch.

"Hey, Wanda?"

The fright made her jump a mile and caused the phone to slip from her hand. She turned to face Nuke looking, she felt sure, incredibly guilty. He didn't seem to notice. Nor did he notice his phone seemed to have duplicated itself on the table.

"You seen my jacket?"

Wanda shook her head. Nuke headed back towards the bedroom. Any relief she felt was only momentary.

Two phones stared up at her from the table. Two identical phones. She had done too good a job. There was no way to tell them apart.

"Fuck."

She should have put some sort of distinguishing mark on the replica. Something only she would recognise. Except she hadn't. Too late now. Come on. There had to be a way to figure out which was which. If she had some time maybe. As it was she only had about three seconds or so until Nuke came back in.

"Fuck."

Quick, quick. No time. Nuke was coming. Wanda needed to make a decision. Right now.

Judging from the angle of the fall and... Whatever. She grabbed one of the phones and took a few steps away. The gravity of the situation weighed down on her. Wrong decision and they were fucked. Well, she had made her choice. Nothing she could do —

"Fuck."

With a burst of speed, Wanda dashed back to Nuke's pile. She switched phones, not because she knew, she simply changed her mind. Wanda just managed to slip what she hoped was Nuke's phone into her dressing gown pocket as he strode back into the room.

"Right. I'm off."

If Nuke had any suspicions, he was good at hiding them. He scooped up his keys, wallet and the phone, kissing Wanda on the forehead as he passed.

The front door slammed behind him.

Wanda made herself wait and it was torture. Only ten minutes and yet it seemed to last forever. Nuke had been surprising her a lot of late, walking in and catching her doing something. She didn't want it to happen again.

Once ten minutes had passed and Wanda was as confident as she could be Nuke had left the building she took the phone from her pocket, holding the thing like it was radioactive.

She switched it on. Success. This was Nuke's. Not the decoy. Her heart soared with relief... for about half a second, before crashing back to earth with the reality she actually had to go through with this now.

She attempted to type a text. Her hand shook so violently the message came out a jumbled bunch of letters.

"Fuck."

Taking as deep a breath as she could manage Wanda told herself to calm down. This was the easy part. With concerted concentration she typed out a message.

Swap. I'll babysit today. You own me.

Send.

If Wanda thought time waiting for Nuke to leave was long, it was nothing compared to waiting for Three's response. She decided to focus on little things. Things she should be able to control, like breathing. And stopping her hands from shaking.

Finally, the phone beeped. A simple two-letter response.

OK

With a little thrill, Wanda ignored the mess of 'what if...' questions plaguing her mind.

She sent a quick simple message to Van Damme.

Running behind. You start. I'll catch up.

She then used her own phone to call Kelly.

"It's me. We're on."

KELLY WAS ALREADY at the car park out the back of Clarence's Discount Safari when Wanda's call came through. No messing about, no chitchat. They were ready. She messaged Jonathan.

All clear. We are good to go.

This was exciting. Kelly had never done anything like this before. After a few moments Jonathan messaged back.

On my way.

Excellent. Everything was going to plan.

34

The day was the longest day Wanda had ever experienced. Time just didn't seem to want to pass. She shuffled through her apartment, moving from room to room with no real purpose or idea of what to do with herself. The apartment felt like a prison at the best of times and now the walls were closing in on her. What had she done? What if the robbery failed and all Wanda managed to achieve was getting Kelly killed?

She couldn't afford to think like that and yet stopping herself was all but impossible. It wasn't like there was anything else she could think about.

Nuke's phone rang, terrifying her. She should have known it would ring at some stage. It was almost impossible that it wouldn't. Somehow this wasn't something that had occurred to her. After a few rings the phone stopped, only to ring again not long after. And again, as though the thing was tormenting her. The sound of each ring like a spike in her heart.

The simplest solution would have been to turn the phone off, although she didn't want to touch it and switching it off seemed like bad luck somehow. Even better than turning it off maybe she should have destroyed the thing. They had no use for it anymore. Its only function now could be an unwanted link between her and the robbery. Indecision paralysed her.

In the end Wanda left the phone on the couch with a cushion over it and walked out of the room. She figured she could decide what to do with it later.

She lay on the bed, trying to find solace. From the other room Nuke's phone rang again. The cushion wasn't enough. She could still hear it. She did her best to ignore it when another phone rang.

The landline.

Hesitant and confused as to what this might mean in terms of the robbery, Wanda picked up.

"Hello?"

"Hey, honey." Nuke's voice was cold and calm.

Wanda sat up, rigid.

"So... What have you been up to today?"

"Ummm," the words died in her throat, not wanting to come out. "Nothing. You know."

"Yes," came Nuke's reply. "I know. I do know."

His tone was chilling. Wanda trembled in the silence.

"Hey, honey? I gotta go. But I'll be seeing you real soon," Nuke said and the phone went dead.

35

You don't know what you don't know, Three told himself. *You don't know what you don't know*. It was one of his father's expressions. The old man had a bunch of them, which annoyed the hell out of Three when he was alive and now stuck in his own mind the older he got.

It takes two not to tango, that was another one of the old man's favourites. Three was older than he should have been when he discovered there was a different version of that one that everyone else seemed to be aware of. *Tomorrow sometimes knows. A bird in the hand is worth a bird in the hand. You don't know what you don't know.*

Three usually avoided thinking about the old man, however today he welcomed the distraction. The stolen shipment frayed his nerves. The theft itself wasn't the problem. More what it meant, both the why and for the future. He and Nuke were supposed to babysit Van Damme together. Except it had become too easy just for one of them to do it. And now this. The Sharks already weren't happy. This wasn't going to help anything.

Three's hands slipped on the steering wheel. His palms

were sweaty, a sure sign of nerves. Just relax, he told himself. There was no point speculating wildly before he had all the information. *You don't know what you don't know.*

The streets around the vacant block were empty and lifeless. Three rounded the corner. Was this even the right place? Why on earth did Nuke want to meet out here?

A surge of relief ran through him as he spotted Nuke's Jag. Good. He was here at least. Three parked behind Nuke's car and jumped out of his Mustang. Looking for Nuke and straining to keep a leash on his agitation.

Three's panic receded slightly upon spotting Nuke, standing in the vacant lot. He clambered through the cyclone fence and hurried over.

"Where the fuck have you been?"

Nuke didn't bother to answer.

"Everyone's looking for you. You don't answer your phone?"

"I do when it rings."

Three shot him a look of impatient exasperation. "We've got a big fucken problem. What happened this morning?"

Nuke turned, strolling idly away, into the knee-high grass. Three stuck close alongside him.

"The shipment was stolen." Fear trickled through his voice. "You were supposed to babysit."

Nothing. Three darted in front of Nuke, trying to get his full attention, searching for any sort of reaction. "Nuke?"

"Hey, Three," Nuke said, his voice sounding vague and detached. "Can I ask you a question? What's going on with you and Wanda?"

"Wait... What?"

"Simple question, Three. What's going on with you and my wife?"

The change of topic took a few moments for Three to

even process. He sighed. "Nuke, your paranoia and your jealousy, it's all fun stuff, but right now we need to focus or we're both fucked."

Nuke nodded looking serious. "Okay."

"You texted me this morning and said you would babysit..."

In amongst the junk, Nuke spotted a discarded toilet cistern lid. Casually he leaned down.

"So I didn't think anything more about it —"

Three never got to finish his sentence. With an explosion of precise violence Nuke swung the porcelain lid, smashing it across the side of his friend's head, sending the big guy tumbling to the ground. Summoning as much anger and force and violence as he could muster Nuke clocked him in the head twice more.

"No, wait. What was I meant to do? Count to five?" Nuke asked the bloody mess in front of him. "One... two... three... four... five... Hmmm. Didn't work. I still want to kill you." He crashed the remains of the lid down on Three again and again, obliterating it in the process. "And you better believe I'm thinking of you."

Nuke bought the remnants of the lid down with last almighty strike. Three twitched slightly, not long for this world.

All done, Nuke turned and strolled casually back to his car, leaving his former friend to die.

CONSTABLE MARKS WAS HAVING a heck of a day. It was a Sunday, which were generally fairly quiet, hence why she had been assigned the shift. She was still new, having only been a police officer a few months now. Except today wasn't quiet. Already this morning there had been several reports of assault and two stolen bicycles. In addition, some youths had obviously taken it upon themselves to smash as many car windows as they could in the surrounding streets, leading to a steady stream of irate car owners parading through the doors.

And now this.

She had asked her superior and only other officer on duty, First Constable Davis how to handle it, but despite having been in the force several years longer than her he was borderline useless as usual.

If there was a God or any common sense in the police force, Constable Marks would soon outrank Davis. He barely seemed equipped to tie his shoelaces, let alone do anything akin to police work. So how to deal with the issue was Constable Marks call and hers alone.

Deep down she suspected she should call Detective Griggs, except she had called Detective Griggs somewhat flippantly on her first Sunday shift and received such a bollocking she was disinclined to do it again.

Griggs had plied her with a full on lecture about the number of hours a detective had to work Monday to Saturday and how Sundays were sacred, not for any religious reason, but because it was the only time Griggs got to spend with her partner and their two girls, uninterrupted. Constable Marks understood all that, she really did, however this was a situation she had no clue how to handle. So she made the call.

An hour later Constable Marks and First Constable Davis loitered awkwardly as Detective Griggs marched into the station.

"This better be worth fucking up by Sunday," she snarled, looking decidedly un-detective like in her tan shorts and a flannelette shirt.

Constable Marks led her to the observation room where she indicated to the monitor. First Constable Davis followed behind. The monitor showed Nuke sitting stone-faced in an interview room.

"Do you know this guy?" Constable Marks asked.

Detective Griggs squinted at the monitor before shaking her head. "Should I?"

"It's the darnedest thing. He just wandered in off the street this morning. Wanted to turn himself in."

"For what?"

"That's the rub. He won't say. He said something about being offered immunity and is refusing to speak to anyone except for..." She checked her notes. "An Agent Harris or a Detective Hunt."

Griggs gave her a sceptical look. Constable Marks handed over Detective Hunt's card.

As these two talked, nobody noticed First Constable Davis slip out of the room and place an urgent call on his phone.

"Yes, yes..." he stressed. "Someone needs to get down here. Right now."

NUKE STARED STRAIGHT AHEAD. He was used to sitting in rooms like this, waiting on cops. Today though was a little unusual, given the circumstances. He had never sat in one of these rooms voluntarily before.

Finally, the door opened and Detective Griggs wandered in, still wearing her shorts and flannel shirt. Nuke scoffed. o

"Nice outfit."

"Blow me. It's Sunday."

Griggs sat and the two stared at one another, sizing each other up.

"Just you? Don't you idiots usually come in pairs? Good cop, bad cop? Talking cop, silent cop?"

"Like I said, it's Sunday. Hang around until tomorrow, who knows? You might get a whole team of people. Today, just me."

"Well, you're wasting your time."

"Oh yeah, why is that?"

Nuke shook his head. "I know you don't have to be too smart to be a cop, but you all must be fucken stupid."

Griggs stared back unfazed.

"I made myself quite clear to the constable." He cupped his hands around his mouth to help amplify the volume of his voice. "I will only speak to Agent Harris or Detective Hunt."

He rested back in his chair, waiting for her to fuck off.

Griggs nodded, in no hurry.

"Yeah, the constable did mention that. But if that's the case, you've got a bit of a problem then."

The two continued to eyeball one another, neither backing down.

"You see, there is no Agent Harris or Detective Hunt."

Nuke furrowed his brow. "What you mean?"

"Did I stutter? We've checked state police, federal police. Harris and Hunt just don't exist."

She waited, watching him as her words sunk in.

"And this?" She held up Detective Hunt's card, before sliding across the desk in front of Nuke. "This isn't one of our cards."

She pulled out one of her own cards placing it alongside the first card.

"This is what our cards look like."

Nuke examined the two cards. Not only were they different designs, when placed side-by-side like this

Detective Griggs' card looked considerably more professional.

"So, what do you want to do here?"

Nuke continued to stare at the cards, his mind galloping.

"You can either wait for your imaginary friends to show up. Or you can talk to me."

The man and his wife had been in the car just that bit too long. What started out as a fun adventure was becoming uncomfortable. He was dressed in a smart casual suit, she was all done up in her floral dress, the two of them much classier than their surroundings.

Easing the car along at about twenty, the man tried to spot something, anything, that would give them a clue as to where they were, whether they were close or not. All they could see was the dark façade of the factories and warehouses.

"We are too far down," he told the woman.

"How do you know?"

The steady stream of cold, lifeless buildings continued.

"There's nothing out here. It's a restaurant. It's gotta be near something."

He tried to hide the tension in his voice. Deserted streets always made him anxious. Not that he would ever admit that out loud. What if they were ambushed? Somebody blocking the road or something? Like in that book by Tom Wolfe. Which one was it again? Vanity Fair? The road blocked by hooligans so that they could rob the drivers that stopped. And look how that turned out. No, these dark, deserted streets were definitely bad news. He preferred the safety of crowds and traffic.

"I don't know," she said. "Obscure is the new black."

"Nah." He slowed the car even more. "Obscure is one thing. This place was featured in Metro. There'd be lights and other people and cars."

He gave it another fifty metres or so and made his decision.

"I'm turning around."

She didn't object. The thing was if they hadn't turned around at that exact moment they would probably have never hit anything.

"What was that?" the woman shrieked wide-eyed, arms splayed out to hold her place in her seat as he came to a stop.

"I don't know," the man said. Impossible to keep the panic from his voice now.

They had definitely hit something. Whatever it was lay on the road behind them. Not moving. The absence of streetlights made it tricky to determine what the thing was, however if he had to guess the man was ninety-nine percent sure the object was a human body.

37

Boss watched the distraught man and woman both talking at once. Both trying to explain what happened. The fear and stress making them talk too fast. The uniformed police officer with his little notepad and pen struggling to keep up. The couple concerned they had to be absolutely in the clear or they would get blamed themselves. Not that they had done anything wrong.

The couple were pretty dressed up, obviously on their way somewhere when it all happened. Dressed up sure, but not a patch on Boss. I'm too sexy for this waiting room, Boss thought to himself. Like the 80s song. It was a game he played. Wherever he was at, Boss strived to be the best-dressed person. Something he learned from NBA players. No matter what the situation, arriving at games and shit, they always look good. Wearing suits. Looking fine.

Boss adopted a similar attitude in his day to day life. If he was out anywhere in public, he made an effort. People tended to take you more seriously if you looked the part. He had his own style. Urban Tough he called it and it was working for him. Rarely did he go anywhere and not feel like the smartest dresser in the room. Hence, I'm too sexy for... *insert location here*. Although in fairness ten o'clock at night in the emergency waiting room was never going to be the toughest competition.

Beside him, String looked sharp too. Not as sharp as Boss of course and really only dressed up because Boss was. Blindingly following the alpha's lead whether he knew it or not. Apart from that there was Mr and Mrs Nobody trying their best and not doing too bad for a middle-aged couple and that was about it. Everyone else other than the doctors, nurses and cleaners (who didn't count cos they were in uniforms) looked dressed more to say do a spot of weekend gardening than go out in public.

The strong odour of cleaning products filled the air. Bleach and disinfectant and whatnot. The smell always reminded Boss of his Gran. Visiting her in the home, those last days. Gran like a different person, inside and out. Shrunken and lifeless and not recognising anyone and shit. Hard to reconcile with the Gran of just a bit earlier that let him have three Arnott's Assorted biscuits for afternoon tea and liked listening to talkback.

The hospital corridor was loud too, man. Busy. Even at this time of night. People coming and going. Patients and public and doctors and nurses and cleaners.

Despite the busyness and the noise Boss could still hear it. The ding, ding, ding.

The dings were soft and everything else loud and yet that's what he could hear. Ever present. There.

He glanced over. String was sprawled in the seat alongside him, leaning forward. Completely engaged in his book. Like a ten-year-old kid who had just discovered Harry

Potter. It wasn't Harry Potter though. It was Sun Tzu's 'The Art of War'. Boss had read it of course, although only once like a normal person. He wasn't sure whether String was either the slowest reader in the history of the universe or if he had read the thing eighteen times already. Boss could understand reading something once not constantly, cover to cover.

In String's other hand were two shiny Baoding balls, which he rotated endlessly in his palm and which, as they revolved around and around and around, let out a slight, unyielding ding.

Ding, ding, ding.

Boss glared at the balls, then the book then String's face and shook his head. String was far too engaged to notice.

"Yo, have they saved the Princess yet?"

"Sorry, Boss?" String said, glancing up.

Boss nodded at the book. A puzzled look flashed across String's eyes.

"Princess? It... It's not that sort of book, Boss."

Over near the man and the woman and the police officer with his little notepad the lift doors opened and out stepped Randall. Randall with his shaggy hair and patterned shirts, always chilled, always looking like he had just come from a beach party.

Boss LED Randall into Saxon's room with String tagging along behind.

Saxon was not in a good way, hooked up to all kind of machines. The trio stood at the end of his bed looking down at the dealer. Saxon wasn't looking back. He wasn't looking at anything 'cept his lids, his eyes taped shut.

"What happened?" Randall asked in a whisper.

"Well…" said Boss, seeing no need to keep his voice down. "They bought him in cos he got run over, but it was getting shot that really fucked him up."

Randall pulled a pained face. "They shot him, then they ran him over?"

Boss shook his head. "Mr and Mrs Nobody out there ran him over. Someone else shot him and dumped him on the road."

One of the machines beeped quietly, letting them know Saxon was still alive, at least for the time being.

"One of yours, isn't he?"

Randall nodded. "Best earner."

"Was," said String. "Now he's your best vegetable."

Good old String, Boss thought. Always knows just what to say. Boss turned to face Randall.

"This shit don't happen by accident, you feel me? Whoever did this, they wanted you to know."

"Flat Stanley here is a warning," said String. "They're sending you a message. We're coming for you."

DESPITE THE HOUR, the hospital café on the ground floor had a decent amount of customers, with a mix of visitors and patients and various hospital staff.

Tucked away in a back corner Boss and String sat opposite Randall in a half booth. Boss and Randall both had coffees. String had an overly elaborate ice chocolate and was struggling with the excessive amount of cream on top.

Why anyone would even think to order such a thing was beyond Boss. And it's not like it was an accident. Like he didn't know what he was in for. There were huge pictures behind the counter. String picked the drink out, like from a line up. Why anyone would ... Anyway...

"This place is depressing," Randall commented glancing about.

"It's a hospital," String said. "What do you expect?"

Boss squirmed. String was spread out against him, sitting too close. String always seemed to occupy more space than necessary. Boss inched over attempting to give himself more room, preferring physical contact with the wall rather than String. The issue was of course that making more room for himself might be futile as String would probably just absorb the freshly created space as well.

"You got an important decision to make."

"Jeez, look at that," Randall said. He indicated towards the counter where a girl of about ten had just entered with her parents. The girl clutched a large teddy bear, almost bigger than she was.

"Look at what? The bear? They sell 'em at the gift shop." String said.

"The girl. It's like, what, eleven o'clock? She shouldn't still be up, not at her age." Randall ignored Boss' glare, focusing on the little girl instead. "Maybe it's to do with her disease."

"Randall..."

"I wonder what she's got."

"You can't just ignore this, Randall," Boss said balancing his voice somewhere between calm and steady, yet also firm.

"I know... I just..." Randall jammed a thumbnail between two of his bottom teeth. "I don't wanna deal with this right now."

"Tough," String said, draining the dregs of his ice chocolate and leaving a little spot of cream right on the tip of his nose. "It's not going away."

Boss thought String must have finally finished his drink now except String discovered some ice blocks in the bottom of the glass which he sucked into his mouth. He proceeded to crunch them loudly between his teeth. Boss glared at him. As per form, String didn't notice and went right on crunching.

"Why does there have to be an issue?" Randall whined. "Why can't we all just play nice? Live and let live? Everybody happy."

String snorted loudly between the crunching. "Hard to have much sympathy with you over this. Since the day you came up with this harebrained scheme Boss has told you repeatedly. He runs the south-east, The Sharks run the west."

"Have you been down there? The university? It's bigger than Chadstone. They've taken over half the suburb. Students everywhere. There's enough customers for all of us. A little competition is healthy."

"Not surprisingly they don't see it that way. You're setting up business in their backyard. You think The Sharks are going to like that? They see that as you pissing on their leg. They don't like people pissing on their legs," Boss said in that same steady tone, reaffirming how serious he was. "One way or another, they will shut you down."

He let his words sink in. At least hoping they were sinking in. It wasn't always easy to tell with Randall. "Like it or not, there's a war coming. A war of your own making."

"A war?" Randall moaned. "I don't want a fucking war, man." He shook his head. "What if I do nothing? Just, you know..."

"There'll still be a war, you'll just lose quicker."

Randall waved him away, frustrated.

"You started it, Randall. This is entirely your doing. Now you either fight or you die."

A pained look sagged Randall's features. "I mean, what the... I don't know... I was never trying to start a war. I just wanted to sell some gear, you know?"

He glanced up for some sympathy. There wasn't a whole lot coming from across the table.

"Will you help me?"

Boss scoffed at him. "Will I go to war with The Sharks? No chance."

"I don't wanna go to war with them either, you know, The Sharks?"

"Yeah, but I'm not the one putting myself in a position where I have to."

Leaning over to the side String tried to get a look at the boards behind the counter. "I might get another drink. What do you reckon? Boss? Should I get another drink? Boss?"

"We're kinda in the middle of something here, String."

"Yeah, I know. Just if we are going to be here for a while I should order it now."

Boss ignored him, focused on Randall. "There's no getting away from this, Randall."

"I don't... I can't..." Randall shook his head in frustration.

"Maybe I should just get coffee this time. I don't usually drink coffee this late though."

"I mean... What do I know about running a fucken war? Please help me, Boss. There's got to be something you can do."

Boss shook his head. He didn't think there was.

"The ice chocolate was okay. A little milky. Not enough chocolate."

And out of nowhere, Boss had a brainwave. It was like the heavens parting, bathing him in sunshine.

"Take String," Boss told Randall, fight to keep the smile from his face.

"What like... A consultant or something?"

Boss nodded.

"You sure, Boss?" String asked.

"Yeah," said Boss. "I can spare you."

Part 4 - A Thousand Victories

(String's Big Idea)

R andall stomped about, hugging himself and blowing on his hands. What the fuck was going on with this weather? It was supposed to be summer. It didn't have to be hot, but a little consistency would be nice. Geez. It wasn't like he could see his breath or anything but still. He should have worn a jacket except the only jacket he had that he liked was his sheepskin one and that would have been way too much for summer.

It hardly seemed worth purchasing an in-between jacket for those few summer days the weather couldn't get its shit together.

There was a misconception around Randall that he was tight. It was a reputation which had followed him all the way from school. A characterisation he felt was a little unfair. Sure he was careful with his money, but he would spend if he had to. It was just common sense to be smart with your cash and not spend flippantly. Which was why working with String was killing him.

Randall wasn't stupid. He knew going to war was going to cost him and once he overcame his initial reluctance to take on The Sharks at all, he was happy to outlay whatever it took. The problem was while to Randall the idea of war conjured up helicopters attacks and Ride of the Valkyries blaring and people loving the smell of napalm in the morning, String seemed to view it more like a covert CIA operation to overthrow the government, with just as much oversight and transparency. String had already started spending on God knows what and didn't seem at all keen to share the details with Randall.

This wasn't going to fly. Randall confronted String and after some back-and-forth String reluctantly agreed to include him a little more. So now they were on their way somewhere to do something although String refused to divulge exactly where they were going or why.

Or they were supposed to be on their way somewhere if String would ever get himself out here. At this rate, Randall was gonna freeze to death before they had even started.

"So, what have we got?" he asked when String finally emerged from the shop. This was better. At least now they could walk. Might warm Randall up a bit.

String took his time, that way he always seemed to do, like every utterance was a fucken fortune cookie of wisdom.

"What's the best way to win a war?"

Randall didn't know and wasn't in the mood for games. Answer questions with answers, not questions.

"Don't fight it," String went on.

"Don't fight it? Don't fight the war? Isn't that what I wanted in the first place?"

"From the recon I have done so far I can tell you The Sharks are a tough organisation."

"We already knew that."

"My recon confirmed it. You take them on you will lose."

"Okay..." said Randall, rubbing his arms, patience dwindling. "So how do we beat them?"

String stopped and put a hand on Randall's shoulder. He raised a finger on his other hand in the air in a pose he obviously thought made him appear wise. To Randall, it looked as though he was appealing to get someone out in cricket.

"In war, avoid what is strong, attack what is weak."

Randall nodded, waiting for more.

"We attack from here," String said, lightly tapping his forehead. "Not here." He pointed at his bicep.

"Right," said Randall, at least able to pretend he had any clue what the fuck String was on about.

String and Randall headed down the street to an apartment building.

"Where are we going, man?" Randall asked as they waited to be buzzed up.

"To see a man about a dog," String said.

Much as Randall wanted to know more, he was fast beginning to realise the sense of suspense and theatrics was part of the cost of working with String. Well, that and the fat fee String was demanding for his 'consultation' services.

They were let into an apartment by a stubbly, half asleep dude who Randall presumed to be the owner or at least tenant of the apartment.

"Randall, this is my main man, Mike," said String after giving Mike a bro hug. "He's helping."

By helping Randall assumed String meant on the payroll as well.

"S'up," said Mike. Was he especially tired or did his eyes always look like this?

They moved into the lounge room which had been converted into a makeshift video edit suite, with a couple of monitors, a variety of computer parts and more cords and wires than Randall had ever seen in one place.

Two chairs waited at the desk, a fancy leather swivel chair which Mike sunk into and a chair which looked like it had been pulled over from the kitchen that String took, leaving no chair for Randall who decided he was meant to stand awkwardly behind.

"How are we doing?" String asked.

"Meh, not great," said Mike.

"Mike's been on a reconnaissance mission as well. Getting us going."

The monitor crackled to life revealing some decidedly unimpressive images. It was a corridor somewhere.

"So, this is it? This is his place?"

"Yep," said Mike. "I got some stuff but I don't know if it is any good."

A man and a woman appeared, poorly framed at the bottom of the screen. A large white circle burnt out a good proportion of the upper right corner of the image.

"That's the guy who lives there."

"Nuke," String said, bringing his hands in prayer position, pointer fingers poking into his lips.

"The other one is his wife," Mike went on.

"Uhuh. And this is what we've got?"

"Umm, yeah," said Mike, hitting the fast forward. "They go in and out of a bunch of times. Another chick comes over to visit the wife quite a bit."

"Hmmm," said String, pondering what he was witnessing. "I'm not gonna lie, Mike. This is garbage. Completely unacceptable." He tapped a pen against the burnt out circle. "What's this?"

"It's cos the camera is in a light."

"The angle is all wrong anyway. I told you putting the camera in the light was a bad idea."

"Yes, and I told you it's not like I can set up a tripod in the middle of their fucken corridor. The camera has to go somewhere and unless you want them to see it, I have to hide it in something."

Mike threw his hands in the air and turned to Randall as if to say 'Back me up here'.

"Hey, man. I don't even know what the fuck is going on, so..."

"Don't look at him," String told Mike. "You're talking to me. Now, I told you what I wanted with this footage, it is up to you to provide it. If that means you have to go back in there and —"

"Yeah, right," Mike scoffed. "I was lucky to get in there once. The place is like Fort Knox."

"Whether you have to go back in there or not," String repeated softly. "We need better footage than this. This is unusable and unacceptable."

Mike pressed some buttons. "It looks better when the light's not on. Maybe some of the stuff at the start. I'm not saying it's good, but it's better."

The footage scrambled into rewind. A sideways image of the door at a much lower angle flashed by, disappearing quickly again.

"Wait," said String. "What was that?"

Mike went back and played the footage through at normal speed. All three of them cocked their heads to one side to watch. On-screen Nuke, Wanda and Three appeared. Although sideways the image was far better quality, with no glaring burnt out light circle to compete with.

"That was fucken scary shit," said Mike. "It was when I

was installing the camera. I was dressed as a fucken repairman, halfway up the ladder and these jokers came out of their place and just stared at me. I thought for sure they were on to me and were coming out to fuck me up. They kept staring. They were off their heads or something."

On-screen Nuke and Three stare about vaguely before bumping fists. All three of them not with it. Three kisses Wanda on the lips before stumbling up the hall.

String sat bolt upright, on the edge of his chair. "Can you rotate that?"

Mike made a few quick adjustments via the keyboard and mouse and the image played up the right way. String sat there for a moment or two too long, either thinking it through or milking the anticipation, Randall couldn't be sure which.

"That..." String said finally, pointing at the screen, "is perfect."

"Oh, okay, cool," said Mike. The pleasant surprise of an unexpected victory.

"Okay, rewind it, stop... There. There."

The image settled on Three and Wanda's peck on the lips.

"There. That's what I'm interested in," said String becoming animated. He indicated to various parts of the screen with his pen. "Now, you need to photoshop it. Get rid of Nuke all together and make the kiss longer. Intimate."

"Wait. You want a still image or video?"

"Video."

Mike shook his head. "Well, I can't photoshop it. Photoshop is for photos. That's why they call it *'Photoshop'*. The clue is in the name."

Once again he looked to Randall to back him up. Randall gave him nothing.

String glared at the editor. "You know what I asked you to do?"

Mike shrugged. String stood, buttoning his coat. Discussion over.

"No, I can't do that," Mike protested. "I mean, of course, I can, but it will look like fucken shit. I'm not ILM. It's a single shot. You can't cut it. And then you will blame me cos it doesn't look as good as you think it should..."

String examined Mike, a curious look on his face.

"What?"

"I'm not sure what gave you the impression this was a discussion."

And with that String strode from the apartment. Randall figured it was probably his cue to leave too.

FIRST FLOOR, String had told him. Randall found the building and let himself in. The stairs creaked and moaned as he made his way up, each step kicking up dust and adding to the decidedly musky odour of the place.

From the landing the office gave the impression of a detective agency out of a film noir, complete with frosted glass in the door window. Inside the illusion was shattered by String's lack of possessions. He had an old desk and a chair, some boxes and not much else.

"What do you think?" String asked, clearly pleased with himself.

"I think you're taking this consulting thing a little too seriously," Randall replied.

Once again there was nowhere for him to sit.

"I don't agree. I reckon there could be something in this consulting. There's a lot of potential. This could be a whole new line of work for me. There are plenty of people out there who could use my expertise."

Randall could see a bunch more issues with what String was saying than positives.

"Plenty of people? Who? How would you ... I mean... how will you get clients?"

"They will find me. It's the way of the universe."

"What do you mean, man? You think they are just going to show up?"

"You did."

Not much Randall could say to refute that. String raised his wise finger again.

"He will win who prepares himself. Opportunities multiply as they are seized."

String tossed a stack of enlarged photos towards Randall. They fanned out as they slid across the desk. All part of the show. You could have just passed on to me, Randall wanted to say, but he bit his tongue.

They were surveillance images of the two guys from the video.

"The big guy is Three."

Big was an understatement. The bloke would likely get mistaken for The Hulk if he were painted green.

"The scary one is Nuke."

Randall wasn't sure. They both looked pretty scary to him. A queasiness swept through his stomach.

"They are The Sharks' main muscle."

True to form the next image showed these two with The Sharks. Randall recognised Ian and Emily.

The final shots showed Nuke sitting at an outdoor table at a café drinking coffee by himself.

"Nuke. He is our target."

Randall shuffled through the photos again.

"Why do they call him Nuke?"

"He's a total nut job. Completely unstable, especially when he's angry.

"And this is your big idea? Piss this guy off?"

"If your opponent is of choleric temper, seek to irritate him."

"What does choleric mean?"

String ignored him, so Randall assumed he most likely didn't know either.

"Out of chaos leaps opportunity. Attack him where he is unprepared, appear where you are not expected."

There was a pause, Randall waiting for String to speak proper sentences again instead of riddles.

"There's no point antagonising someone rational, they'll just act rationally," String went on. "Instability is good, trust me."

He leaned back in his swivel chair, getting into the whole private detective vibe.

"We can't fight The Sharks directly. They're too strong. Too powerful. But if we get them to fight amongst themselves." He gave Randall a mysterious grin. "Then they weaken their own unit. We are winning a war they don't even realise they are fighting."

Looking at String you would believe they had won the war already. Randall wished he had String's confidence. Still, what did he know about any of this stuff? What if String was right? It sounded good. That was a start, he supposed.

So Randall left it at a nod, and hoped String knew what he was doing.

The two of them caught a tram to Mike's place, mostly keeping to themselves, String with his nose stuck in his Sun Tzu book. Not a lot to say if they weren't discussing 'the job' as String preferred to call it.

Mike played them the now doctored images and Randall was surprised what a good job he had done. Impressed even. Nuke had disappeared completely from the footage and Wanda and Three's gentle peck now played out like a full on pash.

"Yes. Very nice," String said with a pleased expression plastered across his face. "I believe it is perfect."

"Then you're an idiot," Mike responded. "Look…"

He played through the footage in slow motion, pointing out its various inequities.

"Look, there's a full-on glitch here. It looks like he's punching her there and then his arm disappears. And who knows what the fuck —"

"They won't be studying this in film school, Scorsese. No one will ever watch it that in-depth. For what we are after, it is perfect."

.   .   .

STRING TOOK them to a classy bar to celebrate. It wasn't like any bar Randall had ever been to before with leather chairs and mahogany tables. He was surprised they let him in or didn't require him to wear some sort of suit coat or something. He and the equally scruffy Mike stood out like a pair of sore thumbs, Mike not helping matters by sitting low in his chair with his feet up inappropriately on the table.

Returning from the bar String had a scotch for each of them. Sure, String may have handed over the money to buy the drinks but Randall imagined he was probably paying for them.

"Gentlemen, to success," String said, raising his glass.

"So, what now?" Mike asked.

"We bring Nuke in and shake him down."

"Who's playing the cops? You two? Nup. No way you two are cops."

"Undercover."

Mike shook his head. "You maybe. Maybe. No way anyone is gonna believe this beach bum mother fucker is a cop."

String looked appraising at Randall. "What if we shave his head?"

"Hey, whoa, do I get a say in any of this, man?" String and Mike kept talking over the top of him, giving Randall the impression he probably didn't.

"Nup. Wouldn't matter. You two aren't cops."

"So, what then?"

"Get an actor."

Randall shook his head. He already wasn't sure exactly what String had told Mike about this whole thing and he certainly didn't want anyone else involved or on the payroll.

Then again he wasn't too keen on playing cop to fool some psycho nutcase either.

AND SO IT was a few days later Randall found himself crowded into String's office, still with nowhere to sit and meeting the toothiest fucken dude he had ever met, Andrew the actor. Fair dinkum, when he smiled it was like a solar flare or some shit.

It wasn't just his smile. Andrew was too good-looking and wore the coolest clothes Randall had ever seen, all of which fitted him perfectly. *No cop is this cool* Randall mumbled in his head, until he caught himself and wondered why he cared Mike thought this guy would make a better pretend cop than him.

"Tell them about *Neighbours*," Mike prompted.

He and Andrew were on the other side of the desk, no chairs for them either.

"Oh, it's nothing..." said Andrew, offering them a new version of that smile.

"It is not nothing. It's a recurring role."

"Eight days at this stage," Andrew nodded, making it clear it was actually quite a big deal despite his modesty.

"And he's got a couple of ads coming up too," added Mike.

"Impressive," said String, clearly enjoying himself. "Well, good to meet you, Andrew. We'll be in touch."

He stood and shook Andrew's hand. Mike walked Andrew out.

Randall took the 8 x 10 headshot Andrew had given them. All teeth. Reminding Randall of a crocodile. A very good-looking crocodile. He didn't need to ask String what he thought. He could feel the excitement radiating from him.

Mike made his way back in. "Hey? What did I tell you?"

"Yes, he's good. Where do you know him from?" String asked.

"Around. I've done a few short films with him. The guy is seriously talented. He is going to be huge. Better than you two."

"Hmmm. That's exciting about *Neighbours*. I'm not convinced though..." He took the 8 x 10 from Randall. "Are you sure he's not a bit too..." His voice trailed away to nothing.

"Up to you, but remember if this guy, Nuke, if he doesn't believe you're cops, your whole deal is blown, right there. Gone."

String nodded thoughtfully.

"Whatever," Mike said. "I don't give a fuck." He moved on quickly. "Now, this van... We're gonna have to get cracking if you want me to build this fucken thing as well."

"Van?" Randall asked, sending a glare String's way.

"Oh, yeah. We're gonna need a bit more cash. We are gonna build a police surveillance van."

"Can I have a word with you, please?" Randall marched out into the corridor outside String's office. He half expected Mike to come too but he didn't fortunately.

"You see these?" String pulled out a fake police ID, like a kid with a new toy. "How cool are they? Freeze, Sucker," he said, shoving the badge in Randall's face.

"A fucken van?"

String shrugged, still focused on the ID. "We need a location."

"This lunacy... It's out of control, man," Randall

complained. "Actors, vans, fake IDs. I'm pissing money here."

"All warfare is based on deception," String said in his sensei voice.

When Randall didn't react, he tried again.

"It is best to win without fighting."

Randall stared back blankly.

"He will win who prepares himself and waits to take the enemy unprepared."

"Stop it."

"You brought me in."

"Yes, to fix the fucken problem with The Sharks, not to build vans and play dress up with your little friend in there."

String's response was measured and calm. He placed a firm hand on Randall's shoulder. "You brought me in, yes? Go with that instinct. Relax. Trust me."

Randall rolled his eyes. A van it was then, he guessed.

40

R andall was annoyed the whole way there. They were
checking out the van Mike had built for them.
Convinced it was a useless, unnecessary expense he sulked.
However, seeing the van, he was grudgingly impressed.
Mike had done a good job.

The old campervan was deceptively large on the inside,
with all interior ripped out and replaced with faux
surveillance gear and a small table, still leaving comfortably
enough room for several adults. Even knowing the van
wasn't real Randall had to keep reminding himself it was a
prop and that it couldn't actually do any surveillance. If it
was this convincing for him, he felt sure the van would fool
Nuke without question.

"And you will sit here," Mike told Randall on the tail end
of their tour. For once someone had remembered a chair for
him, although he wasn't sure he wanted one for this.

"Me? Wait, what? No. Why will I be here?"

"You and Mike are going to sit here, at the back," String
told him. "As... what did Andrew call it again? An extra. You
and Mike will be extras."

"Why?"

"To add an element of realism."

"Wait a sec, man," Randall said. "If I'm not believable enough to be a main cop, why am I believable enough to be a background cop?" He turned on Mike. "What did you say? No way this beach bum mother fucker is a cop?"

Mike shrugged. "This is different. You're surveillance guy. Surveillance guys can be beach bums. It's different from being a regular cop."

"Having a few extra people will give the scene an air of authenticity," String said.

"Or you think it would be better to have four of us here in case this Nuke guy goes berserk," Randall countered.

String gave him a Cheshire cat smile, saying nothing and making him Randall think he was probably right on the money.

Reluctantly Randall took a seat. "So, what am I supposed to do?"

Mike shrugged again. "You're a surveillance guy. Not that hard."

The selection of knobs and buttons in front of Randall was overwhelming. He guessed since most of it wasn't hooked up he couldn't break anything, which was something at least. Still, he had to be believable. If he had to be a part of this scene, the last thing he wanted to do was be obviously faking it and blow the whole illusion. He began pressing buttons and —

"Whoa, whoa. The fuck are you doing?" Mike asked.

"Being a surveillance guy?"

"That's the worst surveillance guy acting I've ever seen. Don't touch anything. Just sit there. That's all you need to do."

. . .

THE BIG DAY FINALLY ARRIVED. String was playing a Detective Hunt while Andrew was going to do all the talking as Agent Harris.

Andrew seemed to be trying a little too hard to look like an undercover detective or agent or whatever he was meant to be. Turnbull-esque leather jacket, mirrored sunglasses, toothpick lolling from his lip. But from the moment they stepped foot in the van, he sold his performance. Transforming into this tough as guts cop before Randall's eyes and Randall could see how Andrew had snagged his eight-day semi-recurring role in *Neighbours*. He was good.

String seemed to be doing a reasonable job as well, although his part was less demanding, sitting there and staring at Nuke and not saying anything.

If indeed String's plan was to have Mike and Randall there as extra help in case things went south, one look at Nuke told Randall it wouldn't have done them that any good. Nuke could have comfortably taken all four of them at once.

Very quickly Randall was pleased they had gone with Andrew after all. Before things had even started Randall felt like there was a golf ball lodged in his throat and doubted he would have been able to talk properly. Sitting there, pretending to operate the machines without touching anything made him nervous enough. He almost shat himself when Nuke addressed him directly, asking something about all the wires in the van and what they did. He was terrified Nuke was watching him, aware he was doing fuck all and he would blow the whole charade.

Everything moved like lightning. Nuke was only in the van for a few minutes and Randall got so caught up in the entire event he failed to see there were problems until it was almost over.

"So thank you for your kind offer," Nuke told the pretend cops sitting in front of him. "But I am afraid I am going to have to tell you to get fucked."

The van descended into silence.

"I'm gonna go unless you wanna try and push some other bullshit on me?"

Andrew dismissed him with a wave of his hand.

"Hey," String said, surprising everyone by breaking his silence and jumping awkwardly to his feet. He handed Nuke another card. "Take the card. You never know."

Nuke stared a good amount of hate in String's direction (or in Detective Hunt's direction, as Nuke thought he was), however didn't toss the card away this time, wedging it in his jeans' pocket on his way out of the van.

A wary silence fell on the occupants as they waited, making sure Nuke was gone.

"And... Scene," said Andrew in a slightly camp voice, switching from his tough cop persona back to his regular actor persona. "Well, that went well. Very well."

Randall shot a quick glance about the van. He was quite impressed but it was clear that nobody shared his enthusiasm. String was fuming. Mike didn't know where to look.

"Luck's a fickle river?" String said, questioning and quoting all in one.

"I know, right? That's one of the things about improv. Sometimes things just come to you like - boom! That lightning strike of inspiration."

It was as though Andrew was high, excitement radiating from him. "I was a little unsure at first, but as it went on, I was really able to capture the essence of that kick-ass, low-grade cop thing. It was raw. Real."

Whatever acting ability Andrew may have possessed, it

was certainly a lot stronger than his ability to read a room. Or in this case, a van. He heartily shook String's hand, slapping him on the back.

"It was good. It was fun. Big fella, you were great too."

He turned and pumped Randall's hand. "Thanks, thanks. I really enjoyed this."

Andrew winked at his mate Mike. "Guess that's it. I'm around. You need anything else, just let me know."

A vacant smile and empty nod was about all String could manage.

With both Nuke and Andrew now gone and only the core group of String, Randall and Mike remaining the stunned silence hung heavily in the air. Randall tried to think of a good word to describe String's expression. Flabbergasted maybe?

"What the hell was that?"

Mike didn't respond.

"I thought he was quite good," Randall said quietly.

"Quite good?" String shrieked. "Are you insane?"

"What was the problem?"

"The monitor. The monitor."

Randall had never seen String this agitated. He looked as though he was about to burst.

"He had one job. All he had to do was get Nuke to look at the monitor. That's what this whole thing was about." String began to pace as best he could in the tight confines of the van. "Going on about bullshit and immunity. Halfway through I whispered to him 'The monitor, the monitor'. Nothing."

String looked to Mike for some kind of explanation, getting little back.

Randall wondered how much of this was actually String's fault. He had been present for all of String's discussions with Andrew about 'the role' and while they had talked at length about the type of cop Andrew should be the monitor was only mentioned in passing. Bad direction. Randall felt it prudent not to share his opinions with String however.

"He offered to take him downtown for goodness sake," String ranted. "What on earth would we have done if Nuke had said yes?"

"At least he took the card," said Mike.

"Yeah, and that was all me. We were lucky to get that." He shoved a chair across the space. Randall guessed it was supposed to be some dramatic outlet of frustration, except the chair simple rolled a few feet on its wheels, colliding gently with the wall of the van.

"Good idea, Mike. Get an actor."

Mike shrugged and mumbled something.

"Sorry, what was that?"

"I said, he works better from a script."

"Oh, really? Thanks. That's good to know. Remember to tell me that last week will you?"

Andrew arrived home still high from his performance. He wanted to act again and right now. That was the problem with acting. It wasn't like painting or writing which you could do it any time, acting required a particular set of circumstances. Primarily an audience of some sort. He had a small role in an upcoming play. He already knew all of his lines but decided to go through them again anyway, just to be doing something.

He took one look at the script and tossed it back down. It wasn't what he needed right now. Feeling energetic and alive he wondered how he could have forgotten what fun improvisation could be. Sure, he would always love chewing over a good script, but improv had that extra element of excitement and danger. Like jumping out of a plane with no parachute or something. Driving super fast with your eyes closed. Maybe they weren't good analogies. Whatever, he decided he might get back into improvised theatre or even do a little theatre sports. Get those juices flowing again.

Maybe he could ring Liam? Liam still did improvised theatre regularly, Andrew was sure. He could point him in the right direction. Maybe there would be something on tonight.

As he searched his apartment for Liam's number, he spotted something out the window. A familiar face sitting in a black Jaguar out on the street, watching his apartment. Andrew didn't really think too much about it until it registered this wasn't just any face, it was Nuke, the dude from the van. How could that be? It would have meant the guy followed him home.

However, Andrew must've imagined it, because when he looked back through the window the familiar face and black Jaguar were both nowhere to be seen.

STRING sunk back into his chair, bringing his hands to his head. "What a disaster. All that work."

"Jesus, quit moaning," Mike said.

"Quit moaning? You realise I put the blame for this squarely at your feet."

"Whatever," said Mike, waving him away dismissively. "Just figure out what you want Andrew to say and fucken bring Nuke in again."

String gaped wide-eyed at Randall. "You believe this guy? Bring him in again?" He turned back to Mike. "What do you mean, bring him in again? Were you not here? He told us to our faces are full of it we are."

"Yeah, he thinks we're inept. So what? He still thinks where cops though."

String opened his mouth to respond and stopped. He had thought of that.

41

"That doesn't mean we are not watching, that we don't know all about your cornball stunts," Andrew told Nuke when they brought him in for the second time.

The van was crackling with tension. No messing about this time. They had to get this right. Randall could feel the pressure, pushing down on him. How was Nuke not picking up on it? Or maybe all encounters between cops and crims were tense like this.

If nothing else Randall was pleased the van was getting a second use, considering all he had outlaid for it.

"We've got you under twenty-four hour surveillance," Andrew went on, indicating to the monitor. On cue, Mike brought the screen to life.

"This is live."

Nuke snorted. "Genius. This is fucken genius. What's that? Outside my apartment?" He chuckled. "Well, you'll learn a lot having a camera out there. That's where all the shit goes down, out there in the corridor. I'm sure you have cracked the case wide op ..."

His voice trailed away. Randall resisted the urge to turn

and look. He wanted to watch so much. To see Nuke's reaction. It wouldn't really be in character though. He reminded himself he was an extra in this little scene.

"What the fuck...?"

Watching his wife kiss another man caused Nuke to lurch to his feet, like a person without complete control of his cognitive functions. There was a horrible moment where Randall feared Nuke was about to go berserk and kill them all, but after a few seconds he staggered out the door.

Once again the 'cops' in the van waited for Nuke to get clear and when he did the mood could barely have been more of a contrast to last time. They jumped to their feet, bro hugs and fist bumps all around.

String stood by the doorway of his office engaged in the ancient, mystical art of Tai Chi. He had considered doing yoga instead today, except there wasn't quite enough room in his office and he didn't fancy moving the desk out of the way.

The slow, gentle Tai Chi movements relaxed him significantly. He had studied the art form enough to have a forty-five minute routine locked away in his brain without the need for instruction. He had even invented a few moves of his own. Maybe he should consider becoming a Tai Chi instructor himself? Take classes as a side business. For pleasure, not money. To give back to the community.

True to Randall's prediction no new customers had surfaced for his consulting business as yet. String wasn't worried. He knew all about manifesting. The customers would come, he just needed to want it enough.

As his hand rippled through the air, a phone rang from his desk. A phone with an unfamiliar ring. Not just any phone, the burner phone he had purchased for this very moment.

"Know thy enemy, know thy self. A thousand battles, a thousand victories," String muttered quietly.

Standing tall and sucking a deep breath he pushed the button on the phone.

"Detective Hunt speaking," he said to Nuke in his best cop voice.

"COME ON, ANDREW. WHERE ARE YOU?"

Randall and String were sitting in String's car waiting. Randall shuffled nervously in the passenger seat.

"What did he say exactly?"

"Who? Andrew?"

"Nuke. On the phone when he rang you."

"That he was worried. He wanted to talk. Straight away."

"And you think he sounded scared?"

"Yeah, why? What's wrong with that?"

"Is he the type to get scared? Everything we know about this guy, he gets mad... But scared?" Randall glanced out the window. The meeting place loomed alongside the car. A dark warehouse. "And he wants to meet us here?"

"That's what he said. I'll give Mike a quick buzz, see if he knows where Andrew is at."

String pushed a button and waited.

Randall could hear the soft beeps emanating from String's phone.

In Mike's apartment the ringing phone was loud in the otherwise silent space. After a few rings the machine picked up.

"This is Mike. Leave a message. Beep."

"Hey Mike, it's String. We're looking for Andrew. Are you home? Pick up…"

Mike was home but there was little chance of him picking up. Andrew was there too, neither of them likely to answer. The friends had been fed head first into the editing equipment by someone with a particularly bad and somewhat explosive temper.

"Guess not. Give us a call when you get this message," String told the machine.

He hung up and looked at Randall. "No answer."

Part 5 - All Together Now

42

Constable Marks' day had done a complete one-eighty, the dull, overly busy Sunday having morphed into something else entirely. She studied Nuke on the monitor, carefully observing every skerrick of body movement. This wasn't simply some crackpot off the street, this guy was part of something. She was certain of it. Something that was going on, something that was big and something that she was now a part of too. Sure, she been lucky and just happened to be on the desk when he walked in but she felt involved. This was how careers were made, wasn't it? Being in the right place at the right time? Career might be overstating things, but it couldn't hurt.

"Any luck?" she asked Detective Griggs, even though she knew full well Nuke had said nothing, having been glued to the monitor in the observation room.

"Nah, not talking," said the detective. "We'll keep him for a while longer and see."

A million questions popped into the constable's mind about who this guy could be and what he was doing here, but she was conscious of playing it cool too, not wanting to geek out in front of Detective Griggs. For her part, Griggs didn't seem overly engaged, at least not to the extent Constable Marks was, and yet she wasn't hurrying back to her Sunday either.

The women watched Nuke on the monitor until the door to the observation room burst open and in marched Senior Sergeant Billings. Of course, Marks knew who Billings was immediately, even if she had never seen him up this close. He was shorter than she imagined yet big. Wide. Built, as the expression went, like a brick shithouse.

Marks launched into an awkward salute. "Sir."

Billings snarled back. "Get. Both of you."

Constable Marks didn't need to be told twice. Detective Griggs though wasn't used to being spoken to in such a manner and didn't move.

"Excuse me?"

Billings pointed at the door. "Out. Now. I'm not gonna say it a third time."

Griggs gave the Senior Sergeant a good glare but did as she was told.

On the monitor Nuke's image turned to static and disappeared.

NUKE WASN'T SURPRISED when the door to the interview room opened, expecting Detective Griggs to return to attempt to wheedle something out of him, so it was quite a surprise to see Ian and Emily flutter in. Same old Ian and Emily, poking each other and giggling and generally having a good time. Senior Sergeant Billings strode in behind them, closing the door and snarling fiercely at Nuke.

Ian and Emily sat opposite Nuke, barely registering him, too engaged in their own tomfoolery.

"Let's ask Nuke," Ian said eventually. "He'll know."

Ian turned and smiled across the table. "Nuke, settle something for us, please. Is Three a magician?"

Nuke wasn't sure if this was a real question. Ian and Emily regarded him as if they were serious.

"Be exciting if he was," Emily said.

"It would be exciting. It would be a surprise too if he had magical abilities that he was keeping from us."

The silence put its hands around Nuke's neck and squeezed.

"You see, why we ask is we were talking to Three before."

"Earlier today," clarified Emily.

"Yes, earlier today... And then, whoosh. He disappeared."

Ian stared across the table.

Nuke felt he should probably say something, except that nothing came to mind. Well, the image of Three's dying body in the vacant lot came to mind but that wasn't a whole lot of use to Nuke right at this second.

"I am... sure he's not dead."

Ian and Emily furrowed their brows.

"Why would Three be dead?" Emily asked.

"I don't know. I'm just sure he's not," Nuke asserted, acutely aware of the sound of his own voice.

"You funny, Nuke," Emily said with a burst of giggles.

The laughter dissolved away, leaving behind an uncertain tension. Nobody seemed quite sure what to do. Or possibly just Nuke wasn't sure what he should do. Ian and Emily appeared perfectly calm and relaxed.

"Phew," Ian said eventually. "What a day."

Emily turned to the brutish Billings standing behind her. "Can we talk freely?"

"Say what you want. Everything is turned off."

"There we were, minding our own business, enjoying our Sunday, when we got a call saying that someone had stolen the shipment. Nonsense, I said."

"You did," Emily agreed. "You said nonsense. I remember because I thought who would Ian be saying nonsense to on a Sunday morning."

"Nonsense, I said. The shipment could not have been stolen. Our two best men are on it. That should have been the end of it. But then the Buyer called to say the shipment never arrived."

"Da, da, daaa," sang Emily, imitating a dramatic music cue. "The plot thickens. Our first thought was it was probably just some misunderstanding. But we thought if anyone would know what's going on it will be our Nuke. So we call you and you don't answer, which is just plain weird."

"So we call Three and he seemed a bit sketchy on the phone. Anyway, he says he'd sort it, except now he is MIA." Ian's eyes bored into Nuke. "But listen to us banging on about our day. I can't even begin to imagine the sort of day you must've had to end up here."

Nuke waited. He knew better than to open his mouth, at least, not right now.

Reaching across the table Emily put her hand on Nuke's. "I hope we haven't done something to offend you. That would be terrible."

There was a look of genuine concern in her eyes. It was an odd mix with the usual psychotic mania.

"It would be sad, it would be," Ian agreed. "If after all this time you felt you had to turn against our happy little family. Work with the police."

Emily faced Ian. "He's gotta do what he's gotta do, Ian. And that is what he feels is right in his heart. We have to support him."

"It's true. You have to be true to yourself. That's the most important thing in life."

Emily turned back to Nuke with a plaintive look. "I just… I would worry about you in a place like this." She gripped his hand hard, driving her fingernails in. "Prison is tough, even for a tough boy like you, Nuke." She looked around and leaned forward whispering, as though she had a secret that was just for him. "People die in prison," she said with a look over her shoulder to Senior Sergeant Billings. "Don't they?"

Billings' eyes didn't leave Nuke. "Sure. If they make it to prison. Some people don't survive their first night in lock-up."

An exaggerated shiver ran through Emily. "Uugggh. I hate the thought."

The trio paused, giving Nuke a few moments to digests what he was being told.

"But, Emily," Ian said after a bit, "it doesn't have to be this way."

"It doesn't?" She said, raising her hands to her cheeks in mock amazement.

"Not at all. See, right now, you're scrambling, aren't you, Nuke? Thinking what can I say? How do I justify being here? But see, the thing is, we don't care. Do we, Em?"

"Nope. Couldn't care in the slightest."

"How you came to be here, whatever happened, it's in the past. It's done. It's what you do now that concerns us."

"What's your number one skill, Nuke?" Emily chimed in happily.

Unsure what he was supposed to say, Nuke didn't respond.

"Fixing things, silly. You are so good at fixing things. So fix this. Be nice if you could recover the shipment today."

"That would be nice," Ian agreed.

The senior sergeant moved forwards and leaned on the desk between Ian and Emily, close enough Nuke could smell the stale coffee on his breath.

"Otherwise I might have to find you and bring you back in here on a less voluntary basis."

43

Completely unbeknownst to any of them Jonathan, Kelly and Wanda were all in remarkably similar predicaments. All three of them were stuck waiting, with little to no idea what was going on, only that whatever was going on was not what they had planned. Worse still, there was nothing immediately evident they could do to make things right, so to an extent they were stuck.

And the waiting was killing them.

It was like sitting in a darkened room waiting for someone to turn on the light. Each quite fearful of what they might see when that finally happened.

Jonathan was the first to break the deadlock. He came to the conclusion he had to call Kelly. He desperately didn't want to. He had been thinking about this all day and avoiding it. Trying to come up with some other option. Anything. The reality was that there were no other options.

His phone told him he had 36 missed calls, all from Kelly, so he was pretty confident she would talk to him.

. . .

KELLY SAT up against a wall in the car park of Clarences's Discount Safari. The sun had moved sufficiently behind the surrounding buildings to afford her some shade in the barren lot.

There wasn't a whole lot of point still being here at the car park and yet she had little idea where else to go. Kelly's day had been an utter shambles.

Everything had appeared to be tracking fine at first. She had organised to meet Jonathan here which had seemed logical, although retrospect helpfully informed her was actually an enormous mistake. She had been in contact with him and all seemed A-OK. It never occurred to her he might not make it until suddenly it was go time and Jonathan was nowhere to be seen.

Van Damme appeared, bewildering Kelly completely. Should she try and take him by herself? She had no weapon and doubted her only advantage, the element of surprise, would do much good. Before she had really had the chance to process things or consider trying to take the bag by herself, Van Damme was gone and she was left standing in the car park out back of Clarence's Discount Safari like an idiot.

Her first thought was that she was going to kill Jonathan. Of course, he would fuck this up. Of course. How did she not see this coming? He was a complete fuck up, always with everything. Why should this be any different?

She ranted and raved into her phone with expletive filled tirades, questioning how he could be so stupid as to be late, today of all days. It wasn't until her third or fourth unanswered call that it occurred to her that Jonathan wasn't late at all and in fact, she had been set up.

Jonathan had fucked her.

A small piece of Kelly was begrudgingly impressed. She

never would have thought he would have had the balls. However, a much larger part of her was fuming with rage and determined to rip those same balls off and feed them to him when she finally caught up with him.

The wrinkle in all of this was that the bag wasn't what Jonathan thought it was and Kelly knew the drugs would completely freak him out and he would come scurrying back to her. So she waited for him, periodically trying to call him and leaving increasingly abusive messages on his voicemail.

Finally, he called her back. Seeing Jonathan's name on her phone prompted a tired sneer.

"What?"

"You fucked me," Jonathan told her from the spare room of the hideout.

"Pot, kettle, my love."

"Yeah, but you planned this from —"

"Jonathan. Did you just ring to bitch and moan or did you have something to say?"

44

Andrew the actor walked the streets in his regular clothes, not looking remotely cop-like any more. He had his phone crammed between his shoulder and his ear, chatting to his long-suffering agent Sally.

"Andrew, I worked hard to get to this role..."

"Sally, you're not hearing me. I'm thrilled with the role. I love the role. The role is great."

"You just don't want to be called Victim Number Two."

Andrew let himself into his building.

"The character would be so much better if he had a name. A real name. Stronger on my CV especially. You should know better than anyone. If I say '*Yeah, I'm in that film. I played Barry Barrison*', it sounds like an actual role. It sounds so much better than if I say '*Yeah I'm in a film I play Victim Number Two*'."

His stiff door stuck as usual, forcing Andrew to use both hands to make his way into his apartment.

"I don't know if the producers will change it," Sally informed him.

"Sal, I'm doing this for you." He walked in. "It's going to be so much easier for you to get me work if —"

His voice trailed off. Something wasn't right. The apartment felt off. He wasn't alone. He turned to see an imposing figure sitting casually on his couch.

"Hi there, Agent Harris," Nuke said.

Andrew's phone slipped off his shoulder and broke on the wooden floor at his feet.

WANDA WAS in her apartment cooking. She merely needed something to occupy her mind, anything to take her thoughts off whatever was or wasn't happening. Cooking food that she guessed no one was ever going to eat was decidedly odd. It was a challenge, focusing solely on what she was doing, chopping down any other thoughts she might have before they had a chance to take root in her mind.

Prior to cooking the thoughts she had engaged in were useless and destructive and answerless. Should she have left her apartment? Except where should she go? Funny how you could run every conceivable scenario for something through your head before it happens and not realise the reality will always be vastly different. No, she had to stay now. Running would only delay the inevitable if everything had all gone wrong.

Finally, the phone rang.

"Hey, babe," came Kelly's calm voice down the line. Wanda felt her heart flip.

"You didn't have to call."

Kelly strode through a park in the late afternoon sun. "I didn't?"

"If you're taking the drugs, cutting me out. You didn't need to call."

"Yeah, well, if I was ripping you off, I probably wouldn't have."

"So, what's up?"

"Right idea, wrong person," Kelly said, a slight puff to her voice from her quick pace. "Jonathan tried to screw us."

"He would have got a surprise when he opened the bag."

"Drugs are useless to him, so he wants back in."

Wanda tried to calculate what this could mean. "So, we're back on? Still on?"

"Maybe," Kelly replied. "Depends what's up with Nuke."

"Yeah, I guess it does."

"Is he onto us?"

Wanda paced the floor of her kitchen. "Not sure. Can't really ring and ask him."

Kelly looked both ways before crossing the road. "Kind of the critical factor at this point, babe."

Wanda knew she should probably put more thought into this, except there was nothing to think about. "Make the deal."

"You sure?"

"Of course not. But we can't be half pregnant. We're either fucked or we're not."

"All right," Kelly said. "That's what I thought. I'll make the deal with Jonathan."

A pause hung between them. A gap that Wanda desperately wanted to fill with millions of words and yet she could barely think of any.

"Hey, Kel?"

"I know, babe. I love you too."

· · ·

As the night slowly stole away the day's light, String and Randall waited in the car. There was still no word from either Andrew or Mike. Randall had no idea if that was what was unsettling him or if it was the whole situation in general.

"All right," String announced, making to get out. "We can't wait any longer. If we're late Nuke might lose his nerve."

"What about Andrew?"

"Don't need him."

"I don't like it."

String gave him a patient smile.

"It makes no sense, the two of us going in."

String got that look in his eye again. That wise sage look.

"*Great results, can be achieved with small forces.* The two of us turning up makes more sense than if I showed up by myself. Cops always do things in pairs."

"No, I mean... Think about it from a story point of view."

"Story point of view?"

"Yeah. Andrew is like the lead cop. Is it going to make any sense when the other detective and some tech guy from the van show up?"

"Andrew's not here."

"I know. I'm... I can't do this. I'm not going in."

String shook his head. It was the first time Randall had seen String look upset with him.

"I find your lack of faith extremely disappointing. This stuff we're doing, it's mind-blowing. It is so far beyond the usual drug war garbage. I'm giving you top shelf, mind game trickery they can't even imagine. Tactics never seen before."

Randall looked away, embarrassed.

"Everything I have predicted has come to pass and yet every step of the way you doubt me. Every step. You didn't want to bring Mike in. You didn't want him to build the van. You didn't want to involve Andrew the actor. And in all those cases I have been right. None of those steps made sense to you beforehand, but when they were in place you could see I was right. I'm pulling the strings here. You've just got to trust me. You don't get angry at the puppet master just because you can't see the direction the puppets are headed."

Randall grunted. He wasn't sold, although it was quite likely he just didn't have the stomach for all this. He did feel kind of guilty for doubting String. And he had a point. Everything String had said about Nuke had proved to be right thus far.

"*Victorious warriors win first, then go to war.* Right here, right now, we win this war."

"You really think he's scared?"

"Nuke? Totally. Nobody wants to go to jail. He's ready to roll over."

The nail of Randall's thumb was going to be all gone if he continued to gnaw on it like this.

"What are you going to say to him?"

"Dunno. This part is a little different. We'll have to improvise. It depends on what he says to us."

String reached across and put a hand on Randall's shoulder.

"The plan, everything, this is what we have been working towards. What it's all been about. Look, the hard part is done. He's scared. We have landed the big fish. All we have to do is reel him in. *Know thy enemy, know thy self. A thousand battles, a thousand victories.*"

Randall glanced back out the window. The warehouse wasn't getting any less ominous.

· · ·

STRING and Randall made their way inside, able to see where they were going enough to avoid the holes in the floor and bits of the junk lying about but not a whole lot more.

"Hello," String called. "Nuke?"

With a loud bang, a bank of fluro tubes above them spluttered to life, dramatically lighting the space. Ian and Emily stood together in front of String and Randall, happy smiles on their faces. A little too happy, especially Emily.

"Gentlemen."

Nuke stepped out from behind, blocking the exit.

String and Randall couldn't quite hide that slight flicker of panic. String though recovered fast. He whipped out his fake police ID.

"Freeze. We have the place surrounded."

Ian's smile became even broader. He waggled a finger at String. "Nice try. But I'm not sure we would fall for that one even if you were police."

"But," Emily said, "perhaps you can help us with our enquiries."

"Ha. Good one, Em. Help us with our enquiries. That's what the police say."

"I know, right? Anyway," she said, turning back to String and Randall. "What have you two done with our shipment?"

Randall glanced at String. Shipment? Now he was confused and scared. What the fuck were they on about?

SOON AFTER THE warehouse was alive with the hum of power tools. No one was foolish enough to walk these streets at night but if they did, they would have thought the occupants of the warehouse were working awfully late. Who knows what they would have made of the low moans of unbearable pain that were accompanying the power tools. String and Randall may have been gagged and yet a gag can only do so much.

Emily stepped away, trying to avoid the steady trickle of blood running down the floor to the drain. She was quite a sight, in splattered goggles and a butcher's apron which was at one point white but was becoming increasingly red as the evening wore on. In her hands she cradled a large drill, almost as blood-soaked as her apron.

She skipped over to Ian and offered him the drill. He declined, pulling a face.

A happy, bubbly tune chimed out from Ian's phone. "Ian's phone, Ian speaking." He strolled out of the room, with a hand to his ear, straining to hear whoever it was. "Really? That is interesting..."

He cupped the receiver with his hand. "Hey, Nuke. Nuke."

The noise of Nuke's power tool slowly drained to a stop. He came over wearing a matching outfit to Emily's and carrying an electric carving knife. Behind him, the moaning subsided to pitiful groans.

"You'll never guess what. I think I may have the answer as to why these two aren't talking."

He paused for effect, which Emily didn't appreciate. She slapped him lightly on the arm. "Well, go on, don't leave us hanging, doodleberry."

"I just got word some other genius is trying to sell what appears to be our missing shipment."

Nuke glanced from The Sharks to String and Randall and back again, genuine confusion in his eyes.

"But then... What are these fake cops playing at?"

45

Jonathan paced around his small empty room in the hideout and for the first time all day he felt marginally better. The phone call to Kelly was considerably less painful than he had imagined. He should have done it straight away. He was just waiting for a call back for confirmation but he was pretty sure they had a deal of sorts. Good result, all things considered.

Even though he hated Kelly and was unimaginably happy never to have to lay eyes on her again after today, it felt better being honest with her, as opposed to surreptitiously attempting to fuck her over. He could only assume she felt the same.

There were still problems however. Issues that needed to be finessed.

The spare room door was open a crack and Jonathan spied Daz stumble by. He heard the toilet door close. Christ, how were they still standing? The two of them, him and Stevo, had smoked consistently since they made it to the hideout. That was hours ago. Jonathan had never seen so much smoking. One long session with no beginning and no end. They only paused to devour the mountain of junk food Jonathan had purchased. At times the smoke was so thick it appeared as though the lounge room was on fire. The neighbours must have been able to smell it. Hell, you could have seen the smoke plume from the moon.

Come on, he told himself. Hold it together. The day was almost over. Kelly would call and he would never have to see any of these people ever again.

A SINGLE DROP eased its way down Daz's nose. He stood watching it descend in the cracked bathroom mirror, completely captivated. He had just splashed some water on his face and the drop was the final result of that.

Boy, was he stoned. Early onset of Alzheimer's type stoned where you've smoked so much you forget what you're talking about halfway through a sentence. Sure he might have been a dope ninja this morning or whatever the fuck he and Stevo were saying they were, but this was a completely different smoking phase. This was the kind of stoned you could watch an entire episode of something on TV and never see anything except the ads. Or you could watch a drop of water run off your face for as long as it took like it was the most fascinating thing in the entire world.

DAZ STUMBLED BACK OUT into the main room and chuckled. Stevo was sitting there with the giraffe mask on.

"Tryin' to pull a bong through this, but it won't work."

While Stevo raised the latex just far enough to uncover his mouth, Daz sank into the other couch. The gurgling of smoke sucked through water filled the room, just as it had all afternoon.

Daz was so comfortable he wondered how he had ever got up. What was he thinking about again? In the bathroom? He was taking a piss and he thought of something he had to tell Stevo, although now he couldn't remember what it was. Think, Daz, think. Oh, yeah.

"Hey, Stevo."

He snuck a look towards the door to the other room just to make sure Jonathan wasn't listening. He couldn't see him.

"I was thinking..."

"Uh oh."

"Shut up. You think we should hide... the whatever it is... The... the bag we stole. You think we should hide it? Them?"

"Hide them?"

"Yeah. In case things go south... Give us... ya know..." Daz's brain not quite working at its optimal level. At this point, it was a challenge for Daz to remember his own name, let alone converse in coherent sentences.

"Give us... ya know..." He repeated. Stevo didn't know. He had no fucken idea.

"Leverage." Daz finally managed to get the word out with some relief.

Stevo gave him something somewhere between a shrug and a nod and went back to sucking on his bong.

IN THE SPARE room and completely oblivious to that conversation, Jonathan hung up from Kelly. He paused, running through what he was going to say to Daz and Stevo. Getting the wording absolutely right, in his head at least.

When he finally strode out of the room a few minutes later and into the lounge, both Daz and Stevo were wearing masks, both giggling like they were hilarious.

"Right," Jonathan announced, ignoring their stupidity. "It is all sorted."

"What?" came Stevo's muffled voice from behind the latex.

"What we're going to do with the drugs."

Daz and Stevo pulled up the masks. Daz at least had the decency to look a little awkward. Stevo just smirked meanly.

"What?" Jonathan asked.

"Sit down, playa," Daz said. "We got this, 'ey?"

A sliver of ice oozed its way down Jonathan's spine. "What?" he said again, not moving.

"We tried things your way, fuckstick. Look what happened," Stevo said.

Before he had even finished, there was a knock at the door. The ice spread rapidly through Jonathan's body.

"Oh, shit. What have you idiots done?"

46

Daz and Stevo stood.

"Idiots?" Stevo said, making his way to the door.

Daz took up a position behind the couch.

Jonathan's head snapped every which way. Oh, God. He was trapped. There was only one door in or out of this stupid place. Could he try a window? Why did the hideout have to be on the third storey? There was no balcony, so he couldn't even climb —

"It's all right, tough guy, chill."

The person outside knocked again, somewhat more impatiently this time.

Stevo threw open the door. "Hey, man."

For a few moments nothing happened, or that's how it seemed to Jonathan. Stevo joined Daz behind the couch and no one else came in.

Then he appeared, seemingly moving in slow motion. The scariest fucken guy Jonathan had ever seen. Not the biggest or the most tattooed or anything like that and yet something in the guy's dead eyes was pure terror.

He shut the door, not making his way in any further.

Appraising the situation and blocking the only exit. Drinking everything in.

Jonathan clenched his arse so tight it hurt. He couldn't stop though.

"Hey, man. I'm Stevo. This is Daz. That's dickhead," Stevo said sniggering towards Jonathan.

"Nuke," the guy said quietly.

There was a pause. No one seemed quite sure what to do. At least Daz and Stevo didn't. Jonathan got the impression this guy Nuke always knew exactly what to do. And Jonathan knew what he should do too. He should get the fuck outta there. Except he was rooted to the spot.

Sniffing the air Nuke asked: "You guys having a party?"

"Nah, just a choof, bro, ya know? You want some?"

Nuke shook his head.

"You here to buy the two bags of drugs?" Stevo asked impatiently.

Nuke shook his head again, prompting Daz and Stevo to swap confused looks.

"Well, what do you want then?" Daz asked.

"I'm here for the shipment, but I'm not buying anything." Nuke looked at them impassively, his voice still soft. "I'm taking back what you stole from us."

The dynamic in the room shifted so dramatically Jonathan almost got whiplash. Daz and Stevo attempted to catch up through their drug-addled brains. Considering his state Daz recovered super quickly. Maybe he was some sort of smoking ninja.

"We got a problem then, 'ey?" stated Daz.

"I've gotta... I don't need to be here..." mumbled Jonathan, finally gaining some control over his faculties.

A simple hand gesture from Nuke was enough to halt him in his tracks, even if Nuke didn't take his eyes from

Daz and Stevo. Jonathan went back to being unable to move.

"You were saying?" Nuke said to Daz.

"You've got us all wrong, bro. We didn't steal anything. We might have found something though. Something of value."

"Is that right?"

"Uhuh. And usually, if you find something, you get a ... what do you call it ... thing. Reward, 'ey?"

The word reward almost evaded Daz's drug-soaked brain, but he got there eventually. Stevo backed up his friend in his own far less verbose and more economical fashion.

"We want some cash, fuckbag."

Oh, God. Jonathan willed Stevo to shut up with every fibre in his body.

"And what's to stop me just taking it?" Nuke asked. "This valuable object you happened to come across."

"You'd have to know where it is, 'ey. We've hidden it."

"Cough up the cash, you get the stash."

Daz smirked, impressed with Stevo's improvisation.

"Is that right?"

Daz and Stevo nodded, happily deluding themselves that this was going well.

"Daz..." Jonathan spluttered desperately.

"Shut the fuck up, dickbrain. The grown-ups are talking now," Stevo said.

"So, what?" Nuke asked. "Only the two of you know where the shipment is?"

"Yep."

"That's right."

"Well, you have a problem then," Nuke said casually, pulling out his gun from the back of his pants. He clicked the chamber to the side and span it. "Or more specifically, one of you has a problem."

Daz and Stevo stammered incoherently, vague comprehension of the trouble they were in slowly dawning on them.

"Cos if both of you know where the shipment is..." Nuke flicked the gun, locking the cylinder back in place. "I can still kill one of you."

As the gun pointed from Daz to Stevo and back again, time slowed once more. Those few seconds stretched into eternity. Except when they were gone they seemed to have taken no time at all.

Jonathan recalled being told once that real gunshots weren't all that loud. In the movies they made guns sound like cannons going off, but real gunshots were more of a pop, the person had said. It's fair to say this wasn't the case with the shot that hit Daz. In fact, quite the opposite. Jonathan thought the bang was about the loudest sound he had ever heard in his life and it got stuck in his ears, echoing and repeating.

Daz had smoked so much that day Jonathan wouldn't have been surprised to see smoke drift out the hole the bullet made in Daz's chest. His face never registered what happened. He merely stumbled back a step, hit the wall and crumpled into a pile on the floor.

Stevo's face however registered Daz going down all too clearly.

"Whoa! Shit! Whoa! Fuck! Shit!" he yelled, throwing up his hands.

Jonathan could do nothing except watch in silent terror.

"Relax," Nuke told Stevo calmly. "You're cool."

Stevo's hands rattled violently, neither relaxed nor cool.

"I can't kill you, right? You're the only one who knows where the shipment is."

Any certainty in Stevo's voice had been replaced by terror. "Ye...Yes... Yeah."

Before Stevo had any chance to process this or hope he might somehow survive Nuke shot him as well. Like Daz, he collapsed into a heap on the floor.

Nuke stepped past the temporarily paralysed Jonathan and stood over what was left of Daz and Stevo.

"Here's a hint, boys. If you're going to say you hidden something, at least take the time to hide it."

He put another bullet into each of them.

Jonathan didn't want to watch and yet he couldn't look away.

The bags of drugs lay on the floor beside the couch. Nuke walked over. Moving the bong and bowl to make some room he placed the drugs and his gun on the coffee table.

"Fucken stoners. Never work with potheads," Nuke told Jonathan. "That shit does something to their brains."

Jonathan watched Nuke examine the two bags of drugs. He looked weary. "Have you touched these?"

"No..." Jonathan attempted to say. His words got stuck in his throat. He shook his head instead.

"Those two idiots didn't?"

"They wouldn't have known what to do with it," Jonathan managed.

Nuke nodded, continuing to examine the bags anyway.

Jonathan dared a quick look at the door. Not a real look. No head movement. Just a flick of his eyes. He was maybe six steps away. Could he make it out? Nuke's gun was on the table. It would take Nuke a second or two to notice. A second or two more to react. Then what? Even if Jonathan made it out. God, it would be like a horror movie - chased by a terrifying dude with a gun. He would have to take the stairs. Except what if he couldn't find the stairs? What if he couldn't even get the hideout door open? He didn't want to get shot in the back. Or make this guy any angrier than he already was.

"Don't do it," Nuke said, reading Jonathan's mind. "There are ways you can make this very, very much worse for yourself. Running is one of them."

"Yes... Yes, sir."

As it was, it didn't take Nuke a second or two to pick up his gun. It took maybe half a second at best. Without even bothering to look he shot more or less in Jonathan's direction. It missed but not by much. Jonathan felt the wind as the bullet whistled by his throat, his neck coated with little flecks of plaster as the bullet lodged in the wall.

"Call me Sir again and the next one won't miss."

Nuke placed the two drug filled, ziplock bags back in Van Damme's duffle bag.

Panic surging Jonathan began to babble, his words all over the place and coming out that bit too quickly.

"My name is Jonathan Small. My mother's name is April. She has two dogs, Smell and Scratchy. I have a sister —"

"Stop that," said Nuke, looking increasingly tired. "What are you doing?"

"I'm trying to make you see that I'm a real person."

"Why?"

"So you might think twice before killing me."

"That shit's not going to fly. What about those two idiots on the floor? Weren't they real people too?"

Jonathan glanced reluctantly at the two dead bodies.

"Look, you're not the first person I've killed today, as you can see, and the way the day's heading you won't be the last. So save your breath."

He laid the gun back down on the table. "Come sit down."

Jonathan didn't move.

Nuke glared threateningly. "Sit."

He waited for Jonathan to do as he was told. They sat opposite each other, with Nuke's gun, Van Damme's bag and the remnants of Daz and Stevo's bowl of dope and the bong on the table between them.

"I've had a long day," Nuke said. "So I'll tell you how this is going to work. I'm going to ask you what I want to know and you're going to tell me."

"That's it?"

"That's it."

"What makes you think I know anything?"

"What? You expect me to believe Wingus and Dingus were the brains of the operation?"

Despite really not wanting to Jonathan couldn't resist shooting another quick glance over his shoulder at Daz and Stevo. The streams of blood seeping from their wounds was pooling together. Jonathan imagined on some level they would have liked that.

"And if I tell you what you want to know, you won't kill me?"

Nuke shook his head. "No, I'm still gonna kill you. It's pretty simple. If you didn't want to die, you shouldn't have stolen the shipment."

"I didn't know," Jonathan scrambled, talking too quickly again. "I didn't know it was drugs. I was lied to. I thought it was money —"

Nuke raised his hand. "You knew you were stealing something. Consequences. There are always consequences when you do something stupid."

The terror and the fear began to shift from Jonathan,

replaced by a new sensation. A dejected and defeated emptiness. He was going to die and soon. Only one last argument came to mind.

"If you're going to kill me anyway, why would I talk?"

"Well, there's dying and there is dying," Nuke told him. "Trust me, one way or another you are going to tell me what I want to know."

Silence smothered the room. Jonathan stared at Nuke. He believed him. It was an odd feeling, knowing he was about to be killed, sitting here in the crappy surrounds of the hideout. Although a little like his conversation with Kelly earlier it was right in a way. Good to be honest and not to worry about any of the bullshit. Would it happen here? His body piled on the floor with Daz and Stevo? That didn't seem fair, although given the day perhaps appropriate.

"Well," Jonathan announced. "If I'm going to die anyway, I'm going to have a smoke."

He was proud of himself. He didn't ask Nuke. He told him.

47

Meanwhile, having made two dinners and baked some cookies and a cake, Wanda was growing tired of the kitchen. The endless emotional roller coaster of her day wore her down. Despite not doing a whole lot little since Nuke left that morning she had run the whole gamut of emotions; worry Nuke would catch her switching his phone, terror Kelly was in trouble, elation Kelly was actually okay and now back into uncertainty having no idea what the heck was going on.

With no cooking left in her, she was out of distractions and stuck with the poisonous voice whispering in he ear.

The uncertainty was, she decided, the worst because her mind projected onto it. Filling in the blanks. Kelly should be back now. Without a doubt. And if not back, in contact at least. What did it mean that she hadn't been? That she was in trouble?

"She doesn't love you," the poisonous voice whispered. "She never did. She screwed you over."

That was the problem with the poisonous voice; it was merciless, knew all her weak spots and made undeniably good points. It was one thing not to have heard from Kelly, but not hearing from either Kelly or Nuke seemed particularly illogical.

"It's because they are together," the poisonous voice said. "She never wanted to run away with you in the first place, you forced this on her."

Wanda walked around with nowhere to go, the poisonous voice relentless.

"Don't you see? Kelly doesn't love you, she wants to replace you. It's the apartment she loves. All the stuff. That's why she always wanted to come to here. That's why she wanted the red dress. Now she wants Nuke."

Kelly the self-confessed liar. Kelly who loved the twelfth-floor apartment so much. It wasn't like Kelly and Nuke had never met each other. Kelly always reminded Wanda of a younger version of herself.

"And what did you want at the same age? You married Nuke..."

No, Kelly was smarter than that surely.

"Are you sure about that? Kelly hooking up with Nuke is win-win. Kelly gets all your pricey things. The apartment, the lifestyle, the money and Nuke gets to upgrade his wife for a younger, sexier model. One that will willingly fuck him. One that loves him."

Somewhere inside a little part of Wanda wanted to believe Nuke wouldn't do that to her.

"Why? Why would he show even a scrap of loyalty to you? It's not like you've done anything except push him away. Of course he wants Kelly. She's gorgeous. Who wouldn't want her? Yep, win-win. Except for you, Wanda. You lose, as always."

Wanda hated the poisonous voice.

"You're desperate to believe she's on your side, except if that's true, where is she?"

There was no answer for that.

So, leave then, the practical side of her said. Get out.

"Too late," the voice sneered. "If you were going to run, you should have gone already and yet here she are, still sitting about here like a sap."

Trying to shake the mess from her brain she moved to the floor to ceiling windows, staring out into the night. A sea of glistening lights stretched out in front of her. As Wanda watched the cars weaving about way down below, there was a buzz from the apartment's video intercom. She had a visitor. Fleetingly she prayed it was Kelly, even though she knew it wouldn't be because Kelly had her security pass and wouldn't bother to buzz. The same logic told her it wasn't Nuke.

Wanda found Ian and Emily's mouths taking up more of the intercom screen than they should. They were standing too close to the camera on their end, inadvertently cropping their heads off at the nose.

"Hello," said Ian's grotesquely oversized mouth and immediately things became clear as they so often do that moment too late. Wanda should have got the hell out of there while she had the chance.

GOD, why don't you just die? It was a passing thought, one that slipped through before he could stop himself. He didn't mean it all. Of course, he didn't want his dear old mum to die. The thought was merely the frustration boiling over. He had spent far too much time over here today. He and his mum worked best in short, sharp bursts. Today it had been hours and now he was stuck watching telly with her, which he loathed as it brought back endless childhood memories. His childhood was fine, he simply didn't care to be reminded of it.

"I don't understand this. What are we watching?"

"It's just a TV show, Mum. Just relax."

"Who's not relaxed? How is this a TV show?"

How many times had they had this discussion? His mum putting on an act for him. Performing. How many more times was he destined to sit through it?

"A show about people who can't cook pretending to be chefs? How is that a TV show? That's all television is now, people pretending. People pretending to be chefs. People pretending to be models. People pretending to be stuck on a desert island."

Jason rolled his eyes. Her rant was just beginning. He could probably say it along with her, word for word, complaining about all this reality nonsense and asking what happened to good old-fashioned storytelling like '*Sons and Daughters*' or '*The Sullivans*' or '*A Country Practice*'? And then she would start banging on about variety TV and how they should bring Don Lane or Bert Newton out of retirement and put on a good old-fashioned variety show, which everybody would watch, certainly people her age at least, at which point Jason's head may well explode and he would have to kill her.

Fortunately, he was rescued by a knock at the front door. The knock he had been waiting to hear all day. His mum muted the television.

"Is that someone at the door?" she said, stuck somewhere between scandalised and concerned.

"It's okay, Mum," Jason said, getting up.

"Who would call at this time? No one decent. I've been in my dressing gown for two hours."

"It's fine. I'll go see."

Thrilled that he would finally be able to get out of here, Jason threw open the door expecting to see Van Damme and Nuke or Three. Two people. He was planning to tell them exactly what he thought of being made to wait about this long, except there was no Van Damme and Nuke didn't look in the mood to be messed with.

"Wow," the Buyer said, looking at his watch. "You are... late."

Judging from Nuke's snarl, even that was pushing things too much.

WANDA SAT PERCHED on the very edge of the couch, her butt barely scraping the cushion. She was used to feeling uncomfortable in her own home. She felt that way whenever Nuke was around. But this was a whole new level of discomfort.

Emily sat on the couch opposite with her eyes wide and the most unfriendly smile Wanda had ever seen plastered across her face. Wanda wasn't sure Emily had blinked once since she sat down.

Behind her Ian ambled about, going through any cupboard or drawer he came across. It was a complete invasion of her privacy and yet what could she do?

"Are you all right there?" she asked.

"Oh, he's fine," Emily told her with a dismissive flick of her hand.

THE BUYER'S bedroom was an odd mix. The walls like a time capsule for several different time periods. There were faded old posters of cricket and football and basketball stars from years ago, as well as some slightly more recent musicians and numerous nightclub cards and flyers, all stuck to the peeling plaster.

"Nice room," Nuke said.

Jason pulled out a set of scales from underneath the bed.

"I keep telling mum to redecorate or turn it into a sewing room or something. She says she wants to keep it like it is. Remind her of what I used to be like. I'm not sure why. I was a feral teen."

Jason weighed the two ziplock bags, one after the other. As he did, he snuck a glance at Nuke.

"You look tired," Jason said.

"Long day."

Correct weight. Not unexpected, but a relief given the way the rest of the day had played out. Little would have surprised Nuke at this point.

With goodbyes said Nuke left the Buyer's place, now carrying a briefcase in place of Van Damme's bag. It was a relief being rid of the shipment. He hated carrying it around. There was a reason Van Damme was the only one who touched it usually.

Nuke jumped in his Jag. The briefcase sat on the seat beside him as he drove, ready for delivery to the Sharks.

IAN JOINED EMILY on the couch, ratcheting up the discomfort level that bit more. Now Wanda had both of these creepy freaks grinning manically at her. *Go back to pouring through our possessions* Wanda wanted to tell him.

Ian motioned towards the balcony and the patio furniture.

"You've got chairs out there."

"Yes."

"Aren't you tempted to throw them off? See what happens?"

"No."

The brother and sister appeared surprised.

"I would be," Emily said and Ian nodded in agreement.

An icy sick shuddered through Wanda. They were going to throw her off the balcony, just like Nuke did with the table. That was the plan. And just like the table, they'd get away with it too. That was how this was destined to play out.

Her hand slipped under the cushion where she felt something cold and metallic. Oh God, it was a gun. For a glorious millisecond her heart soared, implausibly thinking Nuke's gun had been left under there somehow. Her mind irrationally clinging to whatever bit of hope it could, no matter how illogical.

Of course, it wasn't Nuke's gun. It was his phone. She had forgotten to get rid of it. She giggled. Too late now.

"What's funny?" Emily asked.

"Oh... Nothing."

"No, you giggled just then. Tell us why." Emily's tone managed to be both friendly and combative.

Before Wanda had the chance to think up a response the clinking of keys in the door told them Nuke was home. He strode in, staring hard at his wife.

"Hi, honey," he said in a most unpleasant tone.

Wanda had little idea what to do or say. "Look," she managed eventually with an uncomfortable smile. "Ian and Emily are here." Pointlessly redundant and self evident.

"I can see that." His piercing eyes saying so much more than words. "How was your day?"

"Uneventful."

She did her best but Wanda couldn't quite shake the

nervousness from her voice. Nuke glared at her for a long time and then strode out to the bedroom.

Ian and Emily continued to stare. No one moving, no one saying anything. After the longest few minutes of Wanda's life Nuke re-emerged.

"Come down to the garage with me. I've got something to show you."

Oh well, at least she wasn't getting thrown off the balcony.

48

Nuke's invitation to the underground car park was meant for Wanda, yet it was Emily who responded, clapping her hands.

"Oh, goody. Let's all go."

The Sharks stood. The garage was just about the last place Wanda wanted to go with this trio right now, except what choice did she have? As Nuke headed for the door, Wanda made a beeline for the kitchen.

"Wanda..." Emily called in a singsong voice. "Wanda."

She stopped.

"Where are you going?"

"To get my security pass."

"Oh, you don't need that, sillybilly. Nuke has his."

Wanda looked longingly. The pass was right there on the kitchen table, just out of reach. Emily skipped over happily, entwining her arm in Wanda's.

"Come on."

THE FOURSOME WALKED the small distance to the lift, Emily

and Wanda arm in arm. As usual, the corridor was deserted. Nuke pressed the button. The lift took forever to arrive. No one spoke.

When it finally showed up, Emily refused to turn and face the doors like a sane person would in a lift. Instead, she stood face-to-face with Wanda, grinning at her.

Cheesy elevator music serenaded their descent. A lounge cover of an Oasis song. *Really?* Wanda thought. *This is the last piece of music that I will ever hear?* It didn't seem right.

NUKE, Wanda, Ian and Emily walked out of the lift and through the glass security door into the underground car park. The door clicked loudly behind them, locking them in.

Keeping her head still and trying to appear calm, Wanda's eyes darted about, searching for any possible escape route. Nothing jumped out at her. If she had her security pass, there might have been some hope, no matter how slim. Without it there was nothing.

They made their way down the ramp and along the row of vehicles to where Wanda and Nuke's Jags sat side by side in their assigned spots. Nuke popped the boot of his car revealing Kelly, bound and gagged with gaffer tape.

"Look, Thelma, it's Louise," Nuke said casually.

There was a second or two of nothing before Wanda ran. Not her intention or her plan, it just kind of happened. A gut reaction, even if it was entirely pointless. It wasn't like she could do anything to save Kelly.

"Where is she going?" she heard Ian ask somewhere behind her.

Wanda bolted all the way back to the security door and

tugged on it desperately. Of course the blasted thing refused to open. She crouched beside the nearest car, her mind scrambling. There must be some other way out of here. There had to be.

A loud bang rocked the car park and the side mirror just above Wanda's head exploded, showering her with bits of glass. Wanda scurried between the cars, shaking pieces of mirror out of her hair.

Raising up just enough to peak without getting her head blown off she spied Nuke coming towards her, gun in hand.

Ian had positioned himself in front of the emergency exit.

She couldn't see Emily.

The three of them were on the move. Splitting up to trap her.

There had to be another way out. A way out, somehow avoiding the three psychos.

Emily's voice cut through against the low drone of the plant room motors, echoing slightly. "Hey, Wanda? Tell me, what did you think was going to happen here?"

Wanda crept between the cars.

"Em, shush. This isn't our concern," Ian said.

"This is our concern. It is our shipment she tried to steal. Besides, I just think it's pretty heartless, dumping her husband in it for a bag of drugs."

Wanda moved around as fast as she could staying low and out of sight.

"It is cold," Ian agreed.

Wanda stuck her head up again. Emily had made it to the other end of the concrete bunker and was doubling back. Nuke was getting ever closer. Slowly but surely Wanda was being boxed in.

Another blast rang out, shattering a window right beside

Wanda's face. She ran again, increasingly aware of the futility of what she was doing.

"Here's how this is going to work, Wanda." Nuke sounded tired and fed up. "Come out freely now, or I'm going to drag you out by your fucken hair."

Such a tempting offer. Wanda continued to creep, keeping herself out of sight. She popped up again to see Emily right on top of her, bearing down. Nothing for it. Wanda left the cover of the cars and ran.

An unexpected noise captured everyone's attention. The car entrance opened. Why hadn't she thought of that? If she'd been closer, she might have been able to make it out.

She clambered up the split-level and towards the gate as a little hatchback eased its way in. As suspected the metal closed too quickly for her to make it out. However, the car still provided opportunities. Wanda recognised a miracle when she saw one and wasn't about to let it pass her by.

Darting out she flagged the hatchback down. It stopped and Wanda launched herself into the passenger seat.

Ita sat behind the wheel, awaiting an explanation. "I know you..."

"Get us out of here," Wanda screamed at her. "They're trying to kill me."

Ita didn't move, staring at her unexpected passenger.

"Drive, drive. Go," yelled Wanda, with such force she thought she saw Ita's hair move. She felt bad screaming at the old woman, but desperate times... Ita's hands shook as they gripped the wheel.

"Where am I supposed to go?"

"Out of here. Back to the entrance and drive out."

Wanda ducked as low as possible as the car puttered along making a loop of the enclosed car park.

"You... You're scaring me,"

"Good."

Peeking out the window, Wanda's head swivelled in all directions. Ian, Emily and Nuke seemed to have vanished.

"This is important. There are people in this car park trying to kill me. They may try and stop us leaving. Whatever you do, don't stop this car."

"What if they step out in front of us?"

"Drive straight through them."

"I... I'm not going to deliberately hit someone —"

It was the very last thing Ita thought or said in her long life. The windscreen cobwebbed as a bullet tore through, obliterating more of Ita's brain than she could spare.

She collapsed onto the wheel, which turned, the car ploughing heavily into one of the structure's concrete pillars with a tremendous crash.

The airbags deployed, knocking Wanda backwards.

In the few moments after the crash everything was black and fuzzy. Wanda swayed around groggily. She didn't have a seat belt on, but they hadn't been travelling that fast.

Before she had a chance to recover or figure if she was injured the passenger door was thrown open and two hands wrenched Wanda out.

Looking more or less as furious as he had ever looked, Nuke dragged Wanda by her hair back to the two Jaguars and Ian and Emily.

"Hey, whoa, careful, Nuke," Emily said. "Don't hurt her. You don't want to damage her before we get her back to the warehouse." She tilted her head to an approximate of the angle Wanda's head was at. "Ooh, we're going to have some fun with you, Wanda."

While she could only guess as to what fun at the

warehouse with a furious Nuke and a psychotic Emily might entail, Wanda sensed she probably wasn't going to find it all that fun.

Nuke nodded at Emily, an evil smile invading his face. He clicked open the boot and shoved Wanda in with Kelly, slamming it shut. Hard.

49

Ian and Emily walked out of the apartment block to their waiting town car. For once they were slightly restrained. No giggling or laughing or poking one another. It didn't seem like the right time for that sort of stuff.

The driver hopped out and opened the back door for them, nodding politely as they got in.

Ian jumped straight on his phone while Emily addressed the driver.

"There will be a black Jaguar pulling out of here in a minute. We need to follow it back to the warehouse. Stay as close as you can. There is a chance he may try and make a break for it. Don't lose him."

The driver nodded, ready for action.

Ian chatted away quietly as the town car waited. Finally, the black Jaguar appeared. They pulled in behind it, driving off into the night.

As Nuke drove, he reflected on the whole sorry day.

Everything had been so manic and crazy this was the first chance he'd had to really consider what had taken place.

His mind settled on Jonathan, the man with the plan.

Jonathan, scared out of his wits, about to die, yet ballsy enough to tell Nuke he was having a smoke first. Not ask, tell.

"Why did you do it?" Nuke had asked, genuinely interested in what he might have to say for himself.

Jonathan sucked in the smoke from the bong and held it for a moment before spluttering everywhere. "Took a chance," he said between violent coughs.

"You're about to die. Was it worth it?"

"Might have been, if it had worked."

Nuke studied him.

"It's what you do. Everybody. Look for angles. Roll the dice. Try and get ahead any way you can."

"Not me," Nuke said. "I play it straight."

Nuke glanced in the rearview and continued to drive, replaying the conversation over again in his head.

"It's just life," Jonathan had told him. "Always. You're either playing someone or you're being played."

Nuke's eyes found the Buyer's briefcase sitting on the seat beside him. He pulled out his revolver and set it down on top of the buyer's bag, ready. Just in case. You never knew.

THE TOWN CAR did as instructed, sticking close to the black Jaguar, giving it no chance to escape. Just in case. You never knew.

In the back, Ian flipped his phone shut.

"The Senior Sergeant is ready and waiting at the warehouse."

Emily stuck out her bottom lip, making an exaggerated sad face. "Be a shame to lose Nuke."

"It will," Ian agreed. "But it's too messy. We can't do messy."

"I know."

She held up her hand and he grasped it. They sat in silence, holding hands and each staring out their own window.

THE WAREHOUSE WAS dark and uninviting. That was good, at least as far as Senior Sergeant Billings was concerned. The dark made it easier to hide in the shadows. Hiding in the shadows, a good analogy for his career. Analogy? Metaphor? He always mixed those two up. Standing out front and yet hiding in the shadows.

Much easier all happening here. It would have been feasible to kill Nuke in lock-up, just more risky. More eyeballs, more questions.

How should he do it? Shoot him in the car as he drove in? That would be safest, providing he got a good shot off. Tricky in the semi-dark though. It would need to be a clean kill or to wound Nuke badly. Nuke was volatile. If he sensed something was up he might fight back.

This situation was contained as long as it was in the warehouse. It needed to remain that way. If he shot him in the car that would be two things he would have to dispose of; the body and the car. If Nuke was out of the car all he would have to get rid of was the body. Plus he could sell the car if it didn't contain a dead body and a bunch of blood. Probably get a pretty decent price for as well.

He drew his gun and leaned up against the wall, all good to go.

The black Jag appeared first, its headlights splashing through the dark room. The Sharks' car followed a little behind, keeping its distance now. Billings crouched low so not to be seen and once the Jag passed, he scurried behind it, keeping in the car's blind spot.

The brake light bathed everything red as the Jaguar slowed. Billings threw open the driver's door the second the car stopped moving, giving Nuke no time.

"Hands! Hands!" he screamed. "Let me see your hands."

Two hands emerged. Somewhere behind the town car's doors closed and The Sharks walked over.

"Out of the car, Nuke. Slowly. Hands where I can see them. Don't think I won't shoot you if I have to."

The driver complied, doing precisely what he was asked.

Except it wasn't Nuke.

It was Jonathan.

Billings turned towards Ian and Emily for an explanation. They were just as baffled as he was.

"Hello," Ian said to Jonathan. "Who are you?"

For his part, Jonathan was pleased to have made it to this point. He hadn't been shot or wet himself. He was just taking things one moment at a time and despite the odds, he still wasn't dead yet, so who knew?

50

"What did you decide?" Nuke had asked when he opened the car boot and let Jonathan out. "You wanna roll the dice one last time?"

This was in the underground car park of Nuke and Wanda's apartment. After Jonathan's one last smoke and the talk about how you are always either playing or you're being played.

Jonathan had been convinced it was all over as Nuke took him from the hideout and made him get in the boot of his car, Jonathan sure Nuke was taking him somewhere dark and quiet to kill him. Nuke though still had other stuff to do.

First, he went and exchanged the shipment for the briefcase full of cash.

Tempted as Nuke was to run right there after he had seen the Buyer, he knew it was the wrong move. Instead, he went back to his apartment where Ian and Emily and Wanda were waiting for him. He found them on the couches.

"Hey, honey. How was your day?" he asked, genuinely intrigued as to how she might respond.

"Uneventful."

A small piece somewhere inside delighted in seeing her squirm for once. Her cool façade cracked. He had to keep moving however. He hurried into their bedroom.

Nuke had fifty K strapped to the underside of the bed. Rainy day money. Today was about as rainy as it was gonna get. He removed the four thick wads of cash, shoving two in his pockets and two more down the front of his pants.

He got in and out in a matter of seconds. The Sharks didn't come in or appear suspicious when he ambled back to the lounge.

"Come down to the garage with me," he told Wanda. "I've got something to show you."

NUKE DRAGGED Wanda by the hair towards his car.

"Hey, whoa, careful, Nuke," Emily said. "Don't hurt her. You don't want to damage her before we get her back to the warehouse."

Throwing her in with Kelly Nuke slammed the car boot shut.

"You did it, Nukey. You fixed it. Yay!" Emily said with a patronising rub of his arms. "Don't worry about that stupid Wanda. The warehouse will cheer you up."

Any lingering doubt Nuke had about The Sharks and their intentions and whether he should run disappeared immediately.

"Our driver is out front," Ian told him. "We'll follow you."

Nuke tossed his security pass to Ian, who caught it with two hands and no coordination.

"Wave that in front of the thing to get out."

Emily headed one direction, Ian the other.

"You can't get out that way, fruit loop. We're not a car."

"Nah, it'll work," Nuke told them. "There's a sensor over there."

Ian stuck his tongue out playfully at his sister as she hurried to catch up.

Nuke watched them exit, waiting for the crunch of the descending metal gate. He had to be quick. Seconds at best. Even the slightest delay would make The Sharks suspicious.

Once Nuke was certain Ian and Emily were gone he popped the boot of Wanda's Jaguar. Jonathan stuck his head out gingerly.

"What did you decide? You wanna roll the dice one last time?"

JONATHAN DROVE Wanda's black Jaguar out of the car park where it was picked up and closely followed by Ian and Emily's town car.

Moments later Nuke exited the car park in the other Jag and peeled off the other way.

AT THE WAREHOUSE, no one was quite sure what to do next, least of all Jonathan, who still had his hands up.

"You didn't think it was odd, him driving around with those?" Senior Sergeant Billings asked, pointing to Wanda's bright pink vanity plates.

Ian and Emily looked at one another.

IT WAS A RISK, having Jonathan drive off in Wanda's car instead of his own, but Wanda and Kelly were in the boot of this car and there was no time to switch them. Not that he had any idea what he was going to do with them yet.

Nuke headed back to the industrial yard. Back to where Three's body still lay undiscovered. Back to where his car waited abandoned.

The headlights lit up the deserted yard. Clear night. The moon shone down on him. Nuke grabbed his revolver and got out.

"Nuke..." Wanda said as he opened the boot.

"Shut it," he snarled with a cold fury. He dragged Wanda out and threw her to the ground. His revolver was enough to stop her running or perhaps it was the more general fear. He grabbed the still bound Kelly out too and threw her down next to his wife.

"I fucken loved you," he spat at Wanda.

She threw her arms around the defenceless Kelly, terror riddling both their faces.

Nuke took a step back, pointing the revolver at Wanda's head.

And for once he remembered to count to five. As he counted, he thought about his friend Three, his dead body lying somewhere in the long grass behind them. And he thought about Kelly. But mostly he thought about his wife and what the point of any of this was. He wondered how he could have got it so wrong. How he could have loved Wanda so much when she clearly felt nothing for him. Less than nothing.

Heat overran his brain, like it was melting.

All their years together. How could she screw him over like this, after everything he'd done for her? How could she? What a bitch. An absolute fucking bitch.

. . .

WANDA SCREWED up her whole body waiting... Waiting...

What was going to feel like? The hot lead slicing into her. Would she die instantly or would it take a while?

After a few moments or perhaps all of eternity she heard footsteps and yet she still didn't peek. It wasn't until she heard a car door slam and zoom away that she dared open her eyes.

Nuke had gone.

She grabbed the still bound Kelly even tighter, determined that she was never, ever going to let her go.

NUKE DROVE Three's Mustang off into the night. Swapping cars seem like a sensible idea. He doubted the cops would think to look for Three's car. At least not initially.

Thoughts of Wanda and Kelly peppered his mind. Would Kelly make her happy? Or would Wanda lose interest in Kelly just as she had with him? Oh well, that was Kelly's problem now.

He opened the Buyer's briefcase, adding the wads from his pants and pockets. All up, a little over half a million. Enough for a new start anyway.

The little motor whirred opening the automatic window, Nuke letting the breeze bash his face as he drove off into the night.

IF YOU HAVE A MOMENT

I hope you enjoyed reading all about Wanda, Nuke, Kelly and Jonathan and their adventures.

Can I ask a small favour? Reviews are vital in the indie publishing world, especially for novelists just starting out, like me. Taking a moment to leave a quick review on Amazon will help me gain visibility and bring my books to the attention of more great readers like yourself.

Thank you.

HAVE YOU READ BLOCKHOUSE BLUES?

Two crims. One schoolgirl. Someone's in trouble.

Sort of like *SCAM's* little brother *Blockhouse Blues* tells the story of two dumb, wannabe criminals who bite off more than they can chew when they kidnap a schoolgirl from a particularly modern, angular suburban house.

Grab it now here at Amazon or get it for **FREE** by signing up to my mailing list (details over).

HAVE YOU READ 18 HOURS TO DIE?

Owing the big boss is bad enough, but doubling down on that debt? Deadly.

When Lucky the thief wakes in Magik's office after an epic bender, he knows he is in serious trouble. Somehow he managed to rack up an insurmountable debt to the one person you never want to owe.

Magik decides to spare Lucky's life if he will steal some rare, exotic eggs. But when the job goes bad and Lucky goes to ground Magik assumes Lucky has ripped him off.

Now Lucky owes Magik twice and his men are closing in fast.

With nowhere to run and even less places to hide, can Lucky somehow figure a way out of this mess? Or will these last few hours be his last?

If you love your thrillers fast-paced, brutally funny and chock-full of nail-biting action, you'll love *Jack Stroke's* **18 Hours to Die.**

Get it now.

JOIN MY MAILING LIST

Sign up for my mailing list and receive *Blockhouse Blues* for free.

As well as free books, members will get updates and fun stuff about twice a month. There will be no spam, I promise, and you can opt out at anytime.

So, sign up today.

www.jackstrokebooks.com

BLOCKHOUSE BLUES AND THE ELMORE BEAST (FREE SAMPLE)

The following story took place in Melbourne, Australia in 2011.

It is a true story.

(Except for the parts that are made up)

1

The car stood out like dogs balls. Of course it did. Why hadn't Brains thought about it before? Looking up and down the street everything else was big family four wheel drives. Volvos and Porsches and BMWs and there was Brains' piece of shit, beat up, old Camry. It was always going to stand out. But so? What was he meant to do about it? It's not like he had some other car he could use and Hammers didn't have any car, of course.

They could have hired a car, except who would pay for that exactly? Not them. Not Floyd. And so they were stuck in Brains piece of shit old Camry. They may as well have had a big neon sign over their heads - Beware! Two dodgy guys, up to no good. The neighbours were probably calling the cops already. Like that time, five years ago when he was buying some dope from Slow Simon. Simon was taking forever, trying not to act suspicious around his mum, leaving Brains and some mates stranded stuck waiting in a car, out the front of Simon's house for ages when they noticed Simon's neighbour sweeping and re-sweeping the same patch of his front veranda over and over. Sure enough about 20 minutes later the cops showed up wanting to know what they were doing, sitting there in their car like that. And that was some eastern shithole suburb. It wasn't a nice area like this.

Brains glanced in the mirror, adjusting the peak of his beat up old lucky Sox cap. Calm down. Nobody was calling any cops. It was the nerves talking, polluting his mind. Nerves were understandable. This was a big job. Wasn't just nerves though. There was excitement mixed in too. This was it. It was finally happening. Things were happening

Hammers voice forced its way into Brains' head, high-pitched and whiny, like a mosquito. And like a mosquito, you could only ignore it for so long. Sooner or later it would drive you nuts and you'd end up turning on the light in a rage, determined to kill the stupid thing.

"I mean, what have these idiots got against roofs, anyway?"

Brains sighed, his focus shot. "What?"

"I said, what have these idiots got against roofs?"

"Roofs?"

Hammers pointed at the house they were watching. The Blockhouse. "Look at that stupid piece of crap."

The Blockhouse was on the cutting edge of architectural design, like some sort of high-tech cube that had got lost in suburbia. The presumably computer-aided shape gave the appearance of a large concrete cube. Very square. As opposed to the more traditional pointy roof style of housing.

"It's got a roof, you idiot. You just can't see it. It's flat."

"Phhfft. Looks like a concrete block spewin' up glass or some shit."

It was true and although Brains didn't particularly care for the house's style, as with most things these days, if Hammers took a position one way or the other, he felt compelled to say the opposite.

"It's contemporary. Modern."

"It's bullshit. Why would anyone want to live in a concrete block? Buy a house, why can't you buy a house that looks like a fucken house?" Hammers shook his head. His delicate architectural sensibilities offended. "These stupid fucken pricks. All the money in the world and they can't just buy a house that looks like a house. They have to buy a statement."

Why didn't Hammers come with a mute button? Don't engage. You've got a job to do. Just sit there, watch the fucken house.

"Betcha it's nice inside."

Hammers glared at him. Traitor.

"That's why you buy a house. To live in, not to look at."

"That's exactly the sort of shit you do, isn't it? Buy some ridiculous shit like that just so you could say 'Ooh, look at my house, everybody'."

A buzzing grabbed their attention. Brains dug his phone out of his pocket.

"Who is it?"

"Me Mum."

"What's she want?"

Like it was Hammers' business.

"Brains? What's she want?"

Brains stared at him. "Firstly, I didn't answer it, did I? So how am I supposed to know what she wants?" He tossed the phone down. It clattered loudly in the cupholder. "Secondly, fuck off. It's my mum. It's none of your business what she wants."

Hammers made a face like it was Brains that was the problem here. Like he was being touchy.

Around them, the street remained quiet. Very few people about and only the occasional passing car. Of course, Hammers being Hammers, the silence couldn't last.

"See? What's wrong with that?" Accusing Brains with his tone. He pointed to a different house a few doors up from the Blockhouse. House was a loose term at best. Like most of the residences in the street, it was large enough to accommodate a small village. Unlike the Blockhouse though it a was a far more traditional house-like design.

"It'd be 'nice on the inside'. And at least it looks like a fucken house."

This opened the floodgates once again for Hammers to blab on and on about the merits of certain architecture. Brains wasn't listening. There was movement outside the car. The movement they had been waiting for.

On the street, a pretty girl wandered home from school. Kat. Kat chatted excitedly into her phone, too caught up in her social world and dramas to notice anything untoward on the street.

Hammers continued blabbering on oblivious. Typical. Brains' leg jittered up and down. This was it. Go time. He eyed the girl the whole way along the street and into the Blockhouse. Once she was gone, he fired up the car.

2

The rear access lane to the Blockhouse and its neighbours was more like an overgrown track, with knee-high grass and bushes and enormous potholes. Brains' beat up old Camry negotiated it with some difficulty, tossing the two occupants around.

"Look at them all. Tennis courts. Pools. All the money in the world and yet these cunts can't fix the lane out the back of their houses."

"Wouldn't be their responsibility. It'd be a council thing."

"Wouldn't be their responsibility," Hammers scoffed. "Probably got the money in their back pockets, the cheap fucks. Why do they all hafta have pools? All hafta have tennis courts?"

"Why can't they have their own pools?" Brains asked.

"It shows what unfriendly people they are."

The car glided to a stop. Brains killed the engine. Was this the right house? He was pretty confident it was, although it was difficult to tell for sure, the back decidedly less cube-ish.

"If they were friendly, one could have a pool and one could have a tennis court and they could share."

Brains was going to wait, but Hammers showed no sign of slowing.

"That's what I'd do if —"

"Hammers."

Hammers stopped ranting and glanced at Brains, who gestured towards the house.

"Oh, yeah. Right."

Tall fences on both sides secluded the lane. Brains watched Hammers get out, open the back gate and make his way onto the property via the tennis court.

With Hammers and his incessant bleating gone, everything became still and quiet. There was nothing to hear, aside from the occasional bird and soft rumbling of faraway traffic. Brains felt he could breathe once more. It was like that with Hammers, like he sucked all the air out of the room. Or in this case, car.

Revelling in his momentary peace, it was a few minutes until Brains remembered his Mum. He grabbed the phone from the cupholder.

"Hi, there. You have one new message," the automated voice informed him.

Brains' Mum's voice crackled on the line. "Hello, this is your mother. Have you done it yet? It won't do itself remember. Love you."

His Mum's singsong voice made Brains smile. She was right, of course. He hung up and everything returned to quiet.

"Listen Hammers..." Brains practised out loud, his leg jittering up and down. "Hey, Hammers, listen..." He picked a bit of fluff of his tongue. "Hey, Hammers. We need to talk about something."

All of a sudden yelling and screaming shattered the peace. A girl's screams. Kat.

Brains turned to see Hammers make his way back out the rear gate. He had the school girl, Kat, still in her uniform slung casually over one shoulder. Hammers carried her with ease, as though she was nothing. For her part, Kat threw herself about, wriggling and kicking and punching Hammers. All of which had absolutely no impact on him.

Brains froze, completely caught up in the moment and forgetting to do his one job, pop the boot. A moment or two passed with nothing happening, other than Kat's fruitless attempts at getting away. Hammers bashed the side of the car with his free hand, jogging Brains' memory. It took Brains a moment to recall where the boot release button was, but he found it, and the boot swung open. Hammers tossed Kat in and slammed it shut.

Her screaming continued, although being trapped in an enclosed space rendered it a good deal quieter.

In no hurry, Hammers ambled around to the passenger side door and climbed in. He pulled the balaclava from his face, revealing a goofy, self-satisfied expression. By contrast, the look on Brains' face was a well-practiced look of disappointment. "Think she made enough noise? You didn't think to gag her?"

Hammers said nothing, a crooked smile stretching all the way to his eyes.

"What?"

"She was getting changed." He nodded, most pleased with himself. "Her shirt was completely open. Saw her bra."

Like this was the best possible thing in the world. Brains rolled his eyes.

"Know something? She's pretty sexy."

Brains fired up his car. "It was nice, wasn't it?"

"Seeing her tits?"

"The Blockhouse. Inside."

Hammers looked away. "Didn't notice."

"Yeah, it was nice inside."

Brains drove off down the lane. From the boot, the muffled yells and banging continued.

3

It wasn't until they were back in the safety of anonymous traffic that Brains' heart rate began to return to normal. He hadn't realised he was nervous, although it made sense. This was a big thing. With it came a flush of excitement. They were doing. It was happening. He was doing. Step one in the master plan.

Brains' favourite Youtuber was a pretty smart guy who did videos about success and how to achieve it. This guy often mentioned the importance of breaking down big tasks into smaller, more manageable tasks. That's what this was, the first smaller task that would lead Brains to big success.

He drove along. There was a bit of afternoon traffic about but it wasn't too bad. They were early enough to avoid the after work crush.

"Hey, Hammers. Got a question. How do they keep all their stuff dry?"

" 'Ey?"

"In the Blockhouse. How do they keep their stuff dry when it rains? If it's got no roof."

"Nah, it had a roof."

"Oh, it had a roof, did it?" said Brains, making a big show of the fact he was right. "Well, that's good. Hate to think the fucken Blockhouse didn't have a fucken roof."

Of course, the Blockhouse has a roof. Hammers had known that all along. He might not be as smart as Brains, but he wasn't that stupid. All he meant was, why didn't the Blockhouse have a pointy roof, like a normal house? And he stood by that. However, now, having been in the Blockhouse, he had a number of other issues and things he would like to talk to Brains about. Things like all the art inside. Except he couldn't. If he did, he would get himself in trouble and he didn't want that.

They drove in silence for a long while. Around them, the houses and streets began to change. Slowly at first, little changes. The streets became less leafy green. The houses less grand and opulent. Much smaller and increasingly crammed together. More mindless graffiti too. Occasional small shopping strips and parks broke up the house lined streets.

"So, Johnny Twice, 'eh?"

Brains rolled his eyes, as he did most times Hammers opened his mouth. His response having a forced reluctance. "Yeah."

"Big time. Brains and Hammers in the big leagues. Know how he got the name? Johnny Twice?"

"Jimmy," Brains replied curtly.

" 'Eh?"

Brains watch the road, not looking at Hammers. "It's Jimmy Twice, idiot."

The cars in front slowed to a crawl, then a complete stop. Some sort of roadworks. A truck going in or out of a construction site. Kat was still yelling and banging up a storm in the boot. Brains chuckled. Lucky they weren't the first car in the queue. Someone might hear her. Like the dude with the stop sign. Back here they were fine.

"You sure?" Hammers asked, furrowing his brow.

"Yes. It's definitely Jimmy."

Hammers shook his head. He didn't agree but left it. "You know how he got the name 'Twice'?" He took Brains' silence as a sign to go on. "When he was a kid, just coming up, he used to kill people twice. Like he strangled them, then when they were dead…" He made a gun with his fingers. "Bang! He'd shoot them."

Brains shook his head.

"Kill 'em Twice. But what I heard."

"That's just stupid."

"Nah, man. It's sweet. Scare the shit outta mother fuckers."

"It's dumb and it's not even right."

"How'd he get the name then?"

"Dunno. Not like that."

"How do you know?"

"Same way I know it's Jimmy, not Johnny."

They stared out separate windows, having had just about enough of each other. The difference was, Hammers would be over it in about two seconds. Brains would carry around all day like an anchor.

Finally, the truck finished maneuvering its way into position and the dude with the stop sign waved the traffic through.

4

As they neared their hideout, Brains felt another surge of excitement. They couldn't get ahead of themselves, of course, but they had done the hard part. They had kidnapped the girl. The rest would be easy.

He had to try and manage Hammers though. Make sure Hammers didn't screw everything up. That he understood how important this was.

"Listen, Hammers," he began as they turned into the street. "This is important. All the shit we have pulled, where has it ever got us?"

"We're doin' alright."

"Bullshit. I'm sick of being at the bottom of the pile. This is our chance to move up."

Brains pulled his old car into the driveway of their hideout, a piece of shit falling down old dump masquerading as a home. The place used to be government housing, located in an appropriately shit neighbourhood.

"This is our shot," Brains went on. "I don't wanna be some knockabout crim my whole life." He cut the engine.

They sat for a sec. "Do this well, we could be working for Twice. Jimmy fucken Twice, man."

Hammers nodded at first but had that Hammers look on his face. "I thought this job was for Floyd."

Brains did his best to keep the exasperation from his tone. Why did he have to explain everything to this stupid moron?

"Floyd is in Twice's crew. This is our way in, okay?"

Hammers nodded, not really listening.

"I'm serious. No messing up. We have to do this one hundred per cent right, okay?"

"I'm sure it's Johnny."

It's almost done, Brains told himself. Just get through today.

BRAINS GOT Hammers to remove Kat from the boot, not taking the chance of having her see his face. For a second Hammers was worried that they had killed her. She wasn't moving. She was okay though. She was just keeping still. It meant she was scared. She probably should be scared, Hammers thought. They were bad dudes. He put a blindfold over her eyes and carried her through the house with no fuss and down the stairs into the basement.

The basement had the perfect setup. The space was divided into two rooms. They took Kat into the junk room which they had prepared earlier. Well, 'prepared' is probably a little strong. They took Kat into the space where they'd shoved a bunch of old junk out of the way and moved the chair into the middle of the floor. The dank, stale room had no windows or natural light. Exposed wires hung from the ceiling, connected to the old naked halogen globe.

The blindfolded Kat trembled as Hammers secured her to a chair. Brains watched on from the doorway, the only way in or out. The room was full of old junk that hadn't made it to the tip yet. Or stuff that had been used once then abandoned. Tools, bits of old cars, some skis, a cricket bat and other long-forgotten pieces of sporting equipment.

Hammers finished and joined Brains by the doorway. The two of them eyeing their victim, before switching off the light.

Kat flinched as the heavy door slammed closed. Alone and vulnerable. No idea where she was or why.

The adjoining room was decked out like a crummy office/workspace, with a desk and an old computer, a couple of ancient Playboy centrefolds stuck up around the walls and more random junk. The door between the two basement rooms had a rectangular window, about head height, offering Brains and Hammers a perfect view of Kat on the other side. They watched her through the window for a bit, extremely pleased with themselves.

Hammers held up his hand for a high five. Brains reluctantly obliged. Hammers then proceeded to strut about, saying "Yeah", flexing his muscles and making muscle flexing type noises.

"Yeah. Hammers and Brains. We brought the hammers and we brought the brains."

He had hoped Brains would join in and say his bit. He thought it would be cool if the two of them had a catchphrase they could use like he would say 'We brought the hammers,' and then Brains would say 'We brought the brains' part.

Instead, Brains said, "Bought."

"Hey?"

"Bought not brought."

"What?"

"Never mind."

Hammers continued his little singsong chanting. "Hammers and Brains, taking —"

"Hammers, shut up."

Brains always seem to get upset when he called them Hammers and Brains. Hammers didn't care. They could be Brains and Hammers if Brains wanted. Hammers and Brains just sounded better.

Hammers loved his name. He was really proud of it. He had been Hammers since he was the biggest kid in primary school. If he hit you, you stayed hit. That's where it came from.

He had even managed to come up with his own personal catchphrase. These days if he hit someone he would call it 'Bringing the hammers down.' It was cool.

Brains had a cool name too, although it was harder to work into a catchphrase. Brains would probably be able to do it, except when he asked, Brains told him catchphrases were stupid and he didn't need one.

What Brains did have was that hat. Brains always wore an old baseball cap with a B on it. Hammers had always thought that's what the B stood for. Baseball. When he realised it also could stand for Brains, he thought it was about the most genius thing he had ever heard and right there he knew just how clever Brains was.

Ever since he had worked that one out, Hammers had been on the lookout for a hat for himself. One with an H (for Hammers) or even better one with a picture of a hammer. That would be sweet. He hadn't found one yet and couldn't tell Brains he was still looking. He'd told Brains about looking for a hat like that once and Brains went berserk, fully yelling at him for like five minutes. Brains was funny about some stuff. Hammers could never pick what. Oh well, he was going to get a hat anyway and Brains would just hafta deal with it. They'd be known by their hats. 'Oh no, it's the two guys in hats. The tough one and the smart one. Hammers and Brains.' That would be sweet.

Done with his little show of flexing Hammers went back to the window to look at Kat some more.

Brains moved away from the window and glanced about the space. "Hey, Hammers. Where's my bag?"

Hammers eyes didn't leave the girl. "What bag?"

That sinking feeling washed over Brains, fully aware what had happened.

"The fucken bag I told you to bring from our joint."

Hammers shrugged. "You wanted it, you should have fucken brought it."

Brains was about to bite back but restrained himself. What was the point? It was done now. "I'm gonna go grab it. You're okay here?"

Hammer's eyes still hadn't left the girl.

"Hammers?"

"Yeah, yeah."

Brains took the stairs two at a time. The muffled sounds of him leaving floated down from above as Hammers continued to peer at Kat through the small window in the door.

See, Brains, if he was as smart as he thought he was, he should have realised something was up right there, right then. Even if he wasn't that smart, he probably should have realised. Or at least been clever enough not to leave Hammers alone with a poor defenceless 16 year-old-girl.

5

"**B**ecause fucken told you to bring the bag, you stupid cockhead," Brains screamed as loudly as he could, driving his old heap of a car back to his place. Not that Hammers could hear him all the way back at the hideout of course. But getting it out made Brains feel marginally better. His place wasn't too far. The distance wasn't the issue. He shouldn't have had to go at all. That's what annoyed him so much. Stupid Hammers.

He arrived at his house, jumped out and ran inside. His bag was waiting exactly where it was when he told Hammers to take it. He grabbed it and made his way back to the car. The whole thing took a couple of minutes and that should have been that. He should have gone directly back to the hideout. Back to Hammers and Kat. Except he didn't. Brains had another idea. He went to the Blockhouse.

Brains wasn't really sure why he did it. There wouldn't be anything to see. Just a house. Still, the idea of driving past the Blockhouse gave him a perverse thrill. Just to have a look. It's what criminals do, isn't it? Return to the scene of the crime? He could feel himself getting excited. Looking at all these normal people in their cars, going about their normal, boring lives. No one would be able to guess his secret looking at him. He'd kidnapped a girl. Take that world and watch out. There was a new force in town. Brains. A force to be reckoned with.

Any good feeling he had evaporated in a flash before he even made it to the Blockhouse. He was at the other end of the street when he skidded the car to a sudden stop in the middle of the road. For a moment he simply sat, mouth fallen half open, trying to comprehend what he was seeing.

The street was full of cop cars, right outside the Blockhouse. Lights flashing, blocking the road. And the house itself was all taped off with police tape.

Someone beeped from behind Brains, probably wanting him to move from the middle of the road. Yeah, all right. I'm moving. He threw a hand up to acknowledge them and froze again when he glanced in his mirror.

The car that wanted to get by wasn't a car at all. It was a van. A news van. Couldn't be a coincidence. What the fuck was a new van doing here? First cops now news? This was getting worse and worse. Suddenly he had no desire to drive past the Blockhouse. In fact, it seemed like about the stupidest fucken idea anybody had ever had. He wanted to run as fast as he could in the other direction.

Brains slammed the car in reverse and pulled a sharp U-turn, almost crashing into some parked cars on the other side. He told himself to relax and that there was no reason to panic. They were empty words. There was plenty of reason to panic. One thing repeated over and again in his head. A name. Hammers.

DON'T FORGET TO GRAB YOUR FREE COPY
BLOCKHOUSE BLUES

Grab it now at Amazon or get it for **FREE** by signing up to my
mailing list at www.jackstrokebooks.com

Made in the USA
Middletown, DE
30 April 2020